# Berladon Chronicles The Fall of Elas-Tormas

*Grey Book One*

By
M.W. Mathis

Copyright © 2023 by M.W. Mathis

All rights reserved.

No portion of this book may be reproduced in any form without written permission from the publisher or author, except as permitted by U.S. copyright law.

# Table Of Content

Prologue ..................................................................................... i
White Chapter One: The Waning Of Light ............................... 1
Black Chapter One: Glyphs In Stone ...................................... 12
White Chapter Two: Morheim's Council ................................ 17
Black Chapter Two: Forging The Torque ............................... 36
White Chapter Three: Whispers At The Tergian Tower ......... 44
Black Chapter Three: The Torque Of Iron ............................. 59
White Chapter Four: Water And Wine ................................... 69
Black Chapter Four: Silken Gambit ........................................ 82
White Chapter Five: Misses, Missives And Misgivings ........... 99
Black Chapter Five: The Selfish And The Selfless ................ 120
White Chapter Six: The Snapping Of Threads ...................... 135
Black Chapter Six: Intentions Revealed ................................ 145
White Chapter Seven: A Glimmer Of Hope ......................... 161
Black Chapter Seven: The Battle Begins ............................... 169
White Chapter Eight: West Of Elas-Tormas ......................... 177
Black Chapter Eight: Cleansing The Outlands ..................... 182
White Chapter Nine: The Growing Fear ............................... 191
Black Chapter Nine: An Ember Extinguished ...................... 204
White Chapter Ten: Nowhere To Run Nowhere To Hide .... 216
Black Chapter Ten: Threads .................................................. 228

# Prologue

The same year that Vindramion defeated the Darklord at Welryth in the east, he marched his victorious army to the west. Though the lands they traveled through had been devastated by many long years of warfare, now, in the spring, signs of life were returning. The Lepnarions passed through fields of tall grasses and fragrant flowers and past majestic stands of blossoming trees. Flocks of birds filled the sky, and myriad small creatures skittered through the grass. In the distance could be seen herds of wild cattle that somehow survived the destruction of so many towns and villages. Day by day, the horrors of war began to fade, and the men marched with increasing ease, grateful to be heading home after so many years.

Upon learning that the pass at Ajaron through the Raxor Mountains was blocked by prodigious snows, Vindramion turned to the south, following the banks of the mighty Arazor. As he neared the pass at Kalantar, he found it blocked by an armed host and, wishing to avoid further loss of life, continued south toward the passes through Mirion. Now, Vindramion was not a heartless leader; he cared deeply for those he led, and he knew that taking the long path through Mirion would add almost another year to their already long journey home, so he proposed a different solution. He wanted to build many ships and sail home by way of the sea.

As they neared the mouth of the Arazor and the land dipped toward the sea, it became marshy, crisscrossed with many small streams and waterways. When they were less than five miles from the shore, a suitable location was found for an encampment and six thousand men were instructed to build walls and lodging and other such buildings needed for the milling of wooden beams for hulls and masts and oars. The rest of the army continued to the coast and, upon finding an area of stones and hills, set about making a second encampment where a foundry and smithy could be set up for the forging of metal fittings for the ships. The remaining men continued until, at last, they stared out over the vast sea, and here, a bit to the west of the Arazor, they purposed to lay the foundation for a city and harbor where their newly built ships might sail from.

Now, they were not the first people to have discovered this area, for two villages of fishermen already existed where Vindramion intended to build his city. The waters just offshore teemed with life, and the villagers were well-off. The village elders met with the Lepnarion king and refused to give up their lands, nor would they consider selling,

"For where should we go?" they had asked. Vindramion proposed that if they sold him the land, he would decree that they and their descendants would be masters of the docks and harbor for as long as the city should remain, only he asked to be able to build them proper homes of stone. After much-heated discussion and great reluctance, the elders finally agreed to allow the founding of the city to proceed. But they issued a warning to Vindramion not to disturb that which is hidden below for as long as it remains at rest; the harbor and surrounding waters would never become treacherous to any vessel sailing through them. This warning and many other things were chronicled in a tome regarding the founding of Elas-Tormas, but it was quickly forgotten as the city grew.

Word spread that the Lepnarion King was founding a great city, and materials poured in. Oaken timbers from Mirion, ten thousand workhorses from Anar, and great quantities of worked stone, both limestone and marble, from Thagovar. There followed thousands upon thousands of carpenters, masons, engineers, and city planners, all looking to leave their mark on the new city.

It was soon decided that the city should be named Elas-Tormas, which could be interpreted as 'Ellonas Victor overall.' In six months, those of Vindramion's army still desiring to sail for home departed on the newly built ships while Vindramion headed north to the Kalantarn Pass with a thousand hand-picked knights.

# White Chapter One: The Waning Of Light

### The 14th of Lirinn, late morning

"Where are you coming from?" a guard called out of a gate tower window as Paroch led the mantle into Elas-Tormas.

"From the Northern Midwaste," Paroch replied. "Around Talhaven."

"What news?" the guard asked.

Paroch reigned his mount to a stop under the window and, looking up, began to speak. "War is coming."

"This we have heard for some time now, and judging by the refugees we have had pouring into our walls, it is approaching."

"It is very near now," Paroch continued. "We have been hounded and harassed since we left Talhaven many days ago."

"Harassed by who?" the guard asked as another guard poked his head out of the window. "Bandits, brigands…"

"There has been no law in the Midwaste for many years now," the second guard interrupted. "It is no surprise that you would have trouble with bandits and brigands."

"Have the rumors mentioned Dakirin?" Paroch asked patiently.

"Dakirin? What on Kren is that?"

"The winged soldiers of the Darklord. The Falkiri of old."

The guards began to laugh, "Fairy tales come to life, eh?" one said to the other with an elbow to the side.

"War is coming, the Darklord grows in power, and his thirst for vengeance against Lepnar has yet to be quenched. He is slaughtering all

Lepnar that fall into his hands and all who worship Ellonas. Death and destruction approach," Paroch continued.

For those citizens and refugees gathered around behind the mantle, this news was difficult to hear.

"I have heard that as well," someone said. "The lands east of here are littered with the dead."

"Can it be true?" some asked.

"Yes," a few replied. "I have seen first-hand what happens when his armies conquer an area. I only just managed to escape, but many others did not."

"No," others disagreed. "Why would the Darklord single out a specific group for his vengeance? Other peoples joined in and helped overthrow him?"

Both guards laughed.

"I will start to worry about the Darklord's vengeance when his armies are pounding on this very gate." one of them boasted. "Did you not pass through the outer wall? Our defenses are strong and not easily overcome. It will be many long years before his armies approach these walls here."

"Do not put your trust in defense of walls or strength of arms, my friend," Fulcwin advised.

"Is that so," one of the guards laughed. "And what shall we place our trust in? Ellonas? Since he is allowing the slaughter of those who follow him, I can only conclude he is no longer interested in what becomes of them or Lepnar. No, I will trust in my skills with a blade and these thick walls here," he stomped a foot for emphasis.

"You would do well to heed our words," Perin cautioned. "We do not speak idly."

"And you would do well to move on through the gate before we fine you for causing a disturbance," the other snapped as he waved them through.

Paroch nodded and took the lead as he traversed the crowded streets of Elas-Tormas. Much had changed in the past few weeks; armed soldiers were stationed on almost every street corner, and though they took notice of everyone, only a few people were stopped and questioned.

As Paroch approached an inner gate between districts, a soldier stepped forward with his hand held up.

"You all have the look of seasoned veterans. Where will you be staying? If the rumors of war prove to be true, then the king shall certainly have need of your services in the coming days."

"We are staying at the Tergian Tower in the garden district," Paroch replied. "The war is no rumor; it is very near to this city. We will gladly draw swords alongside any who opposes the Darklord and his armies."

"The Darklord?" he shook his head. "He has returned? When? How?"

"That matters little now," Paroch advised, "Just know he has been released from his long imprisonment and seeks his vengeance upon all of Lepnar."

The soldier nodded, "Thank you for the information. Tergian Tower, huh? Good to know." He waved them forward.

Once on the side streets, no one even spared them a second glance as they rode past on their way to the garden district. When they passed the street leading to Endarben's place, Paroch looked to see if Kargen might not be there, but the street remained empty. They entered the familiar gate to the Tergian tower just before noon. Arvendal was on the front steps to greet them.

"Welcome home!" he called out. "All of you, welcome home!"

It did not take long for the horses to be set loose from their saddles, and once free, they set about grazing on the lush grasses around the tower.

"Where is Gilsarn?" Arvendal asked.

"Buried next to Pemogen at Cymbee," Telliken replied curtly.

"He fell at Talhaven," Galortin explained. "We were fortunate to not lose any others," he added. "It was a near thing."

"Gilsarn's death is a great loss, to be sure, but the Herald still lives," Arvendal bowed his head in sorrow.

They talked with Arvendal about their journey both to and from Talhaven, and then talk turned to the Kingsword and the Chantra.

"Were you actually able to retrieve the Kingsword?" Arvendal asked, his hands clasped together in hope.

Paroch produced a leather-wrapped bundle and presented it to Arvendal.

"Is it truly the Kingsword? Abion of old?" Arvendal asked in awe as he slowly pulled back the leather, revealing a four-and-a-half-foot-long broadsword.

The hilt was of gold and inlaid with azure stones, a large sapphire was set in the pommel, and smaller sapphires were set at the end of each guard. The blade itself was four feet long and had five runes etched into the surface.

Arvendal gently touched the sword with both hands and uttered a brief prayer.

"It is the Kingsword of old," Balatiere agreed. "And this means that Paroch is now King of all Lepnar. Right?" he added hopefully.

"I do not wish to ascend the throne in Mar-Storin," Paroch stated.

"You *could* unite all of Lepnar, and with her combined might, we could vanquish the Darklord," Balatiere continued.

Paroch shook his head.

"One thousand years ago, when Vindramion was slain, that would have been true," Arvendal began. "However, much has transpired between then and now. While the Kingsword confers the right to ascend the throne in Mar-Storin to a direct descendant of Vindramion, you also already know the Lepnar of history is now fractured. An uneasy alliance knits the five Lepnars together. It would be quite dangerous to reveal the Kingsword and begin making demands."

"This sword represents the laws upon which Lepnar was founded; they are...," Paroch paused, searching for the right words.

"They are right," Balatiere stated.

"Yes," Paroch agreed, "but they are simply a schoolmaster. It will take more than an ancient blade to bring Lepnar together again."

"Those laws keep order in society. Without them, every man would do what is right in his own eyes. It would be pure chaos."

"Like it is now," Paroch observed.

"Exactly," Fulcwin agreed, "Which is why we need the Kingsword to be made known again."

"It would take time to assemble the rulers of Cul-Amaron, Kir-Esclanin, Bel-Tordanim, Xan-Tarfin and Mar-Storin," Arvendal stated.

"Do not forget Elas-Tormas," Galortin added.

"Elas-Tormas has always been a bit of a separatist," Fulcwin asserted. "Charting her own course. It would be easier to get the other five to agree first, then approach her."

"But it would take time, time we do not have," Paroch insisted. "With so much distrust, there would be fighting amongst the five."

Galortin began to laugh, "Our Herald is right. There would be much bloodshed between the Lepnars, and the Darklord would have an easy time picking them off one by one."

"They would demand an accounting of lineage to ensure that the wielder is truly a direct descendant of Vindramion," Arvendal said, and he looked closely at Paroch and smiled.

"My father Balcryon is not in the royal line, I can assure you of that," Paroch confirmed. He avoided Arvendal's gaze.

"There you have it," Arvendal stated, "a moot point if ever there was one."

"Then why did we retrieve the sword in the first place?" Balatiere asked, frustration evident in his voice.

"Because the blade that Astarlion was supposed to bestow upon the Herald was lost," Arvendal explained.

"Second best is better than nothing, I guess," Galortin added. "What is our next move, Paroch?"

A loud pounding on the tower door echoed through the halls. Arvendal hurried from the meeting room, and the others followed.

When the door was opened, a man dressed in the king's livery stepped back off the stairs and cleared his throat. His pants were dark blue with triple, vertical, yellow stripes; a long-sleeved, dark blue blouse was tucked into the waistband of the pants; its' cuffs were of the same yellow as the stripes. A cape of the same blue hue was rimmed with yellow-dyed fur, and his cap, also dark blue, had a single vibrant yellow plume sticking up from it. He was flanked by four soldiers dressed in similar colors, save the metal armor upon their chests and the helmets upon their heads; they held long pikes. After waiting until everyone had emerged from the tower, he cleared his throat again before speaking.

"Fulcwin of Kire, King Morheim requests your presence this mid-afternoon."

"So now he wants to hear us," Balatiere muttered under his breath, a bit too loudly, for even as Fulcwin gave him an elbow to his side to silence him, the messenger spoke again.

"King Morheim has many concerns and must make decisions sometimes on the scantest of information. Such was the case many weeks ago when you first arrived in our fair city. Much has happened in the intervening days; new information has been revealed since then, and he would speak with you again, at length this time."

Fulcwin looked to Paroch, who gave a slight nod.

"I will be there," Fulcwin stated.

The messenger looked at the other men gathered atop the steps and pointed to Haendorn. "You are no doubt from Mirion. Your presence is required, and any others of you from Anar or Lepnar."

"What of the rest of us?" Gehm asked. "We are from Gorod, Davar, and the Baris Islands and have pertinent information for King Morheim as well," Gehm continued.

The messenger shrugged, "King Morheim only wishes to speak with those from Mirion, Lepnar and Anar at this time. Remember, mid-afternoon. That is all." The messenger turned about on his heels and stalked off, flanked by his escort.

"I will relate your tales as best I can," Paroch said as he looked at those of the mantle who were not invited.

"It may not be a good idea to mention me just yet," Draxin added.

"Probably not at first," Paroch laughed. "But in due time, everyone will know that you stand with us, as opposed to the Darklord."

Draxin bowed low and re-entered the tower.

"Remind him that the Cauldron of Delgeth has already been recovered," Kourakin said as he bowed and followed Draxin.

"And now the staff as well," Reesal added.

"My people are the forgotten ones in this affair," Perin said bitterly. "I would have you inform the king of our plight."

"But you yourself have not returned home to see if, indeed, you have even been attacked," Galortin said with a shake of his head. "The rest of us, at least, are certain that our homes have been destroyed."

"I know in my heart that my people are suffering under the cruel armies of darkness," Perin snapped. He nodded once at Paroch and then entered the tower.

"Perhaps I should not have said as much," Galortin shrugged. He turned to Paroch, "Probably a good idea not to mention the Kingsword either." He patted his shoulder twice and entered the tower.

Gehm smiled at Paroch and saluted before turning to leave.

Elrynn extended his hand to Paroch, "As you speak to Morheim, remember, a word fitly spoken is like apples of gold in settings of silver. May your words fall on listening ears, eager for truth and not falsehood." He smiled and stood atop the stairs beside Arvendal.

"I will speak with them," Arvendal promised.

Paroch sighed.

Telliken, Fulcwin, Balatiere and Haendorn stood nearby.

"I would go see a few of those who survived the journey from Kire with me," Fulcwin said with a salute. "I will meet you at the palace."

"Of course," Paroch said. After a moment, he motioned toward the gate.

"Tell Kulanak I said hello," Balatiere said. "And Shalamar," he added with a punch to Fulcwin's arm as he started toward the gate.

"And the rest of you?" Paroch asked.

Haendorn smiled at him. "I would like to send a message to my people in Mirion, but I shall be back here before you head to the palace." He hurried out the gate after Fulcwin.

"I am with you," Telliken said.

"So am I," Balatiere added. "I doubt anyone else has bested a Chantra and retrieved a sword hidden for a thousand years. I want to see what happens next."

"I do, too," Paroch said as he sat on the steps.

It did not take long for Haendorn to return, and when he did, they began making their way to the palace.

Back at the tower, Arvendal was speaking with those gathered inside.

"Now, why do you suppose that King Morheim has decided not to include the rest of you in his little gathering?" Arvendal asked.

Galortin shrugged, "Makes no difference to me. I find those things boring."

"One can learn many things when one listens with intent," Arvendal replied.

"Intent for what?" Galortin asked gruffly.

"For whatever you are intending to do, hopefully learn, but there are other intentions to be sure," Arvendal answered.

Galortin glowered at him but said nothing else.

"Gehm? Reesal?" Arvendal asked.

"I have no idea, but this is definitely not the Lepnar of old," Reesal stated. "The stories I heard as a young boy mentioned Lepnar righting the wrongs of the oppressed, rushing to the aid of those wrongly attacked, defending the defenseless."

"In some ways, Kren has not changed all that much in the last thousand years, but in those same intervening years, Lepnar has changed. And so have all the countries; look at your Gorod."

"This is true," Gehm stated with a nod. "We have often talked about what might happen if we were able to have Thagovar join with us again. What might we be able to accomplish working together as one Gorod again instead of against one another?"

"Davar is not the same as it was back then either," Kourakin asserted. "And it has recently changed for the worse yet again now that Rudel is seated on the throne. At least with Duros, positive changes were being made to the ruling class in Terjavon. But it is difficult to change the course of an entire country when corruption has become the accepted norm for those accustomed to leading."

"It is definitely easier to float downstream with the garbage than to swim against the current," Arvendal laughed.

"That it is," Reesal agreed, "but it seems more impossible than ever to get help to those trapped inside Thagorod." He sighed.

"At the moment, you are correct," Arvendal agreed. "But that does not mean all is lost for them. I will ask again: why has King Morheim chosen to exclude you all from his meeting?"

"We are too far away to be of concern to him," Perin stated. "That is the easiest answer, but it does not make it any easier to accept."

"A good king must first be concerned about his own country and people and see to their welfare before reaching out to help those countries around him, let alone countries at such distances as we represent," Elrynn explained. "It makes sense then that he would want to speak with his closest neighbors. Perhaps if Anar and Mirion join with Morheim, together they can forge a strong alliance that will be able to stem the rising tide of darkness."

"It will take more than strength of arms to defeat the Darklord," Draxin replied.

A single thump sounded on the tower door. Arvendal smiled, "Allow me," he said, and he made his way to the door. He opened it slowly. No one was waiting on the landing, and no one was seen leaving the gate, but there was a smooth green stone lying near the door. He looked toward a nearby abandoned building; there was a hole under the eaves large enough for a bird to fly through. The opening was dark, but he stared into it all the same. Then, bending down, he picked up the stone. There were scratches on both sides and after reading them, he took one last look at the dark opening and nodded. He closed the door behind him.

"What was that about?" Reesal wanted to know when Arvendal entered the room again.

"Just someone throwing stones at the tower door." He tossed the stone to Reesal. "What do you make of that?" he asked, passing his right hand in front of his eyes.

After inspecting the stone, Reesal shrugged, "Well, it is not from around here that I can tell you for sure. It is reminiscent of the stone we delved into in Thagorod, but it could be from even farther north." He handed it to Gehm.

"A few of the Balar Mountains have stone like this, but this looks to be more like a stone from the Dhurrow Coast. There are very few beaches of sand up north, just stones and pebbles mostly."

"Could be from the Island of Clouds," Kourakin added after he examined it. "But I never paid much attention to the stones of the island."

"Let me see that," Galortin demanded, and he grabbed it out of Kourakin's hand. He inspected it for a moment. "It is an ordinary green stone, is all, perfectly smooth." He handed it to Perin.

"Not interested in stones today, thank you," Perin said sullenly.

Galortin tossed it to Draxin, "What does our resident Dakirin have to say about this stone from up north?"

In one quick motion, Arvendal passed his right hand in front of his eyes again.

The stone landed in Draxin's lap, and he stared at it for a long while. Then, suddenly, he picked it up and looked closely at it. He turned it over and then over again and then a third time before clutching the stone tightly to his chest.

"Well, it looks like Draxin has taken a liking to that stone," Galortin mocked.

Draxin looked to Arvendal; anger and joy played across his face even as tears welled up in his eyes.

# Black Chapter One: Glyphs In Stone

## *The 14th of Lirinn*

As she watched Darxon and the others enter the tower, a slight breeze blew through the opening, and again, she thought of ways in which she might be able to speak with him in person.

"I could always transform, use the scroll one last time and knock on the tower door," she said with a nod. "But somehow, Arvendal would see right through my disguise," she sighed. "He would know."

She ruffled her feathers in frustration as she tried to figure out another way of alerting Darxon. She could think of nothing else short of flying overhead and calling out in Dakirin. She soon drifted off to sleep, and she began to dream.

*"To the left, this way," Darxon called as he banked hard left.*

*She banked to the left, trying to keep up with him.*

*"Now to the right," he called out as he rolled right. When they collided a moment later, Darxon quickly righted himself and steadied her.*

*"I am sorry," she apologized.*

*He laughed. "Let us try that again. Come now, gain some altitude with me." He climbed higher and higher and waited for her to catch up; their wing tips touched momentarily, and their eyes met. "We can do this," he encouraged her. "Come on!" he shouted with joy as he dived straight down.*

*She could not help laughing aloud as she followed after him.*

*"Are you ready?"*

*"Yes!" she shouted.*

*"As we are diving, spin to the right three times, then bank hard left and begin to climb. Got it?"* He called out.

*"Ready when you are!"* she agreed.

*"Now,"* he called out as he began to spiral to the right.

*She followed him spiral for spiral.*

*"Climb to the left!"*

*She climbed up and to the left.*

*"You are doing great!"* he encouraged.

*Inside, she was bursting with joy.*

*"Left!"* he shouted. *She banked the moment he did and stayed close.* | *"Shallow right!"* he shouted again. *She banked again as he called out, remaining in his shadow.* *"Climb!"* he called out. *Once they had reached a sufficient altitude again, he called out to her.* *"You take the lead this time."*

*"Me?"* she asked.

*"Is there anyone else murmuring with us today?"* he laughed. *"Go ahead; it's my turn to become your shadow."*

*"I have no idea where to begin,"* she demurred.

*"Nonsense,"* he laughed. *"Tell you what, close your eyes for a moment."*

*"Why?"* she asked suspiciously.

*"Close your eyes,"* he laughed. *"Trust me."*

*She closed her eyes.*

*"Keep them closed,"* he urged.

*"I am,"* she hollered. *"What are you doing?"* she laughed.

*"Open your eyes,"* he whispered.

*She opened her eyes just as his talons gripped hers. He was upside down underneath her.*

*"Murmur with me,"* he whispered.

She awoke and looked at the tower. It was just after noon, and she saw a lot of people standing around the tower door. Four or five men dressed in blue and yellow clothes, and there was Darxon nearest the door and Arvendal and Galortin and the rest.

She watched with interest as the five men in similar garb left, and then Arvendal, Darxon and six others entered the tower while Paroch and four others remained outside. One of the men, it looked like Fulcwin, left, followed quickly by Haendorn, but Haendorn returned after twenty minutes or so and then all of them, still outside, left the tower grounds.

Suddenly, she dropped from her perch and found the familiar alley where she could transform without being noticed. She did transform and immediately retrieved the bone tube. Her hands were shaking as she removed the leather cap and upended the tube into her hand. But no parchment slid into her hand, only a pile of fine powder that quickly disappeared into the gentle breeze. She threw the bone tube against the ground, and it splintered. Then she sighed and hung her head as a single tear fell to the ground. She stood there for several minutes but eventually transformed and returned to her perch.

She had not been there long when she suddenly cried out and looking at her surroundings, she transformed, careful to stay up on the beam which was her usual perch. What had been plenty of room for a large bird was very cramped for a human, and as she stood hunched over, she felt frantically at the pouches on her belt. Finally, she felt what she had been looking for and carefully brought a green stone out from an inner pouch, which she clutched tightly in her hand. Looking around, she could see nowhere else to go, so she gently crouched until she was able to straddle the beam, her legs dangling down. She breathed a heavy sigh as she studied the stone of dark green and light green speckles. There, on the one side, was the glyph for love from Darxon. She clutched it tightly to her chest for several minutes, then with a nod borne of conviction, she placed it on the beam before her and reached over to her boot for the dagger concealed there. It took a little effort to retrieve the dagger, but she soon had the stone in her right hand and the dagger in her left. She began to carve on the side opposite the message from Darxon. It took time, but she was patient, and she did not give up. When the first glyph was finished, she blew on the stone to clear away any dust. It was legible; that was all that mattered. She nodded as she began to carve another glyph. When she was satisfied with that one, she carved a third. When at last she was finished, she clutched the stone to her chest one more time, then kissed it gently before placing it on the beam. She pushed it as far from her as she could, then transformed. Once the smoke had cleared, she hopped over to the stone and, gripping it in her talons, dropped from her perch and circled the tower.

She landed before the door, laid the stone there and hopped over to and pecked loudly on the door. She turned and leaped into the air, quickly gaining altitude as she circled the tower. She waited for almost ten minutes, but no one came to the door, so she dropped to the landing and, gripping the stone, lumbered into the air. It was difficult to take off with the stone in her talons, but she finally managed to begin climbing. When she was about twice as high as the tower, she dived toward the door and released the stone. She watched as it bounced on the landing and into the moonrose bushes beside the tower.

She landed and hopped over to the bush, and after several minutes of pecking around, she finally was able to find the stone. Using her beak, she was able to push it out into the grass. Once again, she gripped the stone and lumbered into the air, circling the tower as she climbed. Again, she began to dive, and this time, she flew at a downward angle toward the tower door. When she judged she was at the right spot, she released the stone and banked hard left. She watched it bounce on the landing and into the door before coming to rest on the landing. Again, she waited for a long while, but again, no one came to the door. Once again, she retrieved the stone and climbed into the air. This time, she dived to the right side of the tower, and as she drew within ten feet of it, she banked hard left across the front of the door as she released the stone. She heard a loud and hollow thump, and she did not wait around but rather flew immediately to her perch.

She waited breathlessly for what seemed quite a long while and was about to try one more time with the stone when the door to the tower opened. Arvendal looked around and then spotted the stone. He stared right at her and then at the stone in front of him. He picked it up and studied it for a moment before looking at her again. He nodded once, then entered the tower and closed the door behind him.

She waited with nervous anticipation for Darxon to burst from the tower looking for her, but after an hour, the anticipation turned to irritation. She began to wonder if Arvendal really understood what she had written - if he had even given the stone to Darxon. She was trying to figure out another way to contact Darxon when a dark shape flew through the opening.

A Dakirin cocked his head sideways and blinked at her twice, "What are you doing here?" he asked suddenly.

"Watching over the tower, of course," she answered curtly.

"When did you return?"

"What does it matter?" she countered. "I am here now."

"Where is the brooch you were wearing?"

"It fell off when I was struck by lightning," she replied quickly.

"That is odd, is it not?" He stared at her for a moment. "Word on the wing is you died after being struck by lightning."

"An obvious lie," she insisted, bobbing her head and clipping her beak.

"I will need to inform the others of your..." he paused. "Reappearance. They will be most interested to hear of your survival."

"What others? Who will you be informing?"

"Since you have not alerted your superiors regarding this matter, I will do so for you." He turned his head to the left and began to preen his feathers.

It was at this moment that she struck, leaping at him and sinking her talons into his head and exposed neck. He screeched and squawked as he attempted to extricate himself from her fierce grip, even as she pecked his eyes out. When the struggle was finally ended, she hopped from the lifeless Dakirin and shook her head furiously so that great drops of his blood splattered against the far wall. She found she was hungry and so began to feast. When she was finished, she dropped what was left of the carcass into the shadows far below her and resumed watching the tower.

# White Chapter Two: Morheim's Council

### The 14th of Lirinn, mid-afternoon

Elas-Tormas was panicked. The long-doubted rumors of war were proving to be all too real all too quickly. The military was in a state of advanced readiness, and when Paroch and the others approached the palace grounds, they were stopped by crossed pikes.

"What business have you in the palace?" a guard demanded to know.

"We have been instructed to attend King Morheim's council. I am Paroch, and this is Balatiere. We are from Lepnar, Haendorn from Mirion and Telliken from Anar," he introduced them all.

"And I am Fulcwin," he said as he jogged up. "Also from Lepnar. Sorry, I was delayed," he whispered to Paroch.

"Fulcwin is on my list," the guard replied after consulting an unrolled parchment, "but the rest of you are not listed."

"They are with me," Fulcwin insisted. "The messenger clearly stated that any others with me from Lepnar, Mirion and Anar were to attend as well. But you can keep them out here; I will let King Morheim know you have prevented their attendance." He placed his hand on the pikes and pushed against them to gain entrance.

"Hold on!" the guard commanded. "You will wait right there! All of you!" He whispered something to a soldier beside him, who took off running into the palace itself. Moments later, the messenger himself appeared in the doorway, wearing the same outfit but without his hat and shielding his eyes from the bright sunshine.

Fulcwin waved at him and then pointed to the others with him. "They will only let me through. I told them what you said," he hollered.

The messenger stalked over. "Let them through!" he commanded. "All of them."

Fulcwin smiled and shrugged at the guards as the pikes were lifted to allow them passage into the palace. As they climbed the stairs to the entrance, they could hear the messenger berating the guards.

"One of these days, you are going to get yourself in trouble," Paroch observed.

"Perhaps, but not today," Fulcwin smiled. "Let us get this over with."

Paroch shook his head and laughed.

"What did Kulanak say?" Balatiere asked.

"He was out on a mission," Fulcwin replied quietly.

"Then what took you so long?" Balatiere asked.

Fulcwin simply shook his head and smiled.

The five of them approached the double doors to the palace, where a dozen guards dressed in the king's livery were stationed. One of them stepped forward.

"If you will follow me," he said as he turned and led the way into the palace itself. "I will escort you to the meeting."

He led them up a wide marble staircase where alcoves in the wall were filled with relics of past days. A painting of a victory over a Kalantarn patrol and laying in front a notched sword, splintered shield and dented helm, or a painting of a ship fending off a great sea creature and in the front four rusting harpoons and several scales from the creature itself. At the top of the stairs were two half-pillars, one to either side. Atop the one to the left was a fearsome bear standing on his hind legs, mouth opened in mid-roar, and atop the pillar on the right, the figure of a woman in full armor, kneeling with an arrow nocked in her bow, taking aim. They stepped onto a plush carpet of the deepest royal blue, the edges of which were trimmed in gold. This carpet they followed through several wide halls, the first of which had its walls painted with a painting of what the land around Elas-Tormas looked like before the city was founded. The mural continued onto each wall so that it felt like you were standing in one spot and looking at an unbroken view all around you.

Another hall showed the starting and completion of many of the royal buildings, including the palace. They followed the carpet through several narrow hallways filled with portraits of royalty and nobility. When at last they neared the three sets of ornately carved wooden doors, the guard turned on his heels and, giving a slight bow, "The great hall. If you would, please enter and announce yourself so that you may be seated properly." Without waiting for a reply, he hurried back the way he had come.

Fulcwin pushed open the middle doors and walked in. "Fulcwin of Lepnar," he announced.

A young boy, not more than ten, bowed low, "Thank you, Fulcwin of Lepnar. How many are with you?"

"Paroch and Balatiere also from Lepnar, Telliken from Anar and Haendorn from Mirion."

The boy looked at him with eyes wide.

"Four," Fulcwin whispered.

"Thank you, sir, right this way, sirs," the boy said with a bow.

The room was ornately decorated, and the walls were wood-paneled to a height of four feet. Above the panels, there was another continuous mural of a market in Elas-Tormas approaching evening; the ceiling was painted to show the mid-summer sky at dusk. Upon closer examination, each wood panel was expertly carved to continue the mural scene into the wood, or perhaps the painting extended the scene up from each panel - so intricately interwoven was each scene that it was impossible to tell. The floor was comprised of wooden tiles, each two feet wide by two feet long. Most of the tiles consisted of wide bands of yellow wood, but on those tiles leading from the three doors were wide bands of grey wood, or perhaps it was blue. It was difficult to tell in the current lighting.

The young boy led them to an area near the king's table. He pointed to a series of empty chairs, stood at attention and began to speak loudly for all to hear, "Fulcwin of Lepnar," he began well enough, but he opened his mouth to announce the others with him and then quickly shut it again. With his face turning crimson, he looked to Fulcwin, his eyes pleading for help.

"Paroch and Balatiere also from Lepnar, Telliken from Anar and Haendorn from Mirion," Fulcwin obliged before sitting down at the table.

The boy hurried off under the scattered laughter directed at his discomfort.

The seven tables were slabs of white and blue marble, smooth and cool to the touch. Six of them were arranged side by side across the room while the king's table was perpendicular to them. Narrow runners of woven blue silk with silver threaded designs ran down the middle of six of the tables and hung halfway to the floor at either end. The runner on the king's table was of woven blue silk with golden threaded designs. Each seat had a golden plate and a goblet before it, and there were plenty of golden pitchers, some filled with water and others with an aromatic wine, big on flavor with only a hint of alcohol.

Paroch, standing to the right of Fulcwin, looked around before taking his seat. Every chair at the king's table was filled, as were most of the chairs at the other six tables. As other guests entered and announced themselves, the young boy scurried around to make sure every seat was filled. Their table was now full as well. Haendorn sat at the end closest to the king's table, then came Telliken, Fulcwin, himself and Balatiere. Most of the others at his table were engaged in separate conversations, occasionally laughing loudly but not paying attention to anyone else. Most were well-dressed in silks and furs, and few indeed were the fingers that did wear a ring of silver or gold. As Paroch sat down, an elderly man seated across from him smiled and raised his goblet. Paroch nodded in thanks.

When at last every table was filled, King Morheim stood from his seat, "My thanks to you all that are in attendance this day. We have much to discuss. But the mind is sharper if the belly is full." He took his seat once again.

An army of servants entered bearing trays of roasted nuts and breads and jams and honey. These were placed at every table, followed by gasps of delight as those in attendance began to eat. A short while late,r, trays of cheeses and meats, both cold and steaming, were brought forth. As the meal neared its conclusion, the servants appeared and whisked away the platters and plates and reappeared bearing platters of fresh fruits and tarts. Quick as a wink, a new plate was placed before each person and the golden pitchers were filled to the brim.

At this point, Morheim stood again. "That war is drawing near to this city is no surprise to any of you. The rumors have been heard since late Sivrellis and have only grown louder as each day passes. Elas-Tormas has the strength to defend herself…"

"Begging your pardon, Morheim," a lady interrupted as she stood. "You do *not* have sufficient strength to defend against what moves inexorably toward this place."

The voice seemed very familiar to Paroch, and he searched to see where she might be, but he could not find her.

"M'lady," Morheim smiled at her. "You will be permitted to speak in a moment. I would ask that you refrain from interrupting me."

She bowed and, sitting down, tried to hide her blushes with her fan.

"War is upon us, this much we know, but what are our options? This is why you have been called. Our agents have ceased reporting the goings-on to the east and north of us; we only have the word of refugees to rely on, and we are loathe to make decisions based solely on their tales. It has long been a tradition of meetings held in this hall that no lies be told under penalty of death. With that in mind, I would ask that Fulcwin please stand and address those of us assembled."

"Your Highness?" Fulcwin asked as he stood from his seat.

"A short while ago, you and Balatiere shared with me regarding certain events that have transpired in the east," he began.

"It was the twenty-seventh of Durnas, Your Highness," the man seated next to him stated.

"Relate the tale again if you please so that those in attendance can hear it as well," Morheim nodded at him.

"It has been many years ago that King Vindramion was victorious at Welryth over the Darklord. After the Darklord was imprisoned…."

"We know our own history," someone interrupted, and many others laughed.

"You will treat Fulcwin with respect," Morheim demanded, his brow furrowed.

"The Darklord has been released from his imprisonment," Fulcwin stated.

That statement caused an uproar in the room; many voices began clamoring all at once. Some said it was preposterous, others agreed that the timing could be right according to the prophecies, and still others demanded proof.

"He has returned, and he has set up his seat of power in the city of Nekoda."

"There was an Anari garrison there," someone stated.

"There was indeed," Telliken said as he stood. "We were on the causeway marching toward our positions in the Coastal Mountains when Mount Korem erupted, and most of my men were lost in the ensuing destruction. Only I am survived to bring news of the disaster. If you have questions regarding this, ask me now." The look of sadness on his face carried much weight.

There were no questions.

"After the Darklord was imprisoned, Vindramion commissioned a map of gold thread to be woven."

"The Empire Map?" someone asked.

"The same," Fulcwin continued. "And it was housed in the Tower of First Light in Kire along the east coast."

"Again, with the history lesson," several others closer to the back of the room complained.

"All very interesting, to be sure," another said with disdain, "However, we have a war upon our doorstep, and we need to know what we can do about it."

Fulcwin smiled politely and shared how the Empire Map had been stolen.

"Why does this concern us?" an aged man asked as he looked in his empty goblet.

"The Empire Map showed the location of many things, but it concerns us because it also showed the exact locations of each piece of the Dark Trium."

Many grumbles of disbelief were heard around the table.

"You may believe or not as you wish, but what we do know," here Fulcwin motioned to the others with him. "Is that the cauldron of Delgeth was taken from the Island of Clouds shortly after the Map was stolen."

"And exactly how is this known?" another asked.

"Another of our companions stayed behind at the Tower of Tergia; he alone escaped the destruction of the Davarine garrison there."

"Tower of Tergia? Is that the religious place for the worshippers of Ellonas?"

"It is," Fulcwin replied.

"Just great. Why was he not permitted to attend?" the aged man asked without looking up. His goblet had been refilled, and he was swirling the liquid before he took a sip.

"That was my doing," the messenger interrupted as he stood up. "I took it upon myself to limit those in attendance." He turned to Morheim and bowed low. "I can run and fetch Fulcwin's other companions if it is your desire."

Morheim smiled at him, "Thank you, that will not be necessary. We will hear Fulcwin's tale, and if we need further corroboration, we will send for them at that time."

The messenger bowed low again and resumed his seat.

"Shortly after the cauldron was recovered by the Darklord, the city of Kire was attacked, and the same day, we know that Thagorod was also attacked."

"Is anyone here able to corroborate that statement about Thagorod?" the old man asked again.

"We have two companions that survived and have told us the tale, but alas, they also have not accompanied us."

The messenger stood hastily, a concerned look upon his face, but Morheim waved for him to sit down again.

The old man sighed and crossed his arms over his chest.

"Now, I and my companion Balatiere here both survived from Kire." Balatiere stood up and waved to the room. "And here I will tell you that the Darklord has employed the services of a winged army."

"Winged army, like insects? Birds?"

"Like the Falkiri of old. The winged warriors from the tales you heard as a child."

No one responded, though many people were shaking their heads at him, and still others were slowly sipping from their goblets to hide their smiles.

"The Falkiri or Dakirin as they are now called have…,"

"Wait just a minute," the old man interrupted. "How on Kren do you know they changed their names? Wait, do not tell me. You have one of them as a loyal companion, but he stayed back at the tower as well." He laughed at his own joke, and many others did as well.

"We have fought with them many times now," Fulcwin explained. "And on every occasion, they have bragged about no longer being called Falkiri but Dakirin. I am certain if you are patient, you too will be able to ask one in the very near future."

The old man glared at him.

"I will also inform this assembly that the Staff of Abominations has been recovered by the Darklord, found in one of the nights of Thagorod."

"And how did you discern this?" another from the assembly asked, brows furrowed as he stared at Fulcwin. His eyes were dark, and his nose narrow and pointed, a beard of neatly trimmed black whiskers hugged his cheeks and chin.

"We were on our way to Thagorod to see if we could not find the staff and…"

"Claim it for yourselves," the same man finished Fulcinw's statement.

"Our sole intention was to prevent the staff from falling into the Darklord's hands," Fulcwin smiled graciously.

"How noble," he replied. "So we are to understand that your little band of adventurers is seeking to thwart the designs of the Darklord?" he began to laugh and shake his head.

"That is better than sitting behind your walls here doing nothing!" Balatiere shouted suddenly. "We have been entrusted with…" Here, Balatiere stopped as he searched for the right words. "A purpose."

"Yes, I am sure you have been," the man said evenly after a moment. "But for whom do you work? You lack the strength to force your way into *this* palace were you barred from entry, let alone entering a city besieged. And there are other things lost for ages," the man hinted. "Other things that could upset the balance of power." He nodded knowingly.

"Are you suggesting we are agents of the Darklord?" Balatiere asked angrily, hand straying to the hilt of his sword.

"Merely wondering is all," the man replied with a smile. "A just question of strangers in these dark times."

"The race is not always to the swift nor the battle to the strong," Fulcwin replied. "And we are no agents of the Darklord."

Fulcwin leaned down so Paroch could whisper to him.

"Do not mention me being the Herald or having the Kingsword."

"I will not," Fulcwin assured him, "Few people here are ready to hear that truth."

"Fulcwin, did you have anything else to add?" Morheim asked.

"Not at this time, Your Highness. Thank you." He took his seat, finished off his goblet of water, and quickly poured another drink.

"Lord Gedery of the Tav-Tar League," Morheim stated loudly. "If you please."

Paroch watched as a man stood up; his face appeared to have been recently burned, and the hair on his head was mostly missing, and what little remained was heavily singed. His eyebrows were missing, and his arms were heavily bandaged.

He cleared his throat several times and even took several drinks from his goblet before he was ready to speak.

"Thank you, Fulcwin, your tale has filled in much information for me. Please allow me to do the same for you."

Fulcwin stood and bowed in respect.

"I ruled the lands to the west of Tavanie," he began to speak, his voice rough and deep. "Veynohrad was my most beautiful city. We grew some of the finest grapes on the hills surrounding Veynohrad. My wife and five children…" he stopped to compose himself as a tear rolled down his cheek. "Allow me to continue. I had many smaller towns in my lands as well, and I was in the habit of visiting each town or village at least once every year and twice when I could manage it. That morning of the ninth of Durnas, I was secure in my keep near the western border of my lands, tucked between two hills and surrounded by dense forests. Just before noon, a single messenger arrived with news that a rebellion had taken hold in Tavanie and was sweeping across the countryside, along with rumors of a strange winged soldier of some kind. At this point, I allowed most of my guards to return to their homes and make what preparations they could to protect their families. Also, I sent the messenger back to Veynohrad to help escort my family to safety while I remained in the tower with four hundred of my most loyal soldiers. We barricaded the door, but the windows we left open. It was a bit after noon when we first noticed the black-feathered birds circling the tower and when several of them flew through an open window…" he stopped and shook his head at the memory. "I…" he sighed. "I am not certain how to describe what happened next, but the birds…plumes of green smoke appeared around each bird…then suddenly black-clad warriors were standing there."

Many voices began to speak; some expressed a great deal of doubt about what he reported, and others figured him to be mad.

"I know it sounds unbelievable, but I swear by Ellonas that it did happen that way. We did not wait to hear what they might have to say and attacked them immediately. We managed to kill three of them, but the fourth man jumped from the window, and suddenly, he was enveloped by green smoke, and a bird flew out of it."

"Dakirin," Fulcwin stated loudly for all to hear. "Without a doubt, you faced Dakirin."

"They made three additional assaults through open windows, which were all eventually defeated, but more and more of them continued showing up until the flock of them nearly blotted out the sun. There were so many gathered there." He paused again and took a long drink of the aromatic wine. He nodded in satisfaction, and after using his bandaged arm to wipe his mouth, he continued. "Then the nightmare truly began; they began to gather wood and pile it around the tower. Not just a few limbs and logs, mind you, but a pile of wood deeper than the door, and it spread out from the tower on every side. We had a few bowmen with us, and they made several attempts to disrupt the birds or, rather, Dakirin," he said with a nod to Fulcwin. "We managed to kill two of them, but there were literally thousands of them flying to the tower with wood in their talons and flying away again as soon as they had dropped their load atop the growing pile. We bolted every window closed and stationed guards in each room to ensure they remained so; then, I ordered for water to be poured on the wood nearest the door in hopes of keeping it from burning so readily. One hundred men, starting at the spring in the cellar and stretching up three flights of stairs to the three windows thirty feet above the door, began pouring the water as instructed. The first bucket was dunked in the spring, filled to the brim and handed to the next in line, who handed it to the next and the next all the way to the windows where the water was emptied onto the wood below and then the empty bucket was handed back the same way. We had thirty buckets, and though the men worked tirelessly, they were no match for the thousands of birds bringing their loads of wood. Towards evening, I had the men stop and ordered them to prepare to flee through the escape tunnel to safety. When most of the men had already slipped into the tunnel, I went back to an upper room to retrieve something most valuable to me. Once I had it in my possession, I happened to glance out of a crack in the shuttered window; the sky to the west was painted with red and purple hues. Something bright caught my eyes as it streaked past the window much like a firefly, then another bright flash followed by another. I crept to the window to peek out. The birds," he held up a hand. "Dakirin," he corrected himself. "Were circling the tower, and some of them carried lit torches, which were quickly dropped atop the wood. I turned and began to run as the roar," Here he stopped again to compose himself. "The roar of that inferno was terrible to hear. I heard wild screams, shouts of demented glee and evil laughter mixed in. The flames instantly wrapped the tower in unbearable heat, and every combustible thing within the tower began to smolder and smoke. I was initially knocked off of my feet, and I tumbled down quite a few stairs. As I tried to get my bearings, the heat grew intense, and my arms began to burn, as did the back of my shirt, pants and boots. I staggered down the stairs while the tapestries on the stairwell wall above me began to burn, and even as I closed the door to the cellar, flames were already licking the outside of that door. It was good that the others had already begun to escape, or most of us would easily have perished in that fire. Indeed, we hardly needed a torch to light our way; so intense was the fire following behind us that it lit our way through many twists and turns. Fortunately for us, when we reached the end of the tunnel an hour later, it remained unknown to the Dakirin, and we were able to emerge safely. I managed to climb a hill, and looking to the east, the tops of the flames could still be seen as they rose above my now-distant tower. Even as we made our way to Debir, the ever-present orange glow in the eastern sky behind us only faded with the rising of the sun. The people of Debir welcomed us with open arms, and we warned them of the doom behind us. Though they invited us to stay, I decided to continue to Anar in the west, and it is a good thing I did because the rebellion was not far behind. We hid during the day from the ever-present bands of Dakirin and moved as swiftly as possible at night. Eventually, we made it safely to Basgerone, sharing with them the madness that had befallen the Tav-Tar League. I will now let another continue this tale." He turned, bowed to Morheim and took his seat.

"Thank you, Lord Gedery, for your courage and leadership in a difficult time. Please know you are always welcome here in Elas-Tormas." Morheim replied graciously. "Now we shall hear from Anar. Lady Sarahin, queen of Anar." He announced with a smile.

Paroch could scarcely believe his ears, and he sat up a little higher in his chair to see if he could catch a glimpse of her.

"King Morheim, your generosity is well-known and much appreciated." She bowed her head to him and then turned to address the others assembled.

The hushed whispers ceased when she began to speak; so melodic was her voice, and so beautiful was she to look upon.

"Lord Gedery's warnings did not fall upon deaf ears. Anar marshaled her armies and moved to the east to defend the Glyden Pass. We waited for several days, and then word began to trickle in that we had suffered a disastrous defeat. The enemy was advancing on three separate fronts. Abintar was the first city to fall, followed quickly by Pastern and Fetlock. We exacted a heavy price from them, but their numbers proved too numerous for us to deal with. Then we found the western border held against us. It was not long before orders were given for the defending armies to fall back to positions in and around Basgerone and the port city of Loshad. My father ordered for a corridor between the two cities to be kept open at all costs to allow for the transporting of refugees to Loshad and the ships waiting to carry them to safety. Every day, we heard tales of the fighting in and around the corridor, and daily my father urged me to flee to safety. However, my mother could not entertain a journey so perilous as she was desperately sick, and since I was caring for her, I refused to leave her bedside." She paused and dabbed at her eyes with a silk kerchief, then managed a brief smile before continuing. "The morning after she passed away, my father had her buried in the Royal Cemetery. I spent the rest of that day until evening seated beside her grave. A coronation was held after sunset, and I had bestowed upon me the title of Queen of Anar, but there was not much joy nor cause for celebration. The following day, we received word that the corridor was less than a mile wide, and both sides were being pressed mightily. At my father's insistence and against my own wishes, I agreed to undertake the perilous journey to Loshad, where I promised my father I would await his arrival." Sarahin stopped for a moment, and here it was that her eyes met Paroch's again for the first time since their whispered goodbyes outside Elas-Tormas. She smiled, but there was great sadness in her eyes. "I left with a small caravan of five coaches and a heavy escort of over two thousand lancers. The first day out of the capital was like any other; the weather was wonderful, but the breeze carried with it a hint of smoke that left a tang in the mouth. The day after, we passed the first of many ruined caravans, and the smell of death hung thick about the road we were on. There were several skirmishes as the Dakirin attacked, but each time, the lancers were able to drive them off without too much trouble. On our third day, halfway between both cities, we were assailed first from the east. An attack by several thousand soldiers of the Tav-Tar was repulsed with minimal losses. Immediately after, we were assailed from the west. Four thousand soldiers, along with several thousand Dakirin, attacked. In the ensuing chaos, my coach and two others managed to flee to the south, followed by a thin escort of only one hundred lancers. Later that evening, less than a thousand lancers caught up with us, a costly victory. We encountered little in the way of resistance on the fourth day and, thankfully, were able to reach Loshad on the fifth day without further incident. Word soon came that the corridor had finally been breached by the enemy, and despite several attempts to re-open it, there would be no farther caravans coming from the north. I waited for three days to see what might become of my father, and in those three days, I met and befriended Lord Gedery and those with him. When we heard that Basgerone had fallen, we boarded one of the last ships in the harbor and made good our escape in the dead of night. Arriving here just a few days ago." She sighed again. "So you see, though I am a Queen, I no longer have a country to return to."

"Anar has ever been strong and able to defend herself," someone stated.

"What was true of prior conflicts does not matter in this current one. While it is true that our lancers are highly prized or feared on the battlefield depending upon which side you are on, the addition of the Dakirin changes everything. The Dakirin were more mobile and not easily followed; our defensive walls meant nothing to them."

"On behalf of Elas-Tormas," Morheim began, "We are saddened with you at the loss of your parents, and we will do what we can to restore you to your proper place as Queen of Anar."

Sarahin could only nod as she dabbed at her eyes again.

"We shall turn back the evil tide; our walls are strong," several voices boasted.

"Do you not yet understand?" Sarahin asked loudly. "Dakirin have no need for battering rams and scaling ladders or lengthy sieges; whenever they desire, the Dakirin simply land atop a wall or tower, gain control and move on. Gates are opened for the remainder of the army waiting at a safe distance."

The import of her words began to have its effect on those assembled.

"Surely there is something that can be done?" many began to ask.

"Yes, let us triple the wall guard," some suggested.

Sarahin began to laugh, a lovely laugh but filled with sadness and despair, "Still, you fail to comprehend the situation. They will fly over your walls and take what is on the other side."

"Then what shall we do?" many asked. "All is lost!"

"We shall fight with courage like we always do," a few of the older guests suggested.

"And die with honor?" others laughed. "No, rather let us flee and live."

Morheim watched the room with keen interest as three distinct groups formed from those gathered, the largest of which declared that since all indeed seemed lost, surrender was the best course; those opposed to that course were themselves divided into two groups: those that wanted to flee to the west and those who wanted to stand and fight. Those wanting to fight were by far the smallest group, and every time one of them suggested a way in which they might successfully defend Elas-Tormas, they were shouted down.

It was at this point that Fulcwin stood up and raised his voice for all to hear, "Has courage so faded amongst you that you would no longer strive against the approaching evil? Where is the honor required to set things right? Have you not heard what has been said? Do you not realize that the Darklord has been released, and he is exacting his vengeance upon those very peoples that helped imprison him those many years ago?"

"How dare you insult us?" many of the guests clamored. "We have courage!"

"And honor!" others added.

"If my words sting, let them sting as the words of a friend and ally. I am not calling you out; I am calling on you to fulfill your purpose," Fulcwin explained. "To stand firm against the rising tide!"

"Thank you for those stirring words," Morheim said with a nod.

"I did not imprison him," someone stated indignantly.

"Then you are a fool," Fulcwin charged. "In the eyes of the Darklord, if you are of Lepnarion descent, you are just as guilty as the one who placed the chains around him."

"I am no fool," the man retorted. "I simply seek to live."

"And what kind of life will you have in servitude to the darkness?" Paroch asked as he stood up.

The room grew quieter at his question, but the scowls and furrowed brows increased.

"I am Paroch of Cul-Amaron. Though it is true that we face a great darkness, it is also true that Ellonas is a light greater than any darkness."

At the mention of that name, many in the room burst into derisive laughter while others shouted angrily for him to sit down and remain quiet.

"He is no longer concerned with the affairs of men," one stated confidently.

"Just because one chooses to close his eyes to what is true does not suddenly make it false," Paroch replied.

"So now we are blind?" another asked, anger rising in his voice.

"You are here with Fulcwin? Staying in the Tower of Tergia, is it?" the old man asked with disdain as he scratched furiously at the webbing between his thumb and finger.

"Yes, and I have entered the games and emerged victorious," Paroch replied.

The old man shook his head, "What further business do you have here, Paroch of Cul-Amaron? You have subjected yourself to the games; now leave us. We will hear no more from you."

It was at this point that Balatiere stood and raised his voice in anger. "You have no idea who you are talking to. Paroch is the Herald of Light prophesied of old, and he now wields Abion the Kingsword."

Instantly, the room became deathly silent.

"Balatiere!" Paroch hissed as he glared at him.

All eyes in the room fixed their gaze upon Paroch.

"That is impossible," many began to laugh. "That sword was lost many years ago."

"As Ellonas lives, he has retrieved the sword lost to history," Balatiere continued.

"Lies in this chamber are punishable by death," someone yelled. "Yes," others agreed. "Morheim, lies must be punished. Fulcwin and all of those with him should pay for the lies they are telling!" the people began to grow angry.

Finally, Morheim stood and raised his arms to silence the room. When, at last, every voice was silent, he began to speak. "Most everything shared today is without a doubt true. However, being the prophesied Herald and the claim of wielding Abion, the Kingsword must be proven, or those lies must be repaid with your death, Balatiere."

Balatiere looked to Paroch and held forth his piece of the glowing azure cloth.

"My token," he explained. "That reveals me as a true member of the mantle sworn to protect the Herald of Light. We were numbered twelve, but alas, one of us was lost near Talhaven as we battled the forces of darkness."

"A glowing piece of cloth reveals nothing," the old man argued, and he placed his hands flat upon the table.

Telliken stood and showed his piece of the cloth, followed by Fulcwin and Haendorn.

"I have heard ancient prophecies that foretell of a Herald and a mantle of protection," Morheim said slowly. "Paroch, are you truly that Herald?"

"I am, and I have retrieved Abion," Paroch answered. He held the Kingsword aloft for all to see.

The room remained silent for many moments, and then whispered questions began to be heard.

"Is that really Abion?"

"What is it supposed to look like?"

"How do we know?"

"Is he now the king of Lepnar?"

Morheim spoke again, "This news is strange to my ears. The Darklord released according to prophecy, and now the Herald of Light revealed wielding Abion." His eyes lingered ever so slightly on the Kingsword.

"It should come as no surprise that the prophecies of Ellonas are fulfilled exactly as foretold," Paroch stated.

Morheim nodded for a moment, "I have much to contemplate. Advisors, to my throne room. The rest of you may stay or leave as you will. Paroch, do not leave Elas-Tormas. I will speak with you again." As Morheim turned and walked through the double doors behind his chair, ten other men scattered around the room began moving to follow him.

As soon as the doors closed behind them, the room erupted in voices; most were angry, and their anger seemed directed at Fulcwin and Paroch and the others with them. Suddenly, a scream was heard, and a man seated close to Paroch clutched at his neck, gasping for breath before suddenly collapsing face-first onto the table.

As Balatiere moved to assist the man seated next to him, he noticed a small black spider scurrying down the man's arm before dropping to the floor and disappearing in the shadows under the table.

"Did you see that?" he asked as he stomped his foot a few times under the table and quickly stepped back. He searched for a moment under the table, then returned to the stricken man.

"See what?" the old man asked as he bent down to reach under the table. When he finally stood up, he stared at Paroch, and when Paroch met his gaze, a slight smile appeared on the old man's face. He nodded.

"He is dead!" Balatiere announced after feeling for a pulse and finding none.

"What did you do to him?" someone asked Balatiere.

"I assure you I have done nothing to cause his death," Balatiere replied coolly. Nevertheless, his hand strayed toward the hilt of his sword.

"We need to leave now," Fulcwin stated quietly but forcefully.

There were many eyes staring at them and not many friendly. With hands on their hilts, the five of them moved to and through the wooden doors, and following the blue carpet, they retraced their steps to the top of the staircase. After descending the steps, they emerged from the palace, quickly blending in with the evening shadows now covering the streets.

# Black Chapter Two: Forging The Torque

## The 14th of Lirinn, late evening

Tilden took a deep breath before he entered the room where the others were waiting for him.

"Congratulations again on your swift conquest of Anar," Pentar said, and he began to clap. The others, four Dakirin, Burxon, Erelis, Kotkas and Vontar and four humans, Aracelis, Hember, Elisad and Tarbosar, clapped as well.

Tilden laughed, "I almost do not believe it myself, but Anar has officially fallen as of early this morning. Four days ago, we finally managed to collapse the corridor between Basgerone and Loshad; after that, the capital fell easily enough and Loshad the very next day. So tonight, we celebrate our victory of this conquered people."

Everyone present cheered and raised their mugs, with the exception of Pentar.

"Is there a problem?" Tilden asked.

"Not at all. I have just come from my own personal meeting with Mazzaroth and am not inclined to drink anymore this evening," Pentar replied. "But do not let me stop you."

Tilden nodded and raised his mug again. "To our victory over Anar and our coming victory over Elas-Tormas."

Everyone raised their mugs in agreement, even Pentar, and they all drank except for Pentar.

"We will be moving into position to attack Elas-Tormas this very evening after we leave this meeting," Tilden explained. "I know your men are weary, but there is no time to rest, not while Elas-Tormas remains free."

"We were hoping for a week or so to rest and regain our strength," Hember replied. "We have many wounded that…"

"Hember," Tilden interrupted, "You will have your men marching to the Arazor and the rafts awaiting you there on the shore after you leave this meeting. Any of your men so wounded that they cannot or will not march will be dealt with summarily."

Hember glared at him, and he balled his hands into tight fists.

Tilden laughed, "Need I remind you that Mazzaroth has given me my orders, and I am simply relaying them to you. If you have a problem with them, please take it up with Mazzaroth yourself."

"I understand," Hember sighed, and he relaxed his fists. "It is just that my men have fought hard, and they need a rest."

"So have all of us," Tarbosar added. "If I understand correctly, we have one last push to take Elas-Tormas, and then we will have our rest. Is that right?" He looked to Tilden.

"Of course," Tilden replied. "Seven more days is all we need. Then, when Elas-Tormas is in our hands, you shall have your rest and your reward."

"Seven days to take Elas-Tormas?" Elisad said with a laugh. "Are you aware of just how large of a city it is?"

"We are aware," Pentar spoke up. "No need to fear. Dakirin will do the hard and perilous work; the rest of you can clean up after we are finished."

"We are not afraid!" Tarbosar proclaimed.

Aracelis began to laugh, "For a moment, I thought Fintar was here." He shook his head. "He held similar views, and it cost him quite dearly at Kire."

"More than you know," Pentar replied.

"Let me say again, we Dakirin are not questioning your fighting ability or even your will to fight," Tilden began. "The question becomes, are you willing to give all to Mazzaroth or not? If you are willing, then we have no problem, but if you are not, then we have other things to discuss."

"We Dakirin are tired as well," Erelis said as he patted Hember on the shoulder. "We have fought well together, come let us finish what we have started."

"I will have my men marching to the ferries within the hour," Hember said with a nod. He shook hands with Erelis.

"Thank you, Hember. Any wounded that will not be healed up enough in the next week to meaningfully contribute will be moved to Cavalo and cared for in the hospital there," Tilden assured him.

"I will have my men ready as well," Tarbosar agreed.

"As will I," Elisad added.

"Aracelis?" Tilden asked.

"No concerns here. Ready to cross the Arazor and advance upon the outer wall at a moment's notice."

"As of tomorrow, there are to be no Dakirin flying anywhere within eyesight of the outer wall. Is that understood?" Tilden asked.

The other Dakirin were perplexed, but they all eventually nodded.

"There are twenty gates in the outer wall. You will fix your lines in front of each gate, eight thousand men arranged in four lines of two thousand men each. Make certain your lines are visible but outside the range of Lepnarion trebuchets. Hember, you will focus on the four eastern gates. Erelis, you and your Dakirin will remain on the western bank of the Arazor until it is time to attack. Tarbosar, you will do the same thing with the next five gates to the north. The goal is to have eight thousand men facing each gate of the outer wall," He let the import of his words sink in. "The human soldier will be seen by the enemy but not Dakirin; you will hold yourselves out of sight until it is time. Now, Elisad, you will move your men to be in front of the main northern gate, and Aracelis, your men will be marching past that to the western gates. Pentar, if I understand correctly, you and Kinjal are less than a day's march from the main northern gate."

"You are correct," Pentar replied with a yawn.

"Kinjal will need to march his men to the west and south. To be in position for the three gates he is responsible for."

"You are aware that he only has twelve thousand men under his command," Pentar informed him.

"Tell him to defend the gates with four thousand men apiece; I will make certain Elisad and Aracelis each send him six thousand more," Tilden said after a moment's thought.

"I will relay that message to him."

"Any questions?" Tilden asked the rest of those gathered.

"Our lines will be dangerously extended with no reserve to speak of," Hember pointed out. "With our backs to the Arazor, we will be vulnerable to attack."

"And to the north of the outer wall is open country; a successful charge by the Azure Legion might well collapse the entire effort," Elisad surmised.

"It is possible that the Lepnarions may attempt a few attacks on our lines, but I suspect that once they see we have no siege equipment, they will be content to stay behind their walls and prepare to defend against our impending attack," Tilden argued.

"Marching to a destination takes a bit longer than flying," Aracelis pointed out. "When are you planning the attack?"

"The attack will commence when the storm of darkness rolls over the outer wall," Tilden replied. "When the edge of the storm passes over the front of your lines, your soldiers are to begin blowing any horns, beating any drums and shouting. This noise must be kept up until the edge of the storm reaches the outer wall itself; then and only then shall the Dakirin transform and attack the walls."

"Storm of darkness?" Kotkas asked.

"A storm of great power Mazzaroth has created," Tilden shrugged. "I have no idea what it is really, just that we will know when it arrives."

"Do we know when this storm is supposed to be here?" Pentar asked with sudden interest.

"I have no idea," Tilden replied. "Just make certain you are ready."

"What if Kinjal's men are not in position when the storm reaches us?" Pentar asked.

"They must be made to march faster," Tilden growled. "However, I suppose you and your Dakirin could fly there first and set the line just to be on the safe side."

"And what about those of us humans?" Tarbosar wanted to know. "We have no siege equipment, no battering rams to force the gates, not even ladders to scale the walls."

"There will be no need for a lengthy siege. Dakirin will open the gates, and you will simply march in."

"And what then?" Elisad questioned. "If I remember correctly, it is a three-day walk to Elas-Tormas itself."

"You will advance to within bowshot of the walls of Elas-Tormas and await the Dakirin. Once they have cleared the walls and opened the gates, you will advance again."

"Are we expecting any resistance once we clear the outer walls?" Kotkas asked.

"These are Lepnarions," Aracelis replied. "There will most definitely be resistance."

The meeting was interrupted when a late meal was brought in to them. In front of each in attendance was placed a half loaf of bread, a slab of cold meat and a bowl of cold soup.

"I hear this soup is an Anari luxury," Tilden proclaimed as he lifted a spoonful from his bowl and inspected it closely.

"You first," Hember laughed.

Tilden smiled back and popped the spoonful into his mouth. "Not bad," he said after a moment, "Not bad at all."

They engaged in small talk as they ate their meal, bragging about exploits, real and imagined. They shared tactics for combating horsed riders and tactics for facing foot soldiers, and they both marveled at each other, for the Dakirin tactics were foreign to the men and vice versa. It was not long before the Dakirin and humans were talking about how to incorporate the best strengths of each into one cohesive attack.

As the night wore on, Pentar yawned once more and then stood. "Tilden, I shall relay the orders to Kinjal." He nodded once, then walked from the room.

Hember sighed and finished his mug before standing, "I need to get back to my men and get them moving. Erelis, would you mind flying on ahead and relaying the orders for me so we can get a foothold sooner?"

"I will do just that. In fact, the rest of you should do the same," he advised the Dakirin. "This way, our human allies can get into position quicker."

This was readily agreed to, and as the meeting began to break up, Tilden wished them well even as he motioned for Aracelis to stay behind.

"Something amiss?" Aracelis asked.

"No, nothing at all. I simply wanted to share two additional pieces of information with you before you leave."

"Go ahead."

"First, Tigernas have begun cleansing Anar as of this evening. Did you have any men that might want to volunteer to help the Tigernas in their grisly task?"

"I will think on that," Aracelis said slowly. "If I do, where shall I send them?" he asked.

"Send them to me here."

"I will do just that. See you in Elas-Tormas," he said as he turned to leave.

"And Aracelis, one more thing, a contingent of Anari malcontents has been raised. They have been armed and given some of the best horses left in Anar."

"Well, I suppose I am not surprised," Aracelis said after a moment of thought. "War often brings out the best in some men and the worst in others."

"Strange that you should put it that way," Tilden acknowledged. "What do you mean?"

"Only that some men will fight for a cause no matter the cost while their neighbors will fight against the same cause no matter the cost," Aracelis explained.

"Which is the best and which would be the worst?" Tilden wanted to know.

"I suppose that depends entirely upon which side is ultimately victorious," Aracelis laughed.

"Regardless, I have assigned them to your command," Tilden said.

"Really, how many are they, and who are they commanded by?"

"There are one thousand of them, and they cannot wait to tear down the walls of Elas-Tormas," Tilden laughed.

"Should I be concerned with their loyalty?" Aracelis asked.

"They have been given a poison that even now courses through their veins. Most of them will not live beyond the week," Tilden promised. "And they know it."

"I am familiar with this poison. Is there an antidote?" Aracelis asked.

"If they perform well in battle, they will be given the antidote."

"Their leader?"

"I believe you have met before," Tilden laughed. "At least that is what he tells me. He is a Lepnarion, named Rakosa."

Aracelis sighed. "I wondered what had become of him. Where did you find him?"

"Skulking in the Tav-Tar trying to make his way west." Tilden laughed. "I am not sure why those who found him did not kill him, but apparently, he was such a pitiable sight, and he swore he knew you and that you would vouch for him."

"I cannot vouch for him other than to say he is a traitor to his people and very dangerous to us," Aracelis replied. "He remains loyal to no one but himself."

"Be that as it may, he has been given command of the wretches from Anar. Use them however you will," Tilden replied as he turned to leave.

Aracelis looked into the evening sky at the half-moon peeking out from between ragged clouds as they drifted by.

"What are you up to, Rakosa?" he asked aloud. "What are you up to?"

# White Chapter Three: Whispers At The Tergian Tower

## The 14th of Lirinn, late evening

Paroch and the others hurried from the palace through the streets of Elas-Tormas.

"That was not wise, Balatiere," Haendorn stated. "Even if war were not looming on the horizon,, that news you shared would be hard for many to accept."

Balatiere sighed heavily.

"As they say, the die is cast," Fulcwin said. "And word of what was said in that meeting will travel fast."

"My apologies," Balatiere said for the fifth time. "Look, I was incensed at their treatment of Paroch and us. I simply misspoke."

"You spoke hastily and out of anger," Fulcwin corrected.

"So, I have endangered everything now?" Balatiere asked, rising anger evident in his voice.

"Perhaps not," Paroch said calmly

"What does that mean?" Balatiere asked.

"It means that..." he hesitated as a hooded figure drew near and then passed by without paying them any notice. "Are we being followed?" Paroch asked suddenly.

"Not that I can tell," Telliken replied. "But the shadows are deepening on the streets, and they are still quite crowded, so I cannot be certain."

"What were you going to say?" Balatiere pressed.

"I will wait until we see Arvendal," Paroch answered.

They passed through the garden district and soon were at the tower door. As soon as they opened the door, they heard the sounds of fighting.

"Something is wrong," Paroch said, and he attempted to enter the tower, but Balatiere held him back.

"I may have made one mistake this evening, but I will not make another," he said as he unsheathed his sword. "I will go first." He entered cautiously, followed by the others.

"It may only be training," Telliken suggested.

"It does not sound like training," Paroch replied.

They hurried toward the sounds and soon found everyone gathered in the main hall.

"What is happening here?" Balatiere asked as he ran up.

"These two started fighting," Kourakin explained.

"What set them off?" Paroch asked.

"They are both accusing each other," Elrynn replied as he gripped the hilt of his sword. "They have been at this for ten minutes already."

"Draxin is an agent of Mazzaroth," Galortin asserted as he attacked. "And I am going to kill him so he is no longer a threat to the mantle or the Herald."

Draxin laughed and easily parried the strike. "But it is you who are the assassin. Who have you been sent to kill? Is it me or another of the mantle? Perhaps the Herald himself?"

"Perhaps it is you," Galortin laughed, and he swung his blade three times; each time, Draxin parried and stepped away. "I should have killed you the moment I discovered you were against us."

"And when exactly was that?" Draxin asked.

"I figured it out on our return trip from Talhaven. It was that Dakirin that was trying desperately to communicate with you," Galortin stated proudly. "Two nights in a row as I was on watch, a Dakirin landed just outside the ring of firelight. They must have thought I was you because I was wearing a hood, and you always wear a hood."

"Then why are you just now sharing this information with us?" Paroch asked.

"I had to be certain, and I was not until this evening when he attacked *me*!"

"Draxin, can you explain this accusation?" Paroch demanded.

"Galortin, tell us why your piece of the mantle is a slightly different hue than ours?" Draxin asked as he side-stepped around the circle. He made certain Galortin was as far away from Paroch as possible.

"A good agent always turns aside the question and points blame elsewhere," Galortin said as he attacked again. Their swords clanged together, and both men stepped apart for a moment. Galortin moved to ensure there were no others behind him.

"Is that not exactly what you are doing right now?" Draxin asked. He lunged forward, but Galortin parried.

"Then we are both agents?" Galortin asked. "My brothers, come strike down the enemy before you," he urged the others.

"I am an agent of Ellonas, to be sure," Draxin asserted. "Do not strike your brother in the back. Stand with me against Galortin," he called over his shoulder.

"Both of you stop!" Paroch commanded.

Draxin backed away from Galortin but did not lower his guard.

Galortin stared at Paroch for a moment before launching himself toward Draxin again. "You cannot simply accuse me of this and walk away!" he yelled. "You have stained my honor."

"Your honor?" Draxin shook his head. "You have no honor." He parried Galortin's strike and counter-attacked quickly, catching him in the side.

Galortin gasped and staggered back. Without taking his eyes off of Draxin, he reached for the wound and felt around. It was bleeding profusely; Galortin began to breathe heavily, gasping every so often.

"You would let a Dakirin simply kill me? Without coming to my aid?" he asked as he glanced at the others of the mantle gathered in the room.

Many of the mantle had their swords drawn, but they did not move to intervene.

Paroch began walking towards Draxin and Galortin. "My brothers, why do you fight? Our enemy draws near to this fair city, and you bring blackness into this tower. In the name of Ellonas, I command you to stop this at once." He took one more step towards them.

Galortin glanced from Paroch to Draxin and back again; he licked his lips but did not lower his blade.

"Beware, Paroch," Draxin warned. "He is sent to kill you." Draxin lowered his blade just a bit but stepped toward Galortin.

"Draxin, how do you know this to be true?" Gehm asked. "What proof do you offer?"

"I have received a warning," Draxin stated confidently.

"He is found out," Galortin called. "His evil plot is unraveling, and in desperation, he blames me."

"What proof do you offer, Galortin?" Perin asked.

"My blood that he has spilled upon this very floor," Galortin asserted. He took a step away from Draxin and toward Paroch. "Strike him down while he is focused upon me and before he can slay the Herald."

"Both of you," Paroch began. "Swore an oath to protect the Herald. Put down your swords, and let us talk plainly."

"If Draxin will, then so will I," Galortin asserted, and he began to lower his blade.

Paroch looked to Draxin, "Will you also lower your blade so we may talk?"

"There can be no talk with him," Draxin asserted.

"You see," Galortin complained. "He is determined to kill me, and I have done nothing to warrant this."

"You cannot escape your guilt, Galortin," Draxin stated.

"Will no one help me?" Galortin pleaded.

"Draxin will not attack you," Paroch said, and he took one more step toward Galortin. "Put up your sword."

Galortin looked to the others of the mantle, but none of them moved to help him. He glanced behind, but there was no way of escape. He looked from Paroch to Draxin, then suddenly lunged, knocking Paroch to the floor. He dropped his sword and swiftly drew a dagger as he knelt beside him. In an instant, the blade was upon Paroch's exposed neck, pressing against his skin.

"You have been the fool, Paroch, Herald of Light," Galortin whispered. His eyes were wide with madness. "Though I will not live to see tomorrow, I will die knowing you also are dead, and with your death, the prophecy dies with you."

Paroch did not resist; he only smiled at him. "It does not have to be this way, my brother."

Galortin's hand began to tremble. "Do not call me brother!"

As Galortin hesitated, Draxin leaped forward, stabbing him in the side of his chest and driving the blade in deep.

Galortin's dagger fell from his shaking hands as he crumpled to the floor. "A curse on you, Draxin," he managed. As blood pumped from his chest, his eyes closed, and his breathing became shallow.

Paroch knelt beside him and held his head in his hands. "My brother, what can I do?" he asked.

Galortin's eyes fluttered open, and after a moment, he was able to focus. His attempt at laughter quickly turned into a coughing and gasping for breath, "Do not…call me…brother," he finally uttered.

"But why?" Paroch asked, "You have a token of calling just like the others. Do you not?"

Galortin shook his head, and he opened his mouth to clarify, but he found it difficult to speak.

"I have seen it," Paroch insisted.

Galortin fumbled furiously with the pouch at his belt and finally pulled out the glowing blue cloth with his gloved right hand.

"Yes, I see the token," Paroch said.

"Re...move...the...glove...from...my...left...hand," he managed as he held his shaking left hand up.

Paroch grabbed his hand and gently began to remove the tight glove; when it was finally off, Galortin clutched the cloth in his left hand, and instantly, the glow faded.

"What does this mean?" Paroch asked as he looked from the cloth to Galortin.

"It means he is an imposter," Draxin nodded.

"But how? Why?" Paroch wanted to know.

Galortin clutched at the black glove covering his right hand. He spit blood upon it and rubbed furiously until, after a great effort, he managed to reveal a portion of the spider web tattoo on his right hand.

"The weaver's guild," Paroch whispered, and he sat back.

"Yes," Galortin finally said.

"But how did the cloth glow in your right hand?" Paroch asked.

"A...trick...of...the...Darklord," was all he could muster.

"The Darklord sent you to murder Paroch," Draxin said. "You meant to finish him off at Talhaven," he added.

Galortin nodded in agreement.

"Why didn't you?" Draxin asked.

"Change of heart?" He tried to laugh but coughed up blood instead. "A worthy opponent, a worthy companion," he uttered. He managed a half-salute before he closed his eyes and breathed his last.

Paroch bowed his head, then suddenly he looked to Draxin with suspicion, "Are you also an agent of the Darklord? Are any of them?"

"As Ellonas lives, I am not, and I doubt any of them are either," Draxin replied with a nod to the other members of the mantle.

Paroch bowed his head again, and after a few moments, he looked up at Draxin, "Forgive me," he whispered. "And thank you for protecting me."

"I swore an oath," Draxin replied and extended his hand to help him to his feet. "What shall we do with him?" he asked with a nod to Galortin's lifeless body.

"There are many tombs below us," Arvendal stated. "We can find a suitable resting place for him down there."

"Can anyone explain what is going on?" Balatiere asked.

Arvendal nodded, "I believe I can, but let us first tend to the fallen. Then we shall discuss what has happened."

Soon thereafter, Arvendal opened the door to the tombs, and a cold and damp breeze blew forth. He held a lit torch to an unlit torch in a wall sconce, and as soon as it sputtered to light, he pushed his hand toward the darkness and one by one, the torches farther down the hall sprang to light.

"How long has it been since you were down here?" Elrynn asked as he brushed away a thick cobweb.

"It has been many years now since someone died in this tower," Arvendal replied.

The tombs looked much like the hall of testing above, a narrow hallway with offset doors to either side.

"Which door?" Kourakin asked as he, Telliken and Gehm struggled to carry Galortin's body.

"You will know," Arvendal replied over his shoulder as he walked slowly, with purpose, deeper into the tombs. "His name shall appear over the door where he is to be laid to rest."

"But why should he have a resting place in this tower if he were not truly a member of the mantle?" Haendorn asked.

"His piece of the cloth will glow in no other's hand," Arvendal said. "He held a token of calling, and therefore, he was a part of the mantle, even though he tried to kill Paroch."

They followed Arvendal deep under the tower until finally, the name 'Galortin' shone brightly above an ancient wooden door. Arvendal opened the door and entered the small room.

"Here, we shall lay him to rest. May Ellonas have mercy upon him." Arvendal intoned, and after each member had taken a last look at Galortin, he closed the door behind him. "Paroch, Herald of Light, lead the way from these tombs." Arvendal brought up the rear of the procession, and as he passed each lit torch, it was extinguished with a wave of his hand.

Arvendal entered the meeting room, the same room in which Paroch had been revealed as the Herald just over a month prior, the same room that had just seen Galortin slain. There was no blood evidence to be seen anywhere, as if no blood had been spilled.

"What is going on?" Elrynn asked what the others wanted to know.

"A just question. Before I answer, however, I would ask what transpired this evening with Morheim?" Arvendal demanded.

"What could that possibly have to do with what happened here this evening?" Haendorn asked.

"Perhaps nothing," Arvendal replied. "But perhaps everything."

Nodding, Fulcwin related what he had shared and the reaction from those in attendance. Then he shared Lord Gedery's and Queen Sarahin's tales. "It would seem that a majority of the people in attendance were either for fleeing or surrendering without a fight. Only a small minority voiced a desire to resist."

"Which is why I finally spoke up," Balatiere interrupted. "I let them know that Paroch was the Herald as prophesied of old and that he was now wielding Abion, the Kingsword."

At this news, Arvendal covered his eyes with his hand and shook his head. "Balatiere, you have increased the peril under which the Herald and mantle operate."

"I have apologized," Balatiere admitted. "And I wish that I could take back my words."

"Alas, that can never be," Arvendal continued. "The blow, once struck, cannot be un-struck. Still, all is not lost, for we know Ellonas controls all and even your impetuousness may yet serve to further the goals of the Herald." He paused for a moment and looked at each in turn before continuing. "Before Astarlion died, he shared with me what happened with Pemogen on the way to Cymbee. He had a hunch but no real proof. At last, I believe I know what happened. Galortin's right hand was always gloved, yet it was not a glove of leather. Indeed, when his own blood came in contact with it, the glove began to disappear." He paused for a moment.

"What does that even mean?" Reesal asked.

"The Darklord perverts that which is holy and pure for his own evil purposes. The cloth bestowed on Pemogen was not with his body after the battle at Cymbee, correct?"

Both Gehm and Reesal agreed that it was missing.

"Somehow, that cloth and some of Pemogen's blood were brought to the Darklord, and he performed a ritual of great evil in using Pemogen's own blood to form a bloodglove on Galortin's right hand."

"That must have been why the hue of his cloth was not the same as all of ours," Draxin pointed out.

The others began to nod in understanding.

"Before today, I never saw him hold the cloth in his left hand, only his right," Perin said.

"It was rare for him to even bring his cloth out when others had their cloth glowing," Haendorn added.

"He had an opportunity to strike me down when we were all in Talhaven," Paroch said aloud as he remembered back. "I can still see the look of madness in his eyes."

"I wonder why he did not follow through," Kourakin asked.

"We will never truly know the reason," Arvendal said. "But we can rejoice in the fact that he did not follow through. Now, that brings me to some other things that were shared this evening. Balatiere...."

"I know, I know, I need to learn to keep my mouth shut," Balatiere groaned.

Arvendal laughed, as did many of the others. "We will not argue with you on that statement, my friend. However, I was referring to the old man seated across from you at your table this evening."

"Him?" Balatiere asked. "What about him?"

"You mentioned you saw him scratching between the thumb and finger of one of his hands?" Arvendal clarified.

"Yes," Balatiere said after a moment's reflection.

"Then the man seated next to you let out a scream, clutched at his neck and then died?"

Balatiere nodded in agreement.

"You also mentioned that you saw a small black spider on the man's arm right after he clutched at his neck and that the spider dropped to the floor under the table," Arvendal continued.

"Yes, I tried to kill it with my boot. Don't know if I was successful or not," Balatiere replied with just a hint of annoyance in his voice. "And you are simply repeating what I have already said."

"I am simply making certain I have the information correct," Arvendal clarified. "Before I say the following. Given what has happened here this evening with Galortin and Balatiere's words, that old man was also a member of the weaver's guild."

"How can you make that assertion?" Perin asked. "Based solely on what Balatiere has said and the apparent fact that Galortin was a member of this guild of weavers."

"The way in which the old man at their table was behaving, and the spider Balatiere saw, and the sudden death of the one bitten in the neck would be other reasons I make the assertion," Arvendal added.

"What does scratching at his hand have to do with anything?" Gehm asked. He scratched his arm for a moment.

"I have heard that sometimes what appears to be a spider tattoo is not really a tattoo," Arvendal hinted.

"You mean a real spider, not a tattoo?" Kourakin asked as he shivered.

"A gravespider, to be exact," Arvendal stated. "Despite their tiny size, their venom is deadly, as you witnessed this very evening."

"And what, it just lives on that guy's hand?" Reesal asked in disbelief.

"In it, actually," Arvendal clarified. "The one whose hand holds the gravespider must be very careful when they call it forth because they are not entirely immune to the poison."

"Just great," Kourakin sighed. "Well, I, for one, am glad I was not there. I *hate* spiders!"

"I first encountered the weaver's guild on my journey here from Cul-Amaron," Paroch admitted. He then relayed his story of what happened.

"It is clear then that the Darklord has engaged the services of the weaver's guild," Arvendal stated.

"Why should the weaver's guild even care about us at all?" Reesal wanted to know.

"Since their inception, the weaver's guild has sought to control all things of power, blades, rings, thrones, whatever it may be, they covet them," Arvendal explained.

"Are they evil?" Elrynn asked.

"Yes, because they do not follow Ellonas, but not to the same level as the Darklord," Arvendal began. "They are forever on their own side, beholden to no other but the guild itself. And this makes them extremely dangerous as well. They do not accomplish much that you would consider good."

"Then they are allied with the darkness?" Telliken asked.

"At this point, we must consider it so. Most all members have a tattoo of a web on a hand or on their neck; others have a spider tattoo, either in the webbing of the hand between the thumb and finger or behind the left earlobe."

"You would never catch me with the tattoo of a spider anywhere on my body," Kourakin shivered. "I hate spiders," he said yet again.

Haendorn laughed, "A tattoo of a spider would be most difficult to see on me."

Paroch frowned at him.

"I am no member of the weaver's guild," Haendorn laughed again. "Come check me for tattoos."

Suddenly, Paroch burst into laughter, "If any others of you are associated with the weaver's guild, then please weave me a burial shroud before killing me."

There was much good-natured laughter, and talk turned to things less dark. Eventually, one by one, each member excused himself to his room until only Paroch, Draxin, and Arvendal remained. Arvendal was busying himself on the far side of the room and took little notice of the hushed conversation.

"How did you figure out Galortin was a traitor?" Paroch finally asked.

"I had my suspicions long before this evening," Draxin began. "But I had no proof, and then suddenly it landed in my lap."

"What does that mean?" Paroch wanted to know.

Draxin fished a smooth green rock out of his pocket. He smiled as he turned it over in his hand before showing it to Paroch. "When I was a much younger Falkiri, just learning to fly, really," He paused and smiled as he remembered back. "There was a beautiful Falkiri, very shy, mind you, but I adored her. We learned to fly together, and we made plans to be together forever, but then duty called. I was joined to one group that spent most days away from Harkanoph while she was assigned to a different group. Our paths seldom crossed, but our love for each other continued to grow." He paused again and sighed heavily. "One day, I found this rock," he handed it to Paroch. "I found this rock, and I carved a glyph on one side of it."

"So you never gave it to her?" Paroch asked as he examined the rock. He could see carvings on both sides. On one side, the carvings seemed very recent, and on the other, much older.

Draxin smiled and shook his head. "I gave it to her friend and have not seen it since that day until just a few hours ago when Galortin tossed it to me."

"Then where did Galortin get it from?" Paroch persisted.

"I brought that stone into the tower," Arvendal admitted. He walked over to stand before them. "It was some time after you and the others had left for the palace. I heard a loud thump on the door. I opened it and saw this green rock lying in front of the door." Here, he paused for a moment. "Perhaps I should have mentioned this sooner, but I have waited until what I thought was the appropriate time." Both Draxin and Paroch gave him a questioning look. "Where shall I begin? No, too far back. Let me see. Now, in the days before you left Elas-Tormas, I began to notice some strange goings-on. A Dakirin had taken up residence in an abandoned building and was watching the tower closely. I did not give it much thought because the Darklord is always interested in what transpires inside this tower," he chuckled. "But, I noted it nonetheless. Then this stone appeared this evening."

"Anyone could have chucked a stone at the door," Paroch said.

"This is true," Draxin agreed. "But only one Dakirin had the stone I carved on."

Paroch remained quiet.

"Then there was the encounter with a beautiful woman who was peering in through the gate, timid to be sure because I startled her when I introduced myself, so much so that she turned and walked away from me as quickly as possible."

"Beautiful woman?" Draxin asked. "What did she look like?"

"She looked like a Dakirin in disguise," Arvendal answered after a moment's contemplation. "Her skin tone was different, as were the color of her eyes and hair, but her facial features, the pointed nose and chin, so much like yours," Arvendal said as he brought his thumb and forefinger together first in front of his chin and then his nose.

"Is it possible to disguise oneself so completely as to be unrecognizable as a Dakirin?" Draxin wanted to know.

"If a strong enough watcher is involved, then yes, absolutely a disguise can work to great effect."

"Excuse me, but what does this have to do with the green rock?" Paroch wanted to know.

"Perhaps nothing," Arvendal replied, but before he could continue, Draxin began speaking excitedly.

"Do you remember that barmaid in Iverbin?"

"The one with the red hair?" Paroch asked.

"The one so interested in where we were going?" Draxin clarified. "I bet it was the same woman that Arvendal caught peering through the gate."

"Really?" Paroch was incredulous.

"If she were a Dakirin in disguise, she could fly farther in a day than we could ride. Especially if she knew where we were headed."

"So you think this Dakirin is following us?"

Draxin shook his head and took a deep breath before speaking. "I am saying that the woman Arvendal caught peering through the gate is the same woman we met at the inn and the same woman at the bridge who asked to ride with us. I am not sure how she was able to disguise herself, but she was, and I believe she carved on the other side of that rock the glyphs for, 'danger, G, assassin.'"

"You are telling me that your long lost love has somehow found you and, by carving on a rock you gave her many years ago, warned you against Galortin's schemes?" Paroch asked.

"Exactly," Draxin replied.

"It would seem you have an ally on the dark side," Arvendal said.

Paroch nodded, then shrugged and excused himself from the room.

After he was gone, Draxin turned to Arvendal, "I want to see her again."

"You are on a different path than you were before," Arvendal reminded him. "She is part of your past."

"But she is near now, and she cares for me still. Why else would she warn me?"

"Perhaps, but then again, she is in the army of darkness. Maybe she has also been tasked with killing the Herald."

"I won't hear of it," Draxin answered angrily. "Not her." He shook his head. "Not her," he repeated softly.

"Get some rest, Draxin," Arvendal urged. "It is easier to think clearly when the mind is not hampered by lack of sleep."

# Black Chapter Three: The Torque Of Iron

## The 15th of Lirinn, early morning

The sun had not even begun to brighten the eastern sky when Rylabet was awakened by a single knock at his alley door, followed quickly by three more.

"What news then, friend?" he demanded gruffly as he ambled to the backdoor.

"A friend with news," came the muffled reply.

Rylabet smiled ruefully as he unlocked the door and opened it.

An old man entered, and Rylabet, after checking to make sure no one was around, quickly closed the door behind him.

"Were you followed?" Rylabet asked as he scowled. The old man returned his scowl with raised eyebrows and a slight tilt of his head. "Fine, what time is it?" Rylabet demanded. He yawned once and scratched the back of his head.

"Still early yet, or late depending," came the reply.

Rylabet frowned. "So, what is it? What news that requires me to be woken so early?"

"Abion has been found," the old man said excitedly.

Rylabet glared at him, "We have known the exact location of that blade ever since Vindramion lost his arm."

"No, I mean it has been found," the old man insisted. He was gently rubbing the webbing between his thumb and forefinger on his left hand.

"You mean recovered?"

The old man nodded. "I have seen it this very evening at Morheim's meeting."

"Now, that is news, my friend," Rylabet smiled and sat at the table near the door. "Please, take a seat."

The old man did as instructed.

"You used your spider?"

"Yes, I saw an opportunity."

"And? Were you successful?" Rylabet asked.

"In a manner of speaking," the old man replied. "A man lies dead in the palace, but it was not the man I had intended to die."

"And you were able to retrieve your...?"

"Of course, I retrieved my spider," the old man snapped. "However, the one named Paroch seemed very interested in what I was doing."

"How so?" Rylabet asked.

"As I was standing back up from retrieving my spider, I noticed that he was staring at me."

"This means nothing," Rylabet assured him. "So, you have seen this blade, this Abion?"

"Yes, and it is wielded by the very same Paroch that was watching me with such interest," the old man smiled at the sudden change of demeanor on Rylabet's face. "Not what you were expecting to hear?" he asked with a laugh.

"Not exactly," Rylabet said as he stroked his chin. "But we will find a way to make certain it does not present a problem. So, this Paroch wields the blade that has been lost for a millennia? Retrieved from the Chantra?"

"Apparently so," the old man agreed, he was still gently rubbing his hand.

"I should love to hear how this was accomplished. I know of three separate attempts by our operatives to retrieve the sword," Rylabet explained.

"Three?" the old man asked. "I only know of two."

"I am not surprised, really," Rylabet laughed, "Which two?"

"Everyone knows of the first attempt less than a hundred years after the sword was 'lost,'" the old man explained. "And the larger one, four hundred years later. No one ever returned from either expedition."

"Until recently, no one has returned from any attempt to retrieve that sword," Rylabet clarified. "Well, there was that one, a Lepnarion who went mad from his experiences. I have no idea how he managed to escape when not a single one of our operatives ever did. The records do not give much detail beyond his ramblings about the Chantra."

"You mentioned knowing of a third attempt by members of our esteemed association?"

"Ahhh, yes, there was a third attempt made just about a year ago now," Rylabet drummed his fingers on the table a few times. "A rather clandestine business compared to the previous attempts to take it by force. It might have worked too, had we made this attempt early on, but a thousand years later, the Chantra has grown much too powerful."

"It had to have been by stealth," the old man surmised.

"Doubtful, there is little chance this Paroch could succeed where our operatives failed."

"Force?" the old man asked.

"Perhaps, but highly unlikely, we would have already heard of the Chantra's death by now. No, it was something else altogether," Rylabet said slowly.

"What other option is there?"

"A valid question. What all do you know about this Paroch?" Rylabet asked.

"Those with him are claiming he is the Herald, prophesied of old."

"And you are just now telling me this?" Rylabet was a bit agitated.

"My apologies," the old man said with a slight bow of his head. "You were focused on the sword of Abion."

"*You* were focused on the sword," Rylabet corrected. He sat in silence for several moments, drumming the tips of his fingers together. "The Herald, you say?" he finally said.

"That is what they were claiming, and there were plenty of calls to punish them with death for lying, but those calls stopped the moment Abion was revealed."

"Such an antiquated law, death for lying, but very useful when trying to silence someone you do not want to hear," Rylabet observed. "I am tired of looking at you like that. You should really change out of that disguise," he directed.

"Schimbare," the old man said, and Rylabet shook his head and began to laugh. "Akina, you are certainly much better looking without your disguise."

She was curvy and not too tall, with medium-length brown hair. Her green eyes sparkled when she laughed. "You are too kind. Now, what do you propose we do to retrieve that sword?"

Rylabet was silent for a moment, then, with a slow nod, he began to smile, "I think this will work just fine to begin with."

\*\*\*

As the moon began to set in the western sky, alarm bells were heard ringing from the outer wall, and there was much movement to be seen atop the torch-lit wall, helmeted figures pointing and others running to and fro.

Hember smiled at the consternation displayed before him. Just over half of his men had been ferried across the mighty Arazor, not counting the five thousand that had disembarked on a rather large island before determining their error. He could afford to chuckle at that now. Those men would have a long march before them when, at last, they landed on the western shore of the Arazor.

After ensuring that his line before the first gate was secure, he began a leisurely ride to the north toward the second gate. As he went, he gave orders for wooden scaling ladders to be constructed from whatever wood was available and to be made visible to those defending the walls.

"You will advance while the Dakirin are clearing the walls, and if the gates are not opened for you, scale the walls as quick as you can, maybe to help clear the battlements or more than likely just to clamber down the other side and continue your advance toward the main city," he explained time and time again as he rode on.

"Sir," a soldier cautioned as Hember reached the end of his lines guarding the third gate. "We do not know who or what is out there yet. It could be dangerous for you."

"I wish to see what lies ahead. Besides, more men are marching up. Can you hear them?"

The soldier nodded that he could.

"Then you worry about yourself, and let me worry about myself."

"Yes, sir," the soldier saluted.

Hember smiled to himself as he rode away from his line, the waning moon cast wavering shadows and several times he slowed his mount as he looked closely at the darker areas. His mount spooked once, and it was at this point that Hember turned his horse around and began heading briskly back toward his lines. A slight sound to his left and another off to his right brought Hember to a stop. "Who is there?" he demanded. "Show yourself." He unsheathed his blade and turned his mount around in a circle.

A score of armed men sprang from the bushes, surrounding him.

"Come quietly, or you will perish," one of them warned.

Hember glanced around him as he sought to keep his horse under control, they were closing in, but only a few were armed with spears that he could see. "What do you want from me?" he asked.

"Why are you preparing to attack Elas-Tormas?" one of the men countered.

Hember nodded. "My master has asked that I take this city for him. So I am here to take it." His men were marching closer; he could hear the tramp of their booted feet, but they were still too far away to help him. "My men are approaching. You are outnumbered, and none of you will make it back to the safety of your walls," he pointed to the outer wall in the near distance. Whispers amongst the enemy revealed they could indeed hear the approach of his men. "If you surrender to me now, I will make sure you are treated fairly," he added.

"Your men are not here, so we are not outnumbered yet," one of the Lepnarions replied coolly. "Last chance to come with us or perish."

Hember spurred his horse forward and swung at the nearest man with his sword. "Men, to me. I am attacked!" he managed before a well-placed thrust of a spear caught him under the right arm and dislodged him from his saddle. He fell to the ground with a crash, his horse galloping away without him. The sky above was clear, and the crescent moon was sharp as a dagger against a black cloth; the myriad stars glittered like gems, twinkling and winking at him. He blinked a few times and first moved his feet and legs, then his hands and arms, before attempting to sit up. As he looked around, there was no one in sight; the enemy had melted away as quietly as they had appeared. He struggled to sit up, his breath coming in ragged gasps. The shadows around him seemed to grow as he fought to draw breath. A few moments later, he became aware of some of his men surrounding him.

"General Hember, what happened?" the look of concern on the man's face was evident.

"Looks like a spear thrust; perhaps some Anaris are out seeking revenge?" another replied knowingly as he scanned the area.

Hember could only shake his head and point toward the outer wall.

"Are you saying Lepnarions did this?"

Again, Hember could only nod; he opened his mouth to speak, but only blood spilled out. In desperation, his hand clutched the arm of the man beside him, then his head rolled to the side, and he breathed his last.

***

"You are certain he is the same one?" Niven asked.

"I have not seen for myself as of yet, but I assume so," Aracelis replied. "Let us await him here and see."

They waited for about ten minutes before they saw a column of horsed soldiers approaching in the distance. As the head of the column drew close, Aracelis spoke quietly.

"It is him. I want you to keep an eye on our old friend," Aracelis instructed.

"You have no trust for him either," Niven surmised. "Not sure why he was allowed to live, but I will watch him for any signs of treachery."

Aracelis and Niven waved at Rakosa as he drew near.

"No hard feelings from our first meeting at Kire, I hope?" Aracelis called out.

Rakosa gave him a hard stare, "Many things happen in war that we might wish would not have." He reigned his horse to a stop before Aracelis and saluted him. "The enemy of my enemy..." he let his voice trail off.

Aracelis nodded his understanding. "I would ask that you position your men directly across from one of the gates so you can assist our Dakirin in the taking of that gate. Niven will accompany you and lend assistance should the need arise."

"You need not worry about my loyalty," he said as he waved his men forward. "Nor theirs, as far as I can tell. They were the dregs of Anari society. None of us has anything to return to. Our fortunes are before us."

"And what of revenge?" Aracelis asked pointedly. "Against those of us who have left you with nothing?"

"They already have more after joining with you than they did in their own country. As for me," Rakosa replied evenly. "I hold nothing against you despite what you put me through. I can respect what you have done and even what you are doing now. Revenge is a luxury I can scarcely afford. If I survive, then perhaps my desire for revenge against my true enemies can be fostered, but until then, I will content myself with helping to overthrow whatever remains of what they hold most dear."

"Why do you hate him so?" Aracelis asked suddenly. "This Lepnarion you mention?"

Rakosa sighed a heavy sigh, then fixed Aracelis with a haughty gaze.

"Honor was one of the founding principles of Lepnar, something I myself put a great deal of stock in. And yet, when circumstances arose in Kire that demanded honor, there were those who chose convenience instead. Their clever speech convinced many of my fellow Lepnarions to join them and betray our honor. All is lost without honor. I will say no more."

Aracelis nodded and motioned for him to continue after his men. "Niven," Aracelis warned, "do not be swayed by his words. He is dangerous and unstable. Be vigilant."

They watched the Anaris riding slowly past.

"He mentioned true enemies. I suppose that would be us," Niven surmised after a bit.

"That may be, but if he does not survive the coming battle, then we will be left to wonder and not worry."

"Yes, sir. I will see to it personally." Niven saluted and, turning his mount, trotted after Rakosa.

\*\*\*

## The 15th of Lirinn, sunrise

"This is one of those times where I can see a great advantage in being able to transform into something with wings." Kinjal laughed. He was leading his horse and marching with his men. "It would afford me more time for sleep."

"You would think," Pentar replied as he walked beside him. "But you would discover that the sooner you reach your destination, the sooner you find things that need to be done. Truly, there is no rest for the winged."

"You might actually have a point there," Kinjal laughed. "How far do we have to go?"

"You have three gates to guard, and the first is not far from here," Pentar answered. "The other two are much farther. I would guess that you will be at the second gate tomorrow and the last gate the day after that. However, the storm of darkness is already on its way, and we are to attack when it is above the outer walls."

"Mazzaroth conjured up a storm in Nekoda and is sending it here to Elas-Tormas?" Kinjal asked in amazement. "Most of our weather moves west to east..." his voice trailed off.

Pentar nodded.

"What does this storm look like?"

"We will know when we see it," Pentar answered.

"When are we expecting it to arrive?" Kinjal asked.

"Sooner rather than later is all I can say."

"At this rate, we will be in position before the third gate on the eighteenth and not a moment sooner," Kinjal complained.

"And that is if there are no delays," Pentar pointed out. "It is possible the Lepnarions will attempt to block your progress in order to keep their lines of communication open to the west."

"If they do, this is where you and your fellow Dakirin come in," Kinjal replied with confidence.

"Like I said, no rest for the winged."

"Speaking of no rest, perhaps you can send a few of your Dakirin on ahead to scout out a good place to camp this evening and the next?"

"I will make sure we have things ready for you," Pentar agreed.

There followed several moments of silence until Kinjal spoke. "What is it?" he asked.

"Last night with Mazzaroth, I have never seen you like that."

"And?" Kinjal asked.

Pentar shrugged, "Surprising is all."

Kinjal laughed. "Merely a gamble. If I had succeeded, we both would be fabulously wealthy."

"But only if we find the crystal."

"We did this last time," Kinjal chuckled. "The right word is *when*. *When* we find the crystal."

"Finding a map or a cauldron in a tower is fairly easy compared to finding a staff hidden inside Thagorod. But this crystal could be anywhere within Mirion."

"It won't be that bad. We just have to look for the valley of white trees."

# White Chapter Four: Water And Wine

## The 15th of Lirinn, before sunrise

"We have to move quickly," Kulanak urged. He was leading the way, crouched low, and moving as fast as he could from shadow to shadow. "Scribs, why did you have to spear him?" he asked.

"I was trying to prevent our being discovered," Scribs replied indignantly.

"It is ironic that your attempt to avoid being discovered has alerted the enemy to our presence. Had you let him ride back to the safety of his own lines, we could have slipped away into the shadows with no trace of our even having been there."

"I did not think about that," Scribs admitted.

"What is done is done," Kulanak gave him a wry smile. "Let's see if we cannot lead these men to safety."

"What is going on?" another of the men with him asked. "Why is an army preparing for battle against Elas-Tormas?"

"You know as much as I do," Kulanak replied. "You heard what he said; he is following orders."

"Coming from the east, I should think you know more than we do," Scribs countered. "Since early in Sivrellis, we here in Elas-Tormas have heard rumors of war, but you have been through it already. Many have heard your stories of what befell Kire that fateful day and how you and those with you were hounded until you reached the safety of our walls."

Kulanak nodded.

"So what you are saying, is this is the Darklord's doing? This army encamped upon our doorstep?" another man asked.

"It would appear so," Kulanak replied out of breath.

"Where did they come from? Has Anar betrayed us?" someone asked.

"Hardly," Scribs spoke up. "The men of this army have the speech of the Tav-Tar, and the only way they could be here is if Anar has already fallen."

"Impossible!" another stated.

"Do you have a better explanation?" Scribs asked.

"That seems as reasonable an explanation as any," Kulanak added. "And somehow, we find ourselves in the middle of their lines."

Scribs looked to the eastern sky. "The sun will be rising soon. It will be impossible for us to make it to the wall without being attacked in the open."

"Agreed," Kulanak whispered as he signaled for his men to stop. They gathered around, nineteen men looking to their commander. "Men, the enemy now lies between us and the safety of the outer wall. Assuredly, we can slip around their lines unseen, but making it to the gate is another story altogether. They would spot us, and we would be hard-pressed to reach safety. Let us move to the eastern shore of the Arazor and reassess our situation in a place where the enemy is not right on top of us. Hurry to the river; find whatever wood you can that will help you float across."

"The sun will be up long before we make it across," one of the men explained. "Then we shall be visible for all to see, floating targets for archers and slingers."

"The enemy will have their eyes toward Elas-Tormas. By heading east, we may yet escape unseen."

As one, the men stole toward the river bank, looking for and picking up any larger pieces of wood. With one last look behind them, Kulanak and another man waded into the Arazor, carrying a heavy limb between them. Behind, others silently slipped into the current, holding onto dead logs and large branches. Before long, all of them were clinging to whatever they had carried into the river, making slight progress to the east bank while being pulled quickly downstream. A fiery red crescent was just breaking over the eastern horizon when the last of the men stepped onto the shore, dripping and shivering in the cool morning air.

"You see," Kulanak said joyously. "We have successfully braved the river."

"Lead the way," Scribs urged. "I will do what I can to hide our tracks in the sand."

Kulanak turned north and, finding a secluded route, he led his men a little more than a mile before finding a thick stand of old and young trees. Once in and amongst the trees, Kulanak urged the men to form barricades between the larger trunks by tying vines around the young saplings, pulling them into place and lashing them tightly to stakes set in the ground. By the time Scribs found them, there were only two ways in or out.

Scribs nodded appreciatively, "Let us hope they don't have any of those Dakirin you keep talking about."

\*\*\*

## *The 15th of Lirinn, mid-morning*

Arvendal opened the tower door slowly to find four hooded figures standing before him. The closest was also the tallest and spoke first, "It is known that Paroch of Cul-Amaron stays in this tower. We would speak with him who is the rightful king of Lepnar," the figure proclaimed with a slight bow.

"And why do you hide your faces beneath the shadow of your hoods during the daylight?"

"We wish not to be noticed by others who would be keen to know we are here," the figure replied. "We have taken great pains to avoid being followed."

"Who should I say is desiring to speak with him?" Arvendal wanted to know.

"Tell him Queen Sarahin of Anar." One of the figures standing a little behind bowed slightly.

"And you are?" Arvendal demanded of the figure who spoke first.

"I am Leond of the house of Anar."

Arvendal nodded and looked to the other figure holding a large sack over his shoulder, noticing the arms were deeply scarred.

"I am Lord Gedery from the lands near Tavanie. I, too, would speak with Paroch."

"Is the matter urgent?" Arvendal asked.

"Most urgent," Gedery bowed. Behind him, Sarahin nodded in agreement.

Arvendal looked to the figure who had not yet spoken.

"And I am Shalamar of Kire."

"You also desire to speak with Paroch?" Arvendal reiterated.

"I...I wish to speak with Fulcwin," Shalamar clarified.

Arvendal smiled at her, a knowing smile so that she began to blush.

"Come in," he said as he waved them through the tower door. "They are gathered in the meeting room."

"They?" Gedery asked.

"The Herald of Light has his mantle of protection," Arvendal explained.

"Herald?" Leond questioned. He turned to Sarahin. "Are you quite certain this is the same Paroch we met on the road east of Kalantar?" Sarahin nodded.

"I am certain," she replied.

"Before Paroch retrieved the Kingsword of Abion, he was revealed as the Herald, long prophesied to appear when the Darklord was released," Arvendal explained.

"So Paroch is the Herald and the rightful king of Lepnar?" Leond asked.

"It would appear so," Arvendal answered as he led them through the halls until he brought them to the meeting room.

"Who is that with you, Arvendal?" Reesal asked as he looked up from the table. Those seated near looked up as well, and the moment Paroch saw Sarahin, he smiled.

"Paroch, I present Lord Gedery from Tavanie." Gedery bowed low before Paroch and placed the sack on the floor. "I believe you already know Leond and Sarahin, Queen of Anar." Both Leond and Sarahin bowed before Paroch. "And Fulcwin, Shalamar is here to speak with you."

"I told you he was a king now," Balatiere whispered loudly as he gave Fulcwin an elbow to the ribs.

"Please, all of you, take a seat. Are you hungry? Thirsty perhaps?" The four of them took a seat and shook their heads at his questions. "You wished to see me?" Paroch asked lord Gedery.

Gedery stood and cleared his throat as he looked at everyone else in the room. He spoke softly for only Paroch to hear, "I had hoped to speak with you in private."

"These men are sworn to protect the Herald; they are my mantle. Anything you need to say can be spoken freely in front of them as well." Paroch proudly named each member of the mantle. "This is Telliken of Anar, and this is Elrynn of the Midwaste." Telliken bowed to his Queen, and Elrynn waved at them. "Here we have Fulcwin and Balatiere from Lepnar." Fulcwin nodded to them and quickly turned his attention back to Shalamar while Balatiere stood and acknowledged them before re-taking his seat. "This is Perin of the Baris Islands and Kourakin from Davar." Both men bowed and remained standing. "Over there, we have Gehm and Reesal from Thagorod." Gehm smiled and waved while Reesal stood and bowed before returning to his conversation with Gehm. "And here is Haendorn from Mirion and Draxin from Harkanoph." Haendorn stood closest to them, and he shook Gedery's hand and bowed before Sarahin. Draxin bowed low but did not say anything.

"Harkanoph? Where is that? And why is that man's skin green?" Gedery asked with suspicion.

Draxin stood and removed his hood, "I am a Falkiri by birth, a Dakirin by choice and have been saved by Ellonas from both." He looked at each of them in turn, then sat back down but did not cover his face.

Shalamar returned his gaze with a gentle smile. Sarahin looked upon him with pity. Leond smiled and nodded, and Gedery stared at Draxin for a long moment before finally bowing his head, then looking directly at Paroch, he began speaking. "It was quite a shock for many of those in attendance at Morheim's last night. The blade long rumored to be lost was not only found but revealed in such a fashion."

Here, Fulcwin gave Balatiere a hard elbow to his ribs.

"It was not my wish to reveal the Kingsword in such a way as to cause undo duress," Paroch explained.

"I thought not," Gedery continued. "Nevertheless, many men are keenly interested in that blade. I have come to warn you that there are factions within Elas-Tormas. Factions normally contentious toward each other but now seemingly willing to work together to achieve a common goal."

"What factions do you speak of?" Fulcwin asked.

"These three factions are well established within Lepnarion society. The Order of the Blade, the Order of the White Rose, and the Order of…"

"How do you even know this?" Balatiere demanded.

"And the Order of the Hammer," Gedery continued. "I overheard them speaking at a table situated behind me."

"The Order of the Blade would never work with the Rose," Balatiere snorted. "Let alone sit at the same table."

Gedery continued. "I only tell you what I heard. Three were seated at the table behind me and, after a moment, began to consider ways in which recovering the Kingsword might not benefit them all."

"Forgive me," Fulcwin said as he stood. "But how exactly do you know of these three orders? Seeing as you hail from the Tav-Tar?"

"A just question," Gedery began. "In the Tav-Tar, we have our own orders that were similar in nature: builders, growers, warriors. And this is not my first visit to Elas-Tormas. Many times, I have consulted with members of the Order of the White Rose on matters concerning soil, plants and other such things. I have spoken with the Order of the Hammer in regard to building many monuments in Veynohrad. And many were the times both orders mentioned the Order of the Blade, not without some measure of disdain, I might add." He smiled at Balatiere. "Order of the Blade, I presume?"

Balatiere, flustered and red in the face, did not respond; he merely waved him away.

"I am certain you have many more orders than the three I have named," he continued with a slight bow toward Fulcwin."

"Please continue," Paroch urged. "What did you hear them say?"

"First, they were focused on if it was indeed the Kingsword that had been shown to all in attendance. After much debate, they determined it was most likely a counterfeit." Here, Balatiere sighed in frustration. "But they also figured they would take no chances in case it were real. They all agreed that the sword, whether real or not, should be taken by them at the very least for inspection. They knew you were staying at the Tergian Tower, though none of them knew where it was located." Arvendal harrumphed at that admission. "They argued for a bit over where they should take the sword once they retrieved it,"

"If they retrieve it, you mean," Balatiere interrupted.

Gedery paid no attention to the interruption and continued speaking. "One mentioned Mar-Storin, but that was rejected by the other two who favored Bel-Tordanim. It was at that point that one of Morheim's attendants called to me, asking if I needed anything. I replied that I did not, and when I turned around, the three of them were walking out a side door." Gedery nodded. "They know you are staying here in this tower, and I fear they mean to come and take the sword by force."

"It is not unexpected that others would seek to take the Kingsword from me," Paroch stated. "Those who come to steal will find many capable blades in their way. For sharing this information, you have my thanks, Lord Gedery. And I extend my sympathy to you for the evil that has befallen you these past many weeks."

Gedery bowed low before he took his seat.

"Leond?" Paroch asked with a smile. "You have something to tell me?"

"Nothing besides hello again," Leond replied with a wave and a smile.

"It is I who wished to speak with you," Sarahin said as she stood. She bowed for a moment. "Much has happened since we parted ways outside the outer wall. My mother has been buried, and my father did not escape the destruction of Basgerone. I am now Queen of a realm overthrown. Anar lies in ashes, and the enemy marches toward Elas-Tormas. Of this, I am certain, yet I bring far darker tidings to you. More than factions desire the blade that makes one King over Lepnar. Morheim covets the sword and has spoken plainly before me of his intent. He approached me directly, offering to help me regain my throne and rebuild Anar if I would but lend him aid in the taking of Abion. I thanked him for his generous offer and asked for time to speak with my advisors. He has allowed me but two days to make my decision. I have yet to give an answer, but he waits for one, and I suspect when I decline, it will not go well with me or for those with me. Within the fortnight, he intends to surround this tower, and if the sword is not offered to him, he will kill the man who keeps it from him." She shuddered at the thought. "I fear that even if you were to give him the sword he seeks, he would not, no, could not allow you or anyone else present in this room to live."

Paroch smiled at her. "All will be well, for we do not know what tomorrow brings, whether good or ill, and neither does Morheim."

"Still," Gedery spoke up. "Mighty warriors, though you all may be, there comes a point where sheer numbers will inevitably overwhelm you. I have three hundred armed men faithful to me. They are stationed near the docks. I pledge them to you."

Paroch was about to speak when Sarahin spoke first.

"And we have five hundred lancers from Anar," Sarahin spoke quickly. "If it should come to fighting. Though they have no mounts," she lamented.

"The generous offer of support is gladly accepted from both of you," Paroch announced.

"If you do not mind," Gedery spoke up as he grabbed the sack and, gently placing it on the table, he revealed two large bottles of wine. "I think a toast is in order."

Paroch laughed. "Arvendal, do we actually have enough goblets in this tower?"

It was not long after Arvendal left the room that he reappeared bearing a tray on which sat sixteen small golden goblets.

Gedery stared at the bottle a moment before opening it. The instant the bottle was uncorked, a wonderful and slightly intoxicating aroma filled the room.

Moments later, as Gedery poured the last of the first bottle, he sighed, "These are the last of the bottles I was able to take with me when I fled to Debir. They were produced from my vineyard almost seventy-five years ago. This is a most potent wine and, as such, should be sipped and savored."

"There isn't above a mouthful or two in here," Reesal grumbled as he looked in the goblet he had picked up.

"If it is sipped, the effects build slowly, but if you drink all of it at once, you will not remember anything until you wake on the morrow," Gedery smiled broadly. "I can assure you of that." He picked up a goblet and raised it high, and the others did the same.

"To Paroch, the wielder of Abion, the sword that was lost!" Gedery announced, and everyone took a sip, some more than others.

"And the Herald of Light!" Arvendal added as he raised his goblet and took another sip.

"To the mantle!" Paroch hollered.

The second bottle was opened, goblets were refilled, and many more toasts were made so that by the time every goblet was empty, everyone was smiling and filled with cheer.

"I believe Shalamar had something to say," Arvendal exclaimed suddenly.

"Oh yes, I had forgotten. My apologies, Shalamar," Paroch offered. "Please go ahead."

Shalamar stood slowly and bowed to Paroch before speaking, "Fulcwin, I bring word that Kulanak has not returned from his patrol beyond the outer wall. He is overdue."

"Kulanak will be fine," Balatiere promised. "He is quite capable of extricating himself from all kinds of trouble. I should know!"

"Have you not heard the news?" Shalamar persisted. "Early this morning, the enemy was spotted crossing the Arazor and moving into position to hem in Elas-Tormas on land. Every gate in the outer wall will soon have thousands of enemy soldiers facing it. There will be no escape over land."

"The outer wall is over eighty miles in length. Surely there is a portion where the enemy is not entrenched before the wall," Haendorn proclaimed.

"I only know what I have heard," Shalamar answered. "To the east and the north, the enemy advances toward the outer wall, stopping just out of bowshot. Whether they are moving to the western side is unknown to me but seems probable."

"Any signs of Dakirin?" Elrynn wanted to know.

"No," Shalamar shook her head. "They are strangely absent from the enemy ranks."

"Perhaps they are all somewhere else," Perin offered hopefully.

"Elas-Tormas appears to have a large standing army," Kourakin stated. He tipped his goblet once more in a vain attempt to taste the last drop of wine. He placed the goblet on the table before him and sighed. "Perhaps the enemy can be swiftly defeated before the Dakirin return."

"You mean leaving the safety of the walls and attacking? I would not expect that battle to end quickly," Fulcwin contemplated. "Still, you may have a point."

"Have you heard nothing of what has been said?" Sarahin asked in alarm. "Has the wine gone to your heads? Anar has fallen, not just a city or a county but the entire realm! For weeks, Dakirin flew thick over Anar, blotting out the sun and turning the tide of every battle against us. Where they are now, none of us knows, but they will return to take part in the upcoming battle. Elas-Tormas will fall, and it will fall quickly. Let others see to the defense of this city; we should be planning our escape."

"According to you, our avenues of escape appear to be dwindling," Telliken pronounced as he traced his finger around the lip of his empty goblet.

"Then it is fortunate indeed that we have two ships in the harbor," Leond said with a laugh. "We can set sail on the morrow if need be."

"We should head for Mirion," Haendorn offered.

"It would seem that we are indeed being hemmed in," Paroch mused. "And while it remains to be seen how we will leave Elas-Tormas. One thing is now clear to me: we must leave and soon."

"Heading west to Mirion, I presume," Gehm nodded.

"Yes," Paroch replied after a moment. "Yes, I will seek the Council of Elberon. Leond, you mentioned two ships?"

"Indeed, and there is room for us all on them both."

"This is good. However, I need more information before we can make our departure."

"And what of the Lepnarions who made the journey from Kire with Fulcwin?" Shalamar asked. "Is there room for them onboard those ships?"

"How many are there?" Leond asked.

"Shalamar, we cannot take the whole city," Balatiere answered.

"I only ask for those who are loyal to both you and Fulcwin. The same ones who fought for you as we fled from Kire. The same ones who bled defending the defenseless," Shalamar answered softly, tears evident in her eyes.

"Of course, we will try and bring as many as we can," Fulcwin said as he went to embrace her.

Leond cleared his throat, "How many?"

"Maybe four hundred," Fulcwin answered over Shalamar's shoulder. "Almost half of them would be women and children."

"If the journey were not overly long, I think we might be able to squeeze them in somewhere," Leond replied, and he gave Shalamar a reassuring pat on her shoulder.

"We could simply land on the shores of the Blackwood," Haendorn offered. "It might be a four-day journey. Depending on the wind," he added.

"We will go ensure the ships are ready," Leond said with a bow.

"Before we settle on this course of action, I would like a bit more information," Paroch stated again. "I am sure you will all agree that it would be dangerous for me to go traipsing about the city," Paroch began. "And I fear it is now much too dangerous for the four of you to be seen entering or leaving this tower. I can send Perin and Kourakin in your place, Leond. Lord Gedery, I would send Gehm and Reesal in your place. Let these four carry word to your men, alerting them to what is going on. Elrynn, will you and Draxin speak with those who journeyed here from Kire?"

"Those two wouldn't be able to find where they are staying," Balatiere stated. "I will take them there." He thumped Elrynn on the back. "Besides, I will need to explain why this Dakirin is not an enemy. No offense," he added as he looked to Draxin.

"None taken," Draxin replied. "I will wear my hood."

Paroch handed ink and parchment to both Leond and Gedery. Gedery finished his missive first and, after signing and sealing it, handed it to Gehm.

"You will find my men onboard the Hooves of the Sea; it is flying the Anari flag. Deliver this to Orendien only," Gedery instructed.

When Leond was finished, he handed his note to Perin. "Tulikar," Leond said with a nod. "He is on board the Seamane. He will get everything ready."

"Be careful," Paroch added as the seven of them prepared to leave the tower. "May Ellonas guard your steps and deliver you safely to where your journey ends."

# Black Chapter Four: Silken Gambit

## *The 15th of Lirinn, early morning*

Morheim paced in his throne room.

"May I remind you that you gave her two days," a man standing off to one side spoke quietly.

"I know what I said to her," Morheim snapped. "I never should have let her leave the palace."

"That would not have been a wise move, Your Highness. Even though Anar has fallen, there are many here in Elas-Tormas that she can count as allies."

"Yes, yes, you are right." He sighed and sank into his throne. "I want Abion. I would unite all of Lepnar."

"Wielding the Kingsword is but the first step in uniting Lepnar."

"What do you mean?" Morheim demanded.

"The one who would unite Lepnar would need to do so from the throne in Mar-Storin; only there will the Kingsword be recognized and accepted."

"Is there no way to unite Lepnar from here?"

"Allow me to contemplate that," the advisor said.

"In the meantime, I want Abion in my hand!"

"Things like this always take time, my lord," the man bowed. "I have a few others working on a plan to retrieve the sword for you."

"When will this plan be ready?" Morheim asked with sudden interest.

"As I have already said, things like this take time. It would never do to have rumors swirling around the city that *you* had a hand in some untoward behavior. There is plenty of time to weave a web to trap young Paroch in."

"It is the real Abion, right?" Morheim asked.

"Without a doubt, it is the Kingsword of Lepnar. Though it is a shame, it was revealed in such a fashion at your gathering."

"What do you mean?"

"I mean that if it had been revealed to you alone, then we would not be having this conversation," he laughed. "It would have been easy enough to bar the throne room doors and signal your guards to dispatch Paroch and those with him. The sword would have been yours, but now the entire city knows that Abion has been retrieved, and it is here within the very walls of this great city."

"Do not inform me of what could have been," Morheim snapped. "I am only interested in how you are going to bring the sword to me. Have you a plan or not?"

The man cleared his throat and straightened his tunic before looking directly at Morheim. "As I have said numerous times already, Your Highness, these things take time."

"Yes, so you have said, but I want to know what you are planning. How will it be carried out?" Morheim stood and stepped toward his most trusted advisor.

"Perhaps it would be better for you not to know, then you can honestly answer that you had no knowledge of the plan should things go awry." He smiled at Morheim. "You have your royal image to uphold, do you not?"

Morheim frowned, "My royal image? Are you stalling?"

Suddenly, the throne room doors were opened, and a guard entered, bowing until Morheim called to him.

"What is the meaning of this disturbance?" Morheim demanded to know.

"Many pardons, King Morheim, but I bring urgent news." The guard stood but did not make eye contact.

"News of what?" Morheim demanded.

"We are receiving reports from the outer wall that…" the guard stopped for a moment.

"Out with it, oaf," the advisor said. "You must not waste the king's time."

"An enemy army approaches the outer wall."

"Which section?" the advisor asked.

"The entire wall," the guard replied.

"Preposterous," the advisor laughed. "That would take hundreds of thousands of men."

"Well," the guard clarified. "The east wall from the bay all the way to the main northern gate already has enemy soldiers before it. And many thousands more soldiers have been seen marching to the west and turning to the south."

"Perhaps if we sally forth from several gates at once, we can route them before they become entrenched," Morheim contemplated.

"Do they have any siege equipment with them? Towers? Battering rams? Ladders, at the very least?"

"None have as of yet been reported," the guard replied.

"Has there been any sighting of a winged enemy?" the advisor asked.

The guard looked confused.

"A winged enemy, like the Falkiri?" the advisor clarified.

"Falkiri?" the guard was incredulous. "Mentioned in the tales we are told as children?" He began to laugh. "No, not at all. Not a single flying Falkiri has been seen."

"Thank you," the advisor said with a wave of his hand. "You may go back to your post."

Once the throne room's doors closed again, Morheim looked to his advisor. "If we attack from five gates at once, ten thousand men to a gate, we might be able to route the enemy by this very evening."

"That hardly seems necessary," the advisor stated. "There have been no sightings of any Falkiri or whatever they are called. Double the wall guard to be sure and have them prepare to be attacked. But I see no need to waste lives in a spoiling attack. It will take them many, many months to breach the outer wall, and if they do not have siege equipment, it will be nigh on impossible."

"Are they really going to try and besiege us?" Morheim asked.

"It appears that is the case."

"So," Morheim paused. "The reports of a winged enemy from those who spoke last night. Are they all mad? Have they conspired together to lie to us? To sow terror amongst us?"

"All fair questions," the advisor answered with a nod. "I should think none of them are mad, with the exception of perhaps Gedery. However, the things they all mentioned as having been through will certainly tend to produce stress, and stress can play on one's mind and memories. As to your second question, what reason would they have to conspire together? There is no gain in it for them that I can see. As for terror, there are few words or phrases that, when spoken, inspire terror in man, and Falkiri is not one of them."

"What did they see then?" Morheim wanted to know.

The advisor sighed and shook his head, "I have no idea."

"Come now, they saw something, and you yourself have said they would have no gain from conspiring to weave such a fantastic tale." Morheim resumed pacing again. "Do you know what I think?" he asked.

"Tell me," the advisor encouraged.

"I think the winged enemy is real and took part in the subjugation of the Tav-Tar and Anar."

"Fair enough," the advisor agreed.

"I also think they are near even though, at present, they are not making themselves known. And this is because they are trying to lull us into a sense of complacency."

The advisor was nodding, "Go on."

"Therefore, it would be foolhardy for us to sally forth only to have the walls taken behind us."

"I agree completely, and furthermore, we can minimize our…"

"My assessment is not finished," Morheim said as he turned and stepped toward his advisor.

"My apologies," the advisor said with a bow.

"I can no longer afford to wait for Queen Sarahin's answer. I must move against Paroch with or without her help. I must gain control of Abion before it is too late."

"I see. There may still be time, though. Yes, an enemy sits outside the outer wall, but the wall is not yet breached. The winged enemy has not been seen yet. Our armies are strong and able. I would continue to advise caution. A hasty decision now, when we are so close, might bring ruin upon us all."

"Still stalling, I see," Morheim shook his head. "Have you formulated a plan yet or not? I want to know now!"

"With your permission," the advisor bowed. "I will bring the planners in so that they might tell you how they will go about retrieving the Kingsword for you."

"Make it quick," Morheim grumbled. "Despite your rhetoric to the contrary, time is growing short. I will have that sword!"

\*\*\*

## The 15th of Lirinn, late morning

"So we have agreed," Blade stated.

"Yes," Hammer replied. "We need to take the Kingsword and secret it out of here before the enemy can grab hold of it. But there are always contingency plans or should always be anyway."

"A good plan and lots of thought given to possible outcomes of our actions and how we might deal with each one and, of course, time to see that the plan or plans come to fruition," Rose agreed.

"And this is precisely why the Blades look down upon both of your orders. It is long past time for plans and waiting. We need action, and we need it now!" Blade slammed his fist upon the table so that the mugs and platters jostled and rattled together.

"You show disdain for planning," Hammer laughed. "You yourself should readily admit that before going into battle, plans are drawn up and…"

"Battle plans seldom survive initial contact with the enemy," Blade interrupted. "Think of them as…"

"A garden vine that grows anywhere besides where you want it to," Rose laughed.

Blade stopped and, after a moment's thought, nodded his head. "That makes sense. I never thought about it like that before."

"So, we have all agreed then that the sword must be taken," Hammer reiterated.

"Yes," Blade sighed. "And we have a plan."

"Maybe," Hammer stated. "It may not be the best plan, though."

"Agreed," Rose added. "Only time will tell."

"For this plan to work, it will take lots of time. Have you gotten the smiths to start forging the counterfeit sword? Or the pommel and grip? What about the prismologists and others of their ilk that cut gems?"

"I have been in contact with them, yes," Hammer replied.

"Have they started anything yet?"

"They are consulting their books to find out what the sword actually looks like, its weight, and other things like this," Hammer continued.

"Fine," Blade snapped. "Have either of you been able to find out where this tower is located? The tower of Tergia?"

"After consulting with many maps, I believe it is in the garden district on the western side of the city," Rose said. "It is said to be filled with magic that makes it far larger on the inside than it appears on the outside."

"After looking at maps and blueprints, I would agree," Hammer added. "Though I do not know about being filled with magic."

"I simply asked around in the market this morning and was eventually directed to the garden district," Blade boasted. "There is a decrepit old tower in there."

"Why not tell us this earlier?" Rose asked in frustration.

"I wanted to hear what you had learned about it," Blade explained. "I was not able to find out anything else about the tower."

"It is a tower where the followers of Ellonas go to have their faith tested," Hammer added.

"Well, that is something at least. Do we have anyone watching this tower?" Blade asked.

"I sent two to watch there earlier this morning," Rose said smugly.

"I sent four," Hammer stated. "And they have instructions to follow anyone who leaves the tower."

"Now, this tower, how many ways are there to get inside? How many windows are there, and where are they located?" Blade asked. "I only saw a single door this morning, but I was in a hurry to make it back here to meet with you two."

"A wall with only one gate surrounds the tower. No windows and only one door," Hammer replied. "The tower is in a state of disrepair, not too bad, mind you, but a few Hammers working on it for a week or two would make it a fine tower again."

"There is a wonderful garden surrounding the tower, even if it is a bit overgrown," Rose said. "A little attention, and it would be a beautiful little place."

"That is not going to help us gain entrance to the tower," Blade said with a shake of his head.

"Perhaps you can borrow a trebuchet from the wall guards," Hammer said. "And batter the tower into rubble."

"Perhaps you can build a replica of the tower and fool them into going into the wrong one," Blade snapped.

"We could always just knock on the door," Rose suggested.

"And then what?" Blade was genuinely curious to know.

"Hmmm," Rose thought for a moment. "Why not say we have heard of the sword of Abion and wished to see it for ourselves? To hold it perhaps."

"I doubt that will work," Blade said with derision. "We should batter down the door and force entry."

"Violence is not always the answer," Hammer sighed. "Though I daresay you think it is. All of you Blades are alike, bloodthirsty and spoiling for a fight."

"And you Hammers are all alike, following every plan to the smallest detail with no room for deviation even if it were necessary, even if it would improve the original plan. Stubborn and proud, I name the lot of you Hammers."

"If the wall is not straight, it will not stand," Hammer protested.

"And if a Blade shrinks back from a fight, then the battle is lost," Blade retorted.

"I do hope you both realize that each of our orders serves an important function within Lepnarion society, as do the smaller orders. Where would the Blades be if there were no Hammers to build the walls? And where would the Hammers be if there were no Blades to defend the cities of Lepnar? And where would you both be if the Roses were not there to grow food for the lot of you?" Rose laughed. "We spend entirely too much time arguing about who is the most important when we are all important. Are we not?"

The others grudgingly agreed, and for many minutes, the three of them sat in silence. Then, just as Blade opened his mouth to speak, outside the window to their room, they heard yelling and crying and other sounds of distress from the crowd in the street below.

Rose went to the window and, opening the shutters, leaned out. "What is the matter? Have you lost your minds?"

"Elas-Tormas is doomed," someone cried out.

"What makes you say that?" Rose asked.

"An enemy is at the wall," another added.

"The outer wall?" Rose asked. "Surely you mean only a section of the outer wall."

"All gates in the outer wall will soon have enemy soldiers in front of them," another added as he hurried past.

Rose slowly closed the shutters and waited for her eyes to adjust to the dim lighting in the room before she made her way back to the table. "This news is not good for our plan."

"I agree," Hammer said.

"We simply need to adapt our plan, is all," Blade encouraged. "Instead of waiting for the counterfeit sword and the opportune time, we should strike this evening or, at the very latest, tomorrow morning."

"That makes the plan riskier," Hammer stated.

"It was always risky," Rose added.

"But now it *is* riskier," Hammer noted.

"Let us Blades handle the increased risk," Blade suggested.

"That is fine. However, we Roses will still need to be there, just to make certain," she added.

"As will the Hammers," Hammer added.

"You still do not trust us Blades, do you?"

The other two shook their heads.

"There have been far too many times where things have happened," Hammer began.

"No need to rehash old happenings," Rose cautioned. "What is in the past should remain there."

"At the very least, make certain you send the bravest among you," Blade scowled. "I will not have this opportunity lost because a Hammer or a Rose loses their nerve."

"We Hammers are no cowards. I have yet to see a Blade anywhere near the top of a tower while it is still being built. *That* takes nerve," Hammer nodded.

"So, what do you propose for this updated plan of ours?" Rose inquired.

"I am glad you asked," Blade smiled. "Since we cannot mount a direct assault on the tower itself, here is what we are going to do!"

\*\*\*

## The 15th of Lirinn, just before noon

"Are you certain this will work?" Akina asked.

"No, but it is the best plan I can come up with given the circumstances," Rylabet snapped. "Many may not know it, but the enemy approaches the outer wall. It will not be long until the battle rages in these very streets." He paused for a moment and shook his head. "It is a shame that we have so few agents here."

"So few," she laughed. "The two of us are the only agents in all of Elas-Tormas?"

"There were a few others here at one time, but they have been stationed elsewhere."

"You mentioned I was the replacement?" she asked with raised brows.

Rylabet chuckled, "Why yes, I had forgotten I mentioned that."

"What happened to the previous…assistant?"

"I don't know, really," Rylabet shrugged. "Turi never returned from her last mission. It was over three years ago, and I have heard nothing from her since."

"What were we searching for?" Akina asked.

Rylabet simply smiled.

"It is obvious that we were searching for something here," Akina continued.

"Are searching," Rylabet admitted. "Though its priority has been lowered of late." He shook his head. "How long have you been here?" he asked suddenly.

"Two years now," Akina replied after a moment.

"I have been here ten years, and in all that time, there has never been a storm on the bay large enough to cause major damage to either ships or docks. Do you find that strange?"

"Maybe. Are you saying it never thunders here?"

"It rains and thunders all the time, but ships simply do not founder in the bay."

"That is odd," Akina agreed.

"Did you know that this city was built around two fishing villages?" Akina shook her head. "Apparently, the villagers had hidden something in a cave that protected the harbor from storms."

"Where?"

"Exactly," Rylabet agreed. "Somewhere beneath the streets of this city."

"What is it?"

"A ring of azure," Rylabet shared.

"Surely the archives have a tome with at least some mention of it," Akina sat down.

"There are three that make a passing reference to its probable location and one which details this ring, its supposed properties and a map to its location somewhere under the palace."

"So what is the problem then?"

"The map was missing, torn out. So, the search has continued slowly up until recently. But back to the issue at hand, Abion," Rylabet stated as he stood. "I am reluctant to rely so heavily upon..." he paused for a moment, then he laughed aloud. "Why not? It is worth the gamble. Alert our local supporters and have them meet us in the market plaza near the garden district."

"Why there?" she wanted to know.

"It is on the direct path to or from the tower. While you go and get them ready, I am going to finish loading this cart with a few more lovely things to look at, and I will meet you in the plaza." He carried three cloaks out to his cart and began hanging them from the two eight-foot-tall poles standing up from his cart. Each pole had six hooks placed precisely so that two items could be hung, one above the other, and both could be seen.

"I will meet you there, but what exactly is the plan?" Akina wanted to know.

Rylabet nodded as he retrieved seven additional cloaks, each finely made and a long dress, which he placed gently on the table before turning back to his shelves for several pairs of breeches. "I am guessing Paroch will be on the move sooner rather than later, and since, my dear, we are not the only ones interested in acquiring the sword, we are going to attempt to steal it in broad daylight. You remember what they looked like?"

"Who?" she asked, her eyes lingering on the dress for a moment.

"Paroch and those with him?"

"Of course I do," she snapped.

"It would look very nice on you, Akina," he commented. "Perhaps if it does not sell today, I will let you try it on." He smiled at her.

"It would," she agreed. She let the fabric run through her fingers. The skirt was a pale purple with images of flowers and birds along the hemline, while the bodice was cream-colored and pleated, looping down in front to allow ample room. The shoulders were covered, and the sleeves billowed out and ended just between the elbow and wrist. "You have great skill, Rylabet."

"It has served me well over the years."

Akina looked at him, and he smiled as he folded the pairs of breeches. "I meant with a needle and thread," she clarified.

"So did I."

Akina laughed, "What if I had meant skill as an agent of the guild?"

"Then I would have replied that that, too, has served me well over the years."

"I figured you would say that." After a moment, she grabbed the folded breeches and followed him out the front door to his cart. "So what does this plan entail?"

Rylabet busied himself with arranging his merchandise upon his cart, and when at last he took the breeches from Akina, he answered. "We will need the local support to be mingling in three separate locations in the plaza. I will position myself close to one edge of the plaza. When you spot the mark, Paroch or any others that were with him for that matter, you will…"

"If," she interrupted. "If I spot them."

"When," he continued. "When you spot someone, you will call out to them and wave them over to the cart; meanwhile, I will signal the others, and they will come and crowd around. You know, the usual bumping and jostling, just make sure they know not to let the mark escape until we are through with him. Of course, if it is Paroch, then we will take the sword if he has it with him."

"He will resist," she said.

"Then he will meet his maker," Rylabet stated coldly as he began re-arranging the capes for the third time.

"What if it is not him but another that was with him? What then?"

"We will figure that out as we go along. Come, I need to get into position in the plaza, and you have the locals to gather up." He hurriedly locked the door to his shop.

"How many should I gather?" Akina asked.

"Sixty or seventy should be fine," Rylabet instructed. "No more than one hundred." He began pushing his cart down the lane toward the market plaza. "Make sure they are armed with clubs at the very least," he called over his shoulder. "And make sure your spider is ready!"

\*\*\*

## The 15th of Lirinn, early afternoon

Aracelis stared at the outer wall gate before him. It was well-defended, and had he no Dakirin with him, he would have turned his army around and looked for easier prey.

"Have you ever been here before?" Aracelis asked.

"I have not," Niven replied.

"I have," Rakosa stated. "The gates are strong, and the walls are thick, and it is a good thing that we have the winged as our allies. If we did not, it would require three times our number to take the wall."

"I see you are in a fine mood today," Niven teased.

"I see no need for pleasantries or platitudes. I am speaking the truth," Rakosa replied as he stared at the outer wall.

"What is beyond that gate there?" Aracelis pointed.

"Once we have taken the outer wall, you will find several villages and at least three towns, Acorn, Crudan and Little Tormas. There may be more these days. It has been about twelve years since I set foot inside the outer wall."

"Do these towns and villages have walls? Do they have guards?" Aracelis continued with his questions.

"Walls are not needed in the Outlands, and there are guards, but they are there mainly to keep the peace and to hunt down any bandits or thieves attempting to ply their trade."

"How far is it to the city itself?"

"If you march straight to the city and have no delays, it would take two or three days, but I would not expect that to be the case this time."

Aracelis chuckled, "You have yet to fully appreciate the advantages we have with the Dakirin. Any resistance we meet on the road to Elas-Tormas will be dealt with swiftly and without mercy. We will attack from the front, and when the battle is engaged, the Dakirin will attack from behind. Any survivors will flee the battle dispirited, hunted by Dakirin and haunted by their failures."

"Then Elas-Tormas is stricken already," Rakosa said softly to himself.

Aracelis pretended not to have heard Rakosa. "On the given day, we will begin our assault, and once the outer wall falls, the city will follow quickly."

"When are we to begin the attack?" Rakosa asked.

"You will be told at the appropriate time," Aracelis snapped. "That is all."

Rakosa turned and walked toward where his men were waiting.

"Are you certain you wish for me to follow through on your order?" Niven asked.

"That is one order I will not change," Aracelis nodded. "That man is a snake, and a deadly one at that. He would just as soon bite us as the one he hates all the more."

"Is it up to me when it is carried out?"

"You can kill him after we are successful in the taking of Elas-Tormas."

"Does it matter where this occurs?"

"No, of course not, but I will leave that up to you. Make certain there are no witnesses. And Niven, I implore you to be careful."

"You needn't worry about me," Niven laughed. "He won't even see it coming."

***

## The 15th of Lirinn, just after noon

"Signal the others to slow their speed," the captain ordered. While holding tightly to the rigging, he was leaning over the railing and staring at the northern horizon. "Somewhere just beyond where I can see is our destination," he said to no one in particular. He looked behind at the ships sailing with him; he could personally see over thirty of them, and he knew there were closer to two hundred ships in his fleet. "Oh, to be a pirate, to sail the water and waves, to capture other's treasure, and send many to their graves." He sang softly.

His second in command heard him singing and joined in for the second verse. "Oh, to be a pirate, free as the wind in our sails, plying all the seas of Kren in port to avoid the gales."

"There will be no pirating this time, and more's the pity," the captain said.

"Unless some ship tries to run our blockade. What then?"

"Then let us hope she is filled with treasure!"

"Do you suppose we will see any fighting in the days ahead?" the second in command asked as the wind whipped his long, unkempt hair.

"That will depend upon how swiftly the city falls," the captain replied. "The longer the battle on land, the greater the likelihood we will see action on the water."

"Perhaps we could lend a hand?"

"What did you have in mind?" the captain asked.

"Why not sail in under cover of darkness and see if we cannot capture a few of their ships."

"I shall think on that," the captain stroked his bearded chin. "I would hate to have an enemy ship escape our blockade because we were busy with other things. Still, it would be a great prize, but not without risk," he added.

"Either that or we could set their sails on fire," the second offered.

"You *are* spoiling for a fight," the captain observed. "How long has it been since we had any real fun?"

"It was at least a month before, uh," he paused. "How shall I say it? We were joined to the Darklord's navy."

"Yeah, well, it was necessary to survive. But as soon as we can chart our own course again, we shall part ways. Either alone or with a few of the others we know well," he hinted.

"Land ho!" a voice called from above. "In the distance, I can see the city!"

The captain shielded his eyes and nodded when he, too, could finally see Elas-Tormas in the distance. "We shall sail for another twenty minutes or so to make certain they can see how numerous our fleet is. Then, we shall drop our anchors and watch the coming destruction."

The second in command relayed the orders to the flag master, who signaled the closest ships. Within moments, the orders spread throughout the fleet, and twenty minutes later, two hundred ships lay anchored in a line across the wide harbor mouth.

The captain watched in anticipation as four Lepnarion ships set sail and began to approach his position, but as more and more of his fleet became visible, the enemy ships turned quickly and returned to the city.

"Mind you, they might just attempt to sneak past us in the night. We shall have to be extra vigilant in the dark."

His second in command nodded in agreement, and soon this message, too, was delivered across the fleet.

"Send word only to the five captains that have been with us since the beginning. I wish to meet with them onboard my ship within the hour. I think we are going to have a little fun this evening, after all!"

# White Chapter Five: Misses, Missives And Misgivings

## The 15th of Lirinn, noon

As the seven members of the mantle prepared to leave the safety of the tower, Arvendal spoke quietly to them. "It would be best to stay on the main thoroughfares," he advised. "There are plenty of areas you would do well to avoid, especially as evening draws near."

Both Gehm and Reesal laughed. "We are more than capable of handling any trouble we might encounter in this city," Reesal boasted. "Right?" he asked Gehm.

"I should think so," Gehm agreed. "We can take care of ourselves in a fight against ruffians."

"Do not forget that many others are interested in obtaining the sword," Arvendal persisted. "Stay to the main roads, steer clear of the lesser traveled lanes and avoid the alleyways."

"Even in Terjavon, there are places no one goes unless they have no other options," Kourakin began speaking. "The beggar's haunt is one. Many people live there, few out of choice and most with no other place to go. They are a rough lot, pickpockets, cutpurses, thieves and others of that ilk, and then there are those who are sick, either physically or mentally. It is only three hundred yards wide and a little over two hundred yards long, but I guarantee you, Reesal, if you were to walk from one end of the haunt to the other in the daytime, you would be missing something, a coin-pouch, a hat, your dagger, perhaps even one of your crossbows."

"That bad, huh?" Perin asked as he scratched his cheek.

"And if you traveled through at night," Kourakin shook his head. "I daresay you would leave in a coffin."

"Nothing even close to that in our cities," Perin stated. "However, there is an island that we send convicted criminals to, and I would not set foot on that shore even if Paroch and the rest of you were with me. Too dangerous."

"Alright, fine, you have made your point. Gehm and I will stick to the main road," Reesal sighed. "But we should get started. The sooner we leave, the sooner we can return. Are you sure you do not have another bottle of that wonderful wine stashed away somewhere?" he asked Gedery.

Gedery shook his head. "Unfortunately, I could only bring a few when I fled the Dakirin attack."

"Elrynn? Draxin? Are you two ready?" Balatiere asked. "If I remember correctly, we have a bit farther to go, and I do want to return to the tower this evening."

"I am ready," Elrynn replied. Draxin did not reply, but he stood up and, looking at Balatiere, nodded.

Paroch waved to them as they headed for the door.

Arvendal opened the tower door and turned to face the seven of them, "There is mischief about. Stay to the main roads." He stepped aside, and one by one, they left the tower. Gehm, Reesal, Kourakin and Perin exited the gate, walking together. Balatiere and Elrynn were at the gate when Balatiere turned around.

"Draxin? Are you coming or not?"

"I will be there in a moment," he said. He turned and spoke with Arvendal for several minutes, then nodded and turned toward the other two.

"Let's go!" Balatiere shouted.

Draxin waited another moment longer, looking to the rooftops to the left and right of the tower before pulling his hood over his face and hurrying down the steps to catch up to the others.

\*\*\*

As Gehm, Kourakin, Perin and Reesal stepped from the market plaza, Gehm turned suddenly to the right and darted down a narrow alleyway. It was not very long, and he waited at the far end for the others.

"What are you doing? Arvendal instructed us to stay clear of alleys and less traveled places." Kourakin asked as he caught up to him.

"Yes, what *are* you doing?" Perin echoed a moment later.

"He is making certain that we are being followed," Reesal stated calmly as he brought up the rear. "I have observed two or three people that may be following us, and after alerting Gehm, he took us down here. In front of us lies a main thoroughfare, and we should be able to find our way to the docks without further trouble."

"You managed to spot someone following us in that crowd back there?" Perin asked.

Kourakin shook his head even as he looked back the way they had come. "I see no one," he said after a minute. "Perhaps you were mistaken."

"Even if I was mistaken, it is better to be wary and take precautions than to walk right into a troublesome situation," Reesal reasoned. Kourakin nodded in agreement.

"We should keep moving," Perin urged. "Our messages must be delivered, and the sooner, the better."

With one last look behind, Gehm led the way, followed by Kourakin and Perin. Reesal lingered for a minute longer before leaving the alley and following after the other three.

The road they entered from the alley was called Baker's Way, and with good reason, they passed at least a dozen bakeries with a crowd of people gathered around each one, bartering for and buying bread.

"Smells delicious," Reesal stated as he caught up to the others. "I could go for a freshly baked loaf right about now."

"No time," Perin called over his shoulder. "Perhaps when we are headed back to the tower, we could bring a few loaves for everyone."

"Well?" Gehm asked over his shoulder as they continued walking.

"There are six of them dressed in workman's clothes, and not one of them is very good at being stealthy," Reesal laughed.

"Any idea who they might be joined with?" Kourakin asked.

"Good question," Reesal pondered. "I should think any Weaver's guild agent is able to follow someone without being noticed."

"Unless, of course, they were wanting to be seen," Perin interjected.

"So I would say they are not from the Weaver's guild," Reesal continued. "It is possible they are with Morheim, but somehow, I think they would be wearing different attire. I would say they are with the Orders Gedery mentioned overhearing."

"Seems plausible," Kourakin nodded at the explanation.

They continued on Baker's Way until Gehm turned right onto Straight Street. In the distance could be seen the harbor and many masted ships.

"That was easy enough," Perin stated above the crowd noise. The streets of Elas-Tormas were crowded. When Straight Street ended at Western Gate, they turned left and, a few minutes later, took a right onto Wharf Street. Still, it took another thirty minutes of walking to reach the outskirts of the wharf district.

"They are persistent. I will give them that," Reesal stated. "We should be careful. There are eight of them now, and they are no longer trying to hide their presence."

Gehm began to jog, "We need to find the Hooves of the Sea," he called over his shoulder. "Come on, Reesal, pick up the pace."

"They are now jogging as well," Reesal called out.

"We need the Seamane," Perin mentioned as he jogged along.

When they reached the docks, Gehm stopped in front of an older man seated atop a crate, taking a break.

"My good sir, we are looking for two ships, the Hooves of the Sea and the Seamane. Would you, by chance, know where they might be docked?" Gehm asked.

The man looked up, squinting against the sun, and after shading his eyes with his left hand, he spit onto the dock beside Gehm's boots.

"What's that?" he asked.

"They would be Anari ships," Reesal continued.

"In case you have not noticed, there are a lot of ships docked here."

"Recently arrived within the past two days, perhaps," Perin clarified. The old man shrugged and turned back to his meager meal of fish and bread.

"My name is Perin, and I used to have a ship of my own," Perin informed him.

"Many may say the same thing," the old man answered. "Does not make it true."

"I named it the Iceblade," Perin explained. "She was a grand ship."

"Where did you sail then?" the old man asked with sudden interest.

"I am from the Baris Islands. We sailed the Northern Ceron near Thagorod with regularity and the Dhurrow itself on occasion."

"I am too old to be sailing anymore but in my days, I saw the Northern Ceron once. Twas enough for me," he added. "What happened to your Iceblade?"

"I sold it to settle a debt."

He nodded at Perin with respect. "Hey Pilter!" the old man hollered. "Where are those Anari ships docking these days?"

The worker named Pilter pointed west.

"I would search that way," the old man stated and immediately went back to his lunch.

"Thank you," Perin offered as the four of them hurried along.

"They are still following," Reesal warned quietly. They passed scores of sailing ships, some loading and others unloading cargoes of crates and barrels; some used a hoist, and others used muscle as men maneuvered their loads down narrow gangways. Many ships were anchored a bit farther from the docks, awaiting their turn.

"Looking for a ship named Hooves of the Sea," Gehm called to a group of workers huddled over a few barrels.

"What?" one of them scowled as he looked to Gehm.

"Hooves of the Sea? Where is she docked?" Gehm repeated.

They talked in hushed voices for a moment, and then one of them looked to Gehm.

"Think it is down that way," he answered, pointing to the west.

After another fifteen minutes and asking a few more questions, both ships were finally located. After explaining who they were looking for, Perin and Kourakin were soon standing on the deck of the Seamane delivering their missive to Tulikar, and three slips away, Gehm and Reesal were clambering aboard the Hooves of the Sea to deliver their missive to Orendien.

***

Elrynn and Balatiere slowed down and waited for Draxin to catch up to them.

"Why are you constantly lagging behind?" Elrynn finally asked after the third time. They were nearing the market plaza, and the noise of the crowds was plain to hear. "What would normally take fifteen minutes has taken us nearly an hour."

"Apologies," Draxin mumbled. He kept looking to his left and right.

"Are you concerned we are being followed?" Balatiere asked.

"No," Draxin replied.

"You expecting someone?" Balatiere persisted.

"Just go," Draxin stated. "You need not worry about me; I will be fine."

"It will be safer if we three stick together," Balatiere insisted.

"I suppose you are right," Draxin sighed. "Lead the way. I am here and following closely."

Elrynn stepped into the market plaza, a one-hundred-yard long and eighty-yard-wide paved plaza with permanent shops lining the periphery.

Most of the shops were tiny, a mere ten feet wide with barely enough room inside for a merchant to manufacture whatever wares they peddled, but a few were four or five times the size. These almost always had a crowd of curious onlookers gathered around. Hundreds of carts were spread out in the middle; many were selling foodstuffs, and the smells were delicious. Others sold trinkets of various kinds and questionable value. They passed a cart selling roasted pheasant, "Get them while they are hot! The best pheasant in the plaza!" Nearby, someone was selling garlic roasted mushroom caps stuffed with tangy goat cheese, and from another cart, bits of baked fish and sliced roots.

"Why do we insist on eating in the tower when all of *this* is *here?*" Balatiere asked with a wave of his hands. "After that wine, I am feeling hungry." He stopped at a cart where the lady was selling jelly-filled tarts.

"Hawthorne berry is all I have left," she smiled as she proffered a tart to Balatiere.

"They look wonderful. How much?"

"Five copper each," she answered with a smile. "But for you, I will sell four for fifteen copper."

"Come on," Elrynn urged. "We do not have time."

"I have to try at least one," Balatiere admitted. "You two go on; I will be right behind you," he announced as he fished in his pocket.

"What about sticking close together?" Elrynn leaned in and whispered in his ear.

"Do you see the end of the plaza right over there?" Balatiere pointed to several large red and yellow pennants flapping noisily in the breeze. "I will meet you there." He turned back to the woman and smiled. "I will take four of those tarts." He began counting out fifteen copper coins into her hand.

Elrynn laughed and shook his head as he began toward the pennants. Draxin was about to follow when he saw a curious site atop one of the shops on the right side of the plaza. It looked like a Dakirin was trying to communicate with wing flaps and head bobs. Draxin looked to Elrynn, already blending in with the crowd on his way to the other side of the plaza, then to Balatiere, who was still searching in his pocket for a few more coins. Quietly, he moved behind the cart and intently studied the Dakirin. It took a moment for him to realize what was being said, 'I speak with you. Can meet? Urgent!' He glanced around the entire plaza but saw no other Dakirin. 'Urgent! I speak with you!' the Dakirin continued.

'Do I know you?' Draxin asked with a series of complicated hand gestures.

'Yes,' came the reply. 'Yes. Yes. Yes.'

Draxin stood dumbfounded, mouth agape. He looked up at the Dakirin for a long while, oblivious to the people around him, even those who bumped into him as they hurried past. Then, after several moments, he began to take a few cautious steps away from the cart.

Balatiere finished the first tart and sighed with satisfaction, "That is an excellent tart," he commented even as he bit into his second one. "Are you here every morning?"

"Only the first and third day of each week," she replied. "I will be back in two days. I will try and bring a few different flavors for you if you would like."

"That would be amazing."

Suddenly, Balatiere heard his name being called by a woman.

"Balatiere, is that you?"

He looked around, trying to locate who in the crowd was calling to him.

"Balatiere! Over here."

He heard the voice a little louder now.

"It is you!" a young woman called out as she rushed up to him. Her green eyes sparkled as she smiled. "I was positive I saw you at Morheim's palace last night," she stated. "And now I know for certain I did. You were with a couple of others, let me see; one was Fulcwin, and another one was Paroch…"

"I would remember seeing you," Balatiere interrupted as he finished the second tart. He offered the third one to her.

"No thanks," she replied. "But I do want to show you something. I have a cart right over there." She pointed with her right hand and, slipping her left arm around Balatiere's, she began dragging him toward her cart.

"Who are you, and what were you doing at Morheim's last night?" he asked as he took a bite of his third tart.

"You can call me Akina and mostly observing," she laughed.

"But *where* were you?" Balatiere persisted.

"I already told you I was at Morheim's."

"You were definitely not at my table," Balatiere stated. "I would remember a woman as…" he paused and looked down at her. "Breathtaking as you are." He finished the third tart.

"You are too sweet," she replied. "Almost there."

"Where are we going?" Balatiere asked.

"I want to show you something," she replied. "It is just over there."

Suddenly, Balatiere resisted her efforts at guiding him and pulled his arm free of hers. "What is going on?" he asked. "What is it that you want from me?"

"You *are* a suspicious one," Akina smiled, patted his arm reassuringly and slid her left arm back around his. "I help my father sell capes and cloaks. Look there," she pointed. "You can just see one of the capes hanging from the pole. The green one? Do you see it?" Balatiere nodded that he could see it. "Good, I want to show you something special," she insisted as she began scratching at her left hand.

"Aaaah, Akina!" an older man exclaimed as she and Balatiere drew near. "Who have you brought with you?"

"This is one of the men I was telling you about last night. When I returned from Morheim's," she explained.

"Oh yes, the ones with that special sword, right?" he exclaimed loudly as he clapped his hands together. "So glad you agreed to stop by. What can I help you with?"

"Your daughter had something to show me," Balatiere answered slowly. He was about to take a bite of his fourth tart when he noticed many people beginning to crowd in close; they all seemed to be staring at him.

"I feel I should tell you," the old man began. "She is not *really* my daughter."

"I may have stretched the truth just a little bit," she admitted with a nod.

"What do you mean?" Balatiere asked. He looked to the young woman who was still holding onto his arm, a little tighter, perhaps.

"I barely know the young lady," he revealed with a shrug.

"Now, Rylabet, you are just being mean," she teased.

Balatiere dropped his last tart, and his hand went to the hilt of his sword. "You had better tell me what is going on," he menaced as he jerked his arm free of the woman's grasp.

"Even if I told you, you would not believe me," Rylabet promised.

"Just relax," Akina urged as she placed her left hand upon his arm. "We just want the sword of Abion," she whispered.

Balatiere shoved Akina aside and drew his sword. "Elrynn! Draxin!" he yelled as loud as he could. "Elrynn! Draxin!" He felt something crawling up his neck. And even as he raised his right hand to swipe at his skin, he felt a small pinprick. Almost immediately, he started to feel dizzy. "Elrynn! Draxin!" he hollered one more time. He began to stagger around, his vision growing suddenly blurry. The gathered crowd, thinking he was intoxicated, laughed and jeered until he fell to the ground sweating profusely, eyes open and bulging, and his breath coming in ragged gasps.

Elrynn was the first to arrive, shoving his way through the crowd. He immediately went to Balatiere's aid, kneeling beside him. Draxin appeared a moment later.

"Where were you?" Elrynn asked as Draxin knelt beside him.

"I thought I saw a Dakirin across the plaza and stepped away to investigate," Draxin answered. "What happened?" He saw the uneaten tart on the ground and picked it up to examine it closely. "I heard Balatiere say he wanted four of these. Do you think he was poisoned?" Draxin asked. He began looking around for any other dropped tarts.

"I am not certain, but come, we must get him back to the tower," Elrynn stated as he and Draxin struggled to help Balatiere into a seated position.

Rylabet stepped forward. "Hello there, do you recognize me?" he asked Elrynn. "You and two other men with you all entered my shop during this past springfest. Remember?"

Elrynn glanced up at Rylabet, "You're the tailor," he said with a nod.

"At your service," Rylabet smiled. He extended his hand toward Elrynn. "What seems to be the trouble with your friend there?" he asked as he looked down at him. "Nothing catching, I hope," he added with his hand upon his chest.

"He was fine when I left him not more than five minutes ago," Elrynn answered. "Did you see anything?"

"Only that he was eating several tarts," Rylabet offered. "Perhaps they were bad?"

"Perhaps," Elrynn said. "We need to get him back to where we are staying."

"Here, let us help you. Akina! Come and help," he called over his shoulder as he leaned down and grabbed Balatiere's left arm. Akina appeared beside Rylabet, and she, too, grabbed hold of his left arm. Together, the four of them helped Balatiere to his feet, but he was unable to stand on his own.

"Where are we headed?" Rylabet asked.

"Thank you," Elrynn said as both he and Draxin placed their arms around Balatiere's back. "We have him now. Thank you both for your help."

"I have those blue capes if you are still interested," Rylabet offered as he stepped back, rubbing his hands together.

"Perhaps some other time," Elrynn said over his shoulder. They made their way slowly back to the tower, Balatiere's head bowed to his chest and his feet dragging against the paved street.

"Can you hear me, Balatiere?" Draxin asked as they left the market plaza behind.

Balatiere moaned and attempted to raise his head. "They…are…after…Abion," he managed, and then his head slumped down again.

"Who? Who is after Abion?" Elrynn asked, but Balatiere did not reply except to moan once more.

"Do you have any idea what is going on?" Draxin asked.

"Nothing good," Elrynn answered. "Nothing good at all."

\*\*\*

"Perhaps it would be better for you both to stay for a while longer," Orendien suggested.

"Whatever for?" Reesal asked as he drained his goblet and placed it on the table before him.

"Tavanian wine has a way of," Orendien thought for a moment. "Clouding one's discernment. Stay at least until its effects are lessened," he urged.

"Nonsense," Reesal countered. "I am perfectly fine." He stood up, leaning heavily upon the table to steady himself. "It is past time for us to return to the tower." He took a step sideways into a support beam.

"Not to mention making you walk like you are out to sea when you are anchored in port." Orendien chuckled.

"I will be fine," Reesal growled.

"Some bread then," Orendien suggested, hiding his smile by scratching at his thin beard. "It has been long since we ate."

"I was planning on stopping at several of the establishments along Baker's Way for a loaf or two from each to take back to the tower with me. We need to get going; we want to make sure they are still open," Reesal explained.

"All the bakers will be closed by now, and besides, the bread is better first thing in the morning when it is fresh," Orendien offered.

"Then we will buy some in the morning when it is fresh," Reesal laughed. He struggled up the stairs, swaying precariously with each step. "But we are still leaving."

"Then, if you will not stay on board this evening, will you please allow me time to gather an escort?" Orendien asked. "Many of the roads in Elas-Tormas are dangerous after the sun sets."

"We have no need for an escort," Reesal laughed. "We made it here just fine. I am certain we can make it back the same." He leaned against the railing while he contemplated the narrow gangplank to the dock.

"The escort was not for you but rather for lord Gedery," Orendien explained. "We would ensure his safety on returning to the Hooves of the Sea."

"If you are worried about safety, perhaps it is you who should wait until morning," Reesal replied as he stumbled down the gangplank.

"I will gather up an escort," Orendien said. "And be right behind you. I insist!" He added when Reesal looked back with a scowl.

"I apologize for my friend," Gehm said politely to Orendien, who nodded his acceptance. "Do you have need of directions to the garden district?"

"I know the general location of it," Orendien replied. "But we will be following you."

"Just in case you lose sight of us, take Wharf to Western, turn left, then a right onto Straight and a left onto Baker's Way," Gehm said as he walked down the gangplank.

Gehm and Reesal walked slowly back toward the Seamane.

"I think this is the ship they are on," Reesal said as he stood close to the edge of the dock, staring up at the side of a large ship. "Hello up there!"

A head appeared over the railing. "What do you want?"

"Perin and Kourakin," Reesal replied.

"They are friends of ours," Gehm explained. "They delivered a message to the Seamane for one named Tulikar, I believe."

"This is the Seamane, and yes, Tulikar is here. Your friends are aboard and still conversing," the sailor stated. "Tell me your names, and I will let them know you are here."

"I am Gehm, and this is Reesal," Gehm replied.

The head disappeared and then reappeared several minutes later, "Tulikar says they are almost finished, and you are more than welcome to come aboard and wait." He smiled.

"No, thank you," Reesal replied quickly. "Tell our friends we will meet them back at the tower." He turned to leave.

"Please, let them know we have already left," Gehm said, then he turned and hurried after Reesal. "What is the rush anyway?" he asked.

"I do not trust any of them."

"Who?" Gehm asked.

"Morheim, Sarahin, Gedery, the Orders," Reesal listed them.

"We all are fighting against the Darklord," Gehm reminded him.

"Envy makes bitter enemies of those who should be friends," Reesal replied. "We have been told by our visitors that Morheim and the Orders are after Abion."

"So is the Weaver's Guild, according to Arvendal," Gehm added.

"Have you considered that maybe Gedery is out to grab the sword for himself? Or Sarahin, for that matter?" Reesal suggested as they left the docks behind and continued up Wharf Street.

"What good would the sword do either of them?" Gehm laughed. "They are not of Lepnarion descent."

"Why would Orendien need a hundred men to come to the tower?" Reesal questioned.

"He already explained it was to ensure that Gedery would be safe on returning to the ship," Gehm replied.

"One man against the mantle will surely fail, but a hundred men? We would be hard pressed," Reesal pointed at Gehm. "With a hundred men, he could simply take it."

"Arvendal let them in," Gehm argued.

"He also allowed Galortin in," Reesal reminded him.

"Galortin held the same token of calling we do," Gehm sighed. "We were all fooled by his elaborate ruse."

"Perhaps *this* is just another elaborate ruse," Reesal fumed.

"The wine has gone to your head this evening," Gehm said under his breath.

"I heard that," Reesal growled. "It may be true that Tavanian wine is potent, but I can handle my drink."

"I have seen you do just that many times before," Gehm agreed. "I am simply saying you are not yourself right now. That is all," he explained.

"I have not been the same since the day we fled Thagorod."

"I only meant…" Gehm started to speak.

"You are not the same either," Reesal interrupted. He reached into a deep pocket inside his shirt. Gehm caught the strong scent of burnt wood as Reesal brought his hand out and revealed the charred remains of a tiny doll. "After what the mantle has been through, I doubt any of us are," Reesal admitted as he hid the doll back in his pocket.

As they continued walking, Gehm put his arm around Reesal's shoulder. "Yes, we have been through a lot, but remember who we are fighting for."

Reesal nodded.

"Now we have another pressing matter," Gehm said. "Where exactly are we?"

The two men stopped, and Reesal scratched his head as he looked around. The paved road was lit by an occasional lantern, but the road itself was deserted. "I must admit I have no idea," he said after a moment.

"Nothing looks familiar in this dim light, but we can simply retrace our steps, and we should be fine."

"You two should pay closer attention to your surroundings," a voice suddenly challenged from behind them.

They both turned to find a gang of seven men blocking their way.

"We are looking for the garden district," Gehm offered.

"Obviously, this is not it," one man replied. He was taller than the rest, bald with a long mustache, one end of which he twirled between his fingers.

"I can see this is not the garden district. Which way do we go to get there from here?" Gehm asked.

"You are trespassing here," the man stated coldly. "And there is a fine for trespassing." He smiled and pulled his tunic back to reveal the hilt of a sword. "Pay the fine, and you are free to go."

"We are visitors in this g reat city of Elas-Tormas and were unaware of such places as this," Gehm continued. "You must allow us to pass unmolested."

The man and those with him began to laugh. "We control this neighborhood," he insisted. "And I say you cannot leave without paying the fine."

"That will be a problem," Gehm stated as he reached for the hammer at his belt.

"Are you not curious as to what the fine is?" the man persisted.

"I give you fair warning," Reesal challenged. "If you seek to hinder us in any way, many of you will be hurt, and a few of you may even end up dead."

"Bold words from two men lost and surrounded," the man motioned with both of his hands. The sounds of movement were heard behind them.

Reesal turned and placed his back against Gehm's. "I have eight, make that nine men back here," he said calmly over his shoulder as he loosed the hammer at his belt. "So which one of you wants to be the first to feel my hammer?" he yelled the final three words and took a step toward them. All but one took a step back. "Looks like *you* are the one," Reesal stated. He drew his hammer and advanced slowly. "You are about to pay a steep price for trying to collect a fine."

"Be careful, Reesal," Gehm called over his shoulder without taking his eyes off of the men before him.

\*\*\*

Perin and Kourakin were standing on the deck of the Seamane, ready to disembark, when they saw a large group of soldiers marching to a stop by the gangplank.

"Tulikar," one of the men waved, "I would speak with you."

"Come aboard, Orendien," Tulikar replied. "If you would excuse me for a moment," Tulikar said to Perin and Kourakin as he went to speak with Orendien.

"What do you think this is about?" Perin whispered.

"Orendien is with Lord Gedery on the Hooves of the Sea," one of the deckhands replied. "We sailed from Loshad together."

"That must have been difficult," Kourakin said. "Escaping from the destruction of Anar," he added.

"You have no idea," he replied with a shake of his head. "I can still smell the reek of the burning of Loshad. In the days leading up to our escape, embers were our greatest concern. Day and night, we had the entire crew hauling buckets of water up into the rigging to make sure nothing caught on fire. Then, three days before we left, those cursed winged ones appeared."

"Dakirin," Perin corrected.

"What?" the deckhand asked.

"The cursed winged ones, as you call them, are actually Dakirin," Perin explained.

The deckhand frowned at him for the interruption and then continued, "They would swoop down from the clouds and then disappear again in a puff of green smoke, and one or two more of our crew lay dead or dying. The last day was the worst. Despite our best efforts, a fire started in one of the sails. We managed to put it out, but the sail was damaged beyond repair, as well as some of the rigging. It was a good thing Lady Sarahin made it aboard with her men because as we were attempting to affect repairs so we could set sail, those Da…?"

"Dakirin," Perin added with a nod.

"Yeah, Dakirin attacked again. This time, there was about thirty of 'em. We managed to kill three, I think, before the rest flew away, but it was a hard fight. I lost my best friend in that fight," he added.

"Sorry for your loss," Kourakin replied.

"I am sorry too," the deckhand responded evenly. "But it doesn't change a thing." He was about to say something else when Tulikar and Orendien walked over.

"I apologize for the delay," Tulikar said. "Orendien here is from the Hooves of the Sea, Lord Gedery's ship. He has an escort ready to bring both Queen Sarahin and Lord Gedery back to the docks safely. Would you be willing to take them back to the tower?"

"Certainly," Perin replied. "I am Perin," he stated as he held out his right hand to Orendien.

"You have my thanks," Orendien replied as he shook his hand.

"Kourakin," Kourakin said as he shook Orendien's hand.

"Did you want to add any men to this escort?" Orendien asked Tulikar.

"An armed host marching through the quiet streets of Elas-Tormas might elicit a strong response from King Morheim," Tulikar replied after a moment. "However, if we are escorting Her Highness Queen Sarahin, that would be another story. Yes, I will lead a hundred men of my own. We will meet you at the edge of the wharf district."

"Agreed," Orendien laughed. "If you two would accompany me to the edge of the wharf district, we will await Tulikar there."

As the three men walked down the gangplank, Kourakin observed a figure peering out from between two buildings and quickly hiding again.

"We are being spied upon," he whispered.

"Spies are everywhere in this city these days," Orendien replied with a laugh. "No need to concern yourself. We are breaking no law, and we have nothing to hide."

"That may be, but sometimes it is better to disguise intentions and objectives in the face of hostile resistance," Kourakin replied.

"Hostile resistance?" Orendien asked. "I feel the need to remind you that though the enemy is near, our allies still control this city."

Kourakin was about to reply when Perin gave his elbow a quick tug, and when Kourakin glanced at him, Perin shook his head slightly.

"Point taken," Kourakin replied. "Tell me, Orendien, how long have you been with Gedery?"

"For twenty years now," he said with a shake of his head and a laugh. "I cannot believe it has been that long. Why do you ask?"

They drew near the men waiting on the dock, and while Orendien and Kourakin carried on their conversation, Perin listened and observed. Many of the men had arms and heads and faces scarred by fire.

"Curiosity is all," Kourakin answered. "I have spent more than twenty years in the service of my country."

The two of them carried on their conversation until it was announced that Tulikar was approaching.

"See, that did not take long at all," Orendien said. "Shall we?" He motioned for Perin and Kourakin to take the lead.

The streets were wide and empty in the late evening, and Tulikar and Orendien walked with Perin and Kourakin, their men marching in twin columns ten paces behind.

"You say you took Straight and Western to get to Wharf?" Tulikar asked. Perin nodded. "If we continue on Wharf, it runs into Baker's Way. It is much quicker."

"That is good to know," Kourakin stated. "We should go that way."

"But our friends are unaware of that fact and would have headed back the same way they remembered. We must go that way as well in case something has happened to them," Perin said.

"If we split up, then perhaps it will not be quite as noteworthy for anyone still spying on us," Kourakin offered. "Perin and Tulikar can go the way we went earlier today, and Orendien and I will follow Wharf to Baker's Way."

This was readily agreed to by the four of them, and when they reached Western Gate Perin, Tulikar and the men with him turned left and marched into the night.

"You were saying more than twenty years," Orendien continued. "Where did you serve?"

"Many places," Kourakin began. "Fought a few battles in Beraith, fought a few battles on the road to Rusalka on the Inland Sea."

"Now, that is one place I would really like to visit," Orendien interrupted. "The Inland Sea. I wonder how big it really is."

"It is big, which is why they call it a sea," Kourakin laughed. "I have never been on it myself, only cooled my feet in the waters along the shore. But I hear there are tremendous storms that rage for days and weeks, and there are rumors of water dragons."

Orendien burst out laughing. "Water dragons? In the Inland Sea? Now, that is a tall tale if I have ever heard one."

"I have never seen one, but the humble folks in Rusalka swear they have. Apparently, they are dangerous, and this is why they refuse to sail more than a few miles from the shoreline."

Suddenly, they became aware of the sound of fighting, men yelling and cursing and the heavy thump of hammers on metal shields. By the time they reached the location of the fighting, it had already ended; two men lay motionless in the middle of the street, and in the dim lantern light could be seen several smears of blood where other bodies had presumably been dragged away.

"Probably local gangs fighting over territory, but be careful," Orendien warned as Kourakin went to investigate.

Kourakin came to the first body lying face down in a pool of blood and knelt beside it. He could discern no breathing and went to investigate the other body less than eight paces away. Looking down, he recognized the armor as being Reesal's, and as he motioned for Orendien to come near, he fell to his knees.

"What is it?" Orendien asked as he ran up.

"I know this man."

"Is he dead?" Orendien asked.

Before Kourakin could answer, Reesal opened his eyes and drew a ragged breath. "Help Gehm," he urged before closing his eyes again.

Litters were hastily formed out of capes and spears, and both Gehm and Reesal were gently picked up and carried to the tower of Tergia.

# Black Chapter Five: The Selfish And The Selfless

## *The 15th of Lirinn, evening*

"Tell me," Hammer asked as he paced back and forth with his hands clasped behind his back. "What good did it do to kill those two? Do we have the sword?"

"No," Blade replied testily.

"This debacle has made our position more tenuous," Rose stated.

"How?" Blade demanded.

"When those two do not return, then..."

"Then what?" Blade interrupted. "We killed two of their number. Do you know how many more we face? Either of you?" Both Hammer and Rose shook their heads. "Me neither, but I do know this. There are always casualties in a conflict."

"Yes, three of my Hammers lie dead."

"And a Rose, too," Rose added.

"I lost three Blades as well, but if we can grab that sword, it will be well worth it. Do not lose sight of what we are doing and why," Blade urged. "This mission we are on has implications far beyond what we do here this evening."

"Yes, but to lose so many lives in the process," Rose agonized.

"And this is why we Blades look down on you. You are weak!"

"Having a love for life does not make one weak," Rose protested.

"That is not how I see it," Blade laughed as he twirled the end of his mustache. "If only they would have listened to me, we would not have had to kill them." He looked to his left hand and flexed it, then winced as he moved to straighten his arm.

"We cannot change that now," Hammer intoned. "What is our plan? It has been brought to my attention that one of Morheim's spies saw our confrontation with those two and is probably informing on us as we speak."

"I do not like the sound of that at all," Rose said.

"This certainly narrows our options," Hammer stated.

"It does indeed, but we may still have an opportunity. It will be tricky with Morheim snooping about, however." Blade sighed and twirled both ends of his mustache. "Morheim will make his move quickly now that he is certain the Orders are after the sword as well, which means that we will need to move quicker still. My spies tell me the men we spotted leaving the docks are planning on escorting some folks in the tower back to their ships."

"What good does that do?" Rose asked.

"If we knew the route they were going to take, we could ambush them," Blade mused. "But I am more worried about Morheim's men. They show little mercy to those in their way."

"This is true," Hammer agreed. A knock on their door interrupted him. "What is it?"

"Urgent news," came a muffled reply.

"Enter and speak," Blade commanded.

The door opened slowly, and a man walked in. He was of the Rose, disheveled and shaking. "I bring news of the war. The enemy is at the walls and..."

"We were already informed of this," Hammer replied quickly.

"There are still two gates in the west that do not have any visible enemy before them," the man continued. "But we have seen the enemy marching in that direction, so soon all gates will be blocked. There will be no escape!"

"It does appear our escape routes are dwindling," Rose began. "However, once we have Abion, we can always set sail and…"

"The harbor is blockaded by several hundred ships as of a few hours ago. We are soon to be completely surrounded." The messenger began shaking again.

"This changes things significantly," Rose said as she waved for the messenger to leave and close the door behind him.

"I do not see how," Blade argued. "We still do not have Abion."

"I am thinking about our love of life," Rose laughed. "It would be better to be alive and have another opportunity to try and capture Abion at some later date than to stay in this city and be killed either with or without that cursed sword."

"Your true colors are showing through Rose," Blade mocked.

"Red for the Rose blood shed in the street," Rose replied.

"I was thinking more along the lines of yellow for being a coward," Blade laughed. "Flee if you want, not that there is a safe way to flee, mind you."

"Actually, I may have a way out of here," Hammer spoke up. "There were many ancient tunnels near Crudan, old mining tunnels. Some of them were connected with tunnels leading under the walls of Elas-Tormas, and a few were extended toward the outer wall. I have heard that smugglers used them in the past, and when this was discovered, the king had many of those tunnels collapsed."

"That information does us little good," Blade complained. "Unless you have been working on clearing one out," he added hopefully.

Hammer smiled at him but remained silent.

"Are you not open to other ways of retrieving this sword?" Rose asked.

"When time runs short, the direct way is usually the best way," Blade replied with a nod.

"Usually?" Hammer asked.

"Most always," Blade reiterated. "About that tunnel near Crudan?"

"There is one tunnel still open," Hammer admitted. "It is known only to a few in the Order of Miners and, of course, to myself."

"How do we find this tunnel?" Blade asked.

Hammer smiled again but did not reply.

"Is that how it is?" Blade asked.

"When the sword is in our possession, I will lead you through the tunnel myself."

"How do you propose we get the sword now?" Rose asked.

"There is no need to change our plan," Blade admitted. "We will still have the opportunity when they leave the safety of their tower."

"Then a toast is in order," Rose said suddenly. "Allow me." Rose hurried into the back room and appeared a moment later bearing a tray with three goblets on it. After placing it on the table, she disappeared into the room again, only to reappear bearing a glass decanter and a small flask.

"Is that Tavanian wine?" Blade asked with sudden interest.

Rose smiled. "This wine is very potent," she began as she unstopped the decanter and filled each goblet. The wine had a pale yellow color with a hint of green to it. "Fermented from the berries of the…"

"What's in the flask?" Blade asked suddenly.

"The flask is for those who cannot handle the full potency of this wine," Rose answered and opened the flask, allowing four drops to fall into her goblet. She looked to Hammer, who nodded, and she added four drops to his goblet. Rose looked to Blade with raised brows.

"How potent can a berry wine be?" he scoffed. "I have no need to weaken this drink." He reached over and, grabbing hold of his goblet, tipped it back and downed its contents in one long drink. He sighed in satisfaction. "I am going to take that sword, and when I do, I will remember your cowardice," he promised Rose.

Neither Rose nor Hammer replied, but they watched Blade with keen interest as each sipped from their own goblet.

"What was that stuff anyway?" Blade asked slowly. He blinked his eyes several times and shook his head.

"Just some wine made from the berries of the Nerium bush," Rose answered.

"Nerium? Thothe are poithonouth!" he slurred. He tried to stand but could not and ended up falling headlong onto the floor.

"It can be," Rose replied as she took another sip of the wine. "If you do not have the antidote." Hammer shook his head as he stared down at Blade writhing in pain. "You have overstayed your welcome," he said dryly.

Blade reached a shaking hand toward the table, but the effort was too great, and his arm fell to the floor. He opened his mouth to speak, drew in a ragged breath, and then exhaled long and slow as his eyes rolled back in his head.

"Good riddance! Now, let us discuss our plan as we finish the wine," Rose chuckled.

"Agreed," Hammer stated. "We could follow this Paroch wherever he goes and be prepared to take advantage of any opportunity the moment it presents itself."

"Perhaps we should just travel to Mar-Storin and let the head of our orders know that Abion has been found again," Rose suggested.

"It would have been so much easier to try and grab the sword outside of the city. But first, we need to get safely away from the coming destruction!"

\*\*\*

"The selfish regard the selfless with scorn, and the selfless regard the selfish with pity," Rylabet stated. "I have always found that to be fascinating."

"And which one are you, I wonder?" Akina asked quietly to herself.

"Now, *that* would depend on many things," Rylabet replied. He chuckled and shook his head. "However, let us get back to the problem at hand." He turned to a shelf stacked high with thin scrolls and began rifling through them.

"What are you looking for?" Akina asked as she peeked over his shoulder.

"A specific schimbare scroll. One that will make you appear to be a native healer from the Phayroc region of Antaria." He looked at her for a moment to see if she understood. "This is the area that your gravespider came from," he continued explaining. "The one whose bite has poisoned Balatiere. If an antidote is not administered, he will most surely die," Rylabet said last with mock concern, which quickly turned to laughter.

"A native healer?" she asked.

"Oh yes, you must look authentic if you are to be convincing enough to pull off the next part of our plan."

"And do we have an antidote for the gravespider?" Akina wanted to know.

"In a manner of speaking," Rylabet answered slyly. "You must have developed some immunity to the gravespider venom by now?"

Akina sat down in a chair beside the table and stared down at her left hand. She spread her thumb and fingers wide, staring at the stretched skin, at the spider there. Gently, she rubbed across the spider with her right index finger; the legs of the spider moved in response to the stimulation.

"What does it feel like?" Rylabet asked over his shoulder as he continued searching through the scrolls.

Akina continued staring at the spider while it repositioned its legs. She thought back to when she had first become an assassin for the Weaver's Guild. On the outskirts of the small town of Ormas, nestled amongst three-hundred-year-old oaks, stood the remains of a once grand building. A hermitage, once a bastion of learning for Ellonas, now abandoned and picked over by locals for building materials. The dirt path was not wide but well-worn, packed hard by the countless footsteps of those who sought more from the guild they served. She smiled as she remembered her initial fear when the doors creaked open, and she was beckoned inside by two black-robed and hooded figures. The smell of molder and rot stung her nostrils immediately, but it did not take long before it became familiar to her, even comforting in its pungent odor. Her room was in a dark corner above the main floor. Thirty feet above her bed, there was no roof save the interwoven limbs of the mighty oak trees, and beneath her leather-booted feet, the sagging floor of sodden timbers did nothing to ease her fears. Nearly every morning, she was awakened by the dripping of water from the dew-drenched canopy. Indeed, it took a long time before she was able to sleep while it was raining, and even then, she would stay up and watch the lightning as it played across the clouds, only falling asleep as the last peals of thunder faded into the distance. Everywhere in the hermitage, the hewn stones were covered in hues of green, reddish brown, and black from growing molds and lichens. Most were harmless and some mildly irritating, while a few were quite deadly. Half-rotted timbers jutted from the walls, signifying where the upper floors had been. Remnants of stained glass windows stubbornly clinging to their decaying frames would gleam and sparkle under the beams of any sunlight that managed to penetrate the surrounding oaks. The stones were always cold to the touch, no matter the time of day or year, cold and dark.

Rylabet cleared his throat and turned to look at her.

"Most days, I cannot feel anything," she replied. She rubbed the spider again, this time a little harder than before. She winced momentarily as the spider's fangs pierced her skin. She moved her thumb back and forth a few times, and the spider relaxed its grip, adjusting its legs once again.

"How did they get that in your hand?" Rylabet asked as he turned back to the shelf to resume searching through the scrolls.

Akina shook her head at the memory.

She knew of the ceremony of mating a spider to its host; she had read the books and listened to her teachers, but she felt nervous as she descended the stairs into darkness. Following the instructions given to her, she found the closed door and knocked upon it in the expected manner.

"You may enter," a voice answered, and the door swung open of its own accord. Brilliant firelight streamed into the darkened hall, and she squinted against the sudden light, but the warmth greeted her, beckoned to her. It had been a long time since she had felt real warmth. "Enter or go away, but do not simply stand in my doorway," the voice barked. Akina entered the room and approached the fire slowly. "Over here," the voice sounded on her left. Turning, she saw a stone table, not much longer than her arm extended and not much wider than her torso. There were several large iron rings set in the stone. "Take a seat. Place your left arm on the table and through the rings," the voice said as it drew nearer. Akina stole a quick glance; the figure was robed and hooded like all the other teachers, his face hidden by shadows. She had just placed her arm on the table and slipped her hand through the fourth and final ring when the figure rushed over, manipulating the rings. The one closest to her shoulder was tightened first, then the one by her elbow, then the middle of her forearm and finally the one around her wrist. The rings gripped her arm tightly so that she could not move it at all; only her hand and fingers could she move. Akina tried to pull her arm free but could not.

"There is no need to panic," the voice intoned. "You have been told what to expect. Besides, you volunteered for this." He walked over to the fire and picked up a small device, glowing bright orange at the tip. "I must warn you," he said as he drew near. "It is imperative that you keep still. This is a delicate task, and any movement on your end will cause quite a bit more pain and may even result in the loss of a finger or two." Akina placed her hand flat on the table and gritted her teeth. "You may look on or avert your gaze as you wish," the man continued. He brought the device, a short-handled skewer still glowing red at the end, close to the flesh between her finger and thumb. "I suppose I should ask if you are ready," he began. "But every time I ask, the answer is always the same. Still, it might be a good thing to know." He paused. "Are you..." he started to ask, and then he slowly pushed the skewer into her flesh. The pain was intense, and Akina clenched her eyes closed. She heard the sound of sizzling and the smell of burnt flesh stung her nose, but she did not move the fingers of her left hand. "Impressive, not even a flinch," he said as he worked quickly. "You are a pleasant surprise. I have seen grown men scream out, and yet you have not uttered a sound." The intense pain subsided to be replaced by a sharp throbbing, and presently,

Akina felt a tugging at the skin on her left hand. She ventured a peak. The man was no longer wielding the skewer but rather an odd-shaped instrument that had been inserted into the skin and was tugging as he manipulated it.

"What is that?" Akina asked as she watched.

"I should think the worst part is over," he answered. "But this little device is rolling up the skin around the hole I made. This should, in theory, form a nice circular scar in the middle of which will reside your spider. Ideally, the center will be deep enough for the spider's body to lie flush with the scar while its legs will drape over, giving the appearance of an intricate tattoo."

"And if the hole is not deep enough?" Akina asked.

"I have been told the spider will *make* it deep enough," he chuckled.

"How exactly?" Akina pressed. The pain had subsided to a dull throb.

"It is not pleasant, and that is why I take extra care to make sure it will be deep enough," he explained. After a few more minutes, he removed the tool and inspected his work. "A fine job if I do say so. I will be right back." He left the room, closing the door behind him. Akina looked at her hand but could not see where the hole was. She wiggled her pinky and then her ring finger and middle, all without pain. However, the moment she moved her index finger, the pain increased. She closed her eyes and began moving her thumb in slow circles, bringing it in close to her fingers and then stretching it out again. After a few minutes of this, she made a fist and then clenched it, again painful but not terribly so. She continued moving and flexing her fingers until she heard the door open and the man enter. She opened her eyes and watched him approach the table upon which he placed a small wooden box and a glass vial.

"See, it is not too bad. Before long, you will not even remember that pain." Akina did not respond but continued moving her fingers. "Now, for this next part, I need you to tilt your hand toward the ceiling as far as you can and then hold very still." Akina did as she was asked and watched as he opened the vial and placed it above the hole in her hand. She thought she could smell the faint odor of decaying flesh, but the smell did not linger. He tapped the vial gently several times until a fine grey powder began to fall. It looked like ashes, and it burned when it touched the raw, exposed flesh of her hand. She winced but did not move. He tapped until the entire hole was filled, then after plugging the vial, he took a wet cloth and, using just the tip, he dabbed up all the powder that had fallen onto her skin outside the ring. This took several minutes, but he was thorough and soon was satisfied with the results.

"What is that powder?" Akina asked.

"It serves two purposes; the first is to prevent your body from repairing and filling in the hole I made."

"And the second?"

"The second is to make your spider feel right at home." Before she could say anything else, he grabbed the wooden box, placed it above her hand and slowly slid the top open. A single tap caused a pair of spiders to tumble out onto her hand. Akina held her breath as she watched the battle unfold. Both spiders were about as big around as her pinky nail. She could feel them ever so slightly as they moved around her hand, one positioned itself on her thumb and the other on her index finger. They were both black with a blue area on their backs in the shape of a teardrop; the area around the eyes and the mandibles was bright red, as were the tips of their legs. They began waving their two front legs in the air, taunting, intimidating the other, then quicker than her eyes could follow, the spiders leaped at each other, a mass of legs and fury. One spider tried to retreat, but the other was upon it in an instant. The fight was over quickly, and before Akina could even comprehend what was happening, the victor was nestling into the hole in her hand, the hairs from the spider's body irritating the exposed flesh.

"I found it!" Rylabet crowed as he turned to face Akina, scroll held high in one hand.

Akina shook her head for a moment, "What did you say?" She found herself gently rubbing the skin around her spider.

"You were deep in thought," he commented.

"Mhm," Akina nodded.

"Good memories, I hope."

Akina shrugged.

"I have read about the Cult of Jabitern. The great sacrifices it requires of its adherents."

"It is not that bad once you get used to it," Akina explained. "It can even be rewarding."

Rylabet laughed. "I will take your word for it, but Vapir is enough for me," he explained. "Now, about our plan."

\*\*\*

## The 15th of Lirinn, before midnight

"Every gate in the outer wall is hemmed in by thousands of enemy soldiers, and now word reaches my ears that the harbor mouth is blockaded by several hundred enemy ships. Elas-Tormas is completely surrounded for the first time in her history." Morheim remarked. "I wonder if Vindramion foresaw this at her founding."

"Not every gate, m'lord. Two western gates have no enemy before them as of yet. This city will not fall," the advisor answered confidently. "Her walls are tall and strong and defended by our finest troops."

"Walls, no matter their height, will be of little use against an enemy with wings," the king replied as he paced.

"There have been no reports of any winged enemy in the ranks of the army encamped before our walls. It would appear the reports of winged Dakirin were highly exaggerated."

"The sword of Abion is within my grasp, and it is withheld from me! And to make matters worse, several hundred men have been seen entering the tower of Tergia. Paroch is strengthening his defensive position," Morheim fumed.

"Your Highness, may I remind you, it is only one report. It is possible, indeed highly probable, that the report has been overstated. I would advise caution," the advisor said calmly. He smiled and offered Morheim a goblet of wine. Morheim accepted the goblet and took a drink.

"He is planning treachery against the throne of Elas-Tormas! Against me!"

"You are jumping to conclusions again." The advisor smoothed the wrinkles from his clothes and then looked up at Morheim and cleared his throat. "Mere possession of Abion, Kingsword though it may be, does not confer the right to rule over Lepnar. One must be of noble birth, and this Paroch of Cul-Amaron is most definitely not."

"How do you know?" Morheim challenged.

"I have had some of our best scholars poring over the royal genealogies, and there is no mention of one of royal blood named Paroch." He paused for a moment before continuing. "In fact, Your Highness might want to consider bringing charges against Fulcwin and those who are with him." The king looked at him with raised brows. "For inciting panic," the advisor explained. "And spreading falsehoods, undermining the morale of our defenders. There are a whole host of reasons to pick them up and have them publicly punished or even executed. And, of course, once that is done, the Kingsword will be yours, though I daresay it will not be of much use to you here in Elas-Tormas. Its rightful place is in the throne room of Mar-Storin."

A knock on the throne room doors echoed through the hall. The advisor bowed low and hurried to the door, which he opened slightly. Morheim could hear hushed voices but could not discern what was being said. He finished the wine and placed the empty goblet on the tray beside the still half-full bottle. He scowled as he looked to the doors where his advisor was still engaged in a hushed conversation.

"What thing are you hiding from me now?" he demanded to know.

The advisor looked back at him and then turned toward the door once more. He spoke a few more words, then quickly shut the door and, turning to Morheim, began walking up to him.

"Apologies, my liege," he bowed low and long, waiting for Morheim to bid him to speak.

"Out with it, you snake!" Morheim growled. "What message did he bring?"

"I can assure you it is nothing to trouble you with," the advisor explained.

"You may trouble me with it anyway," Morheim demanded.

"As you wish," the advisor cleared his throat. "It seems there was a disturbance in the city this evening, and as a result, nine men were slain. As I said, there is really nothing to it."

"And why was this matter brought to your attention instead of the captain of the local watch?" Morheim frowned. "Your scheming is going to get you killed someday soon."

"I can assure you I am merely looking out for your best interests," the advisor bowed low again.

"You are, are you?" Morheim stared him in the eyes. "Then tell me why you have kept from me the fact that two of the men slain this evening were staying in the Tower of Tergia and were likely allied with Paroch?" Morheim paused for a moment, then with a wild look in his eye, he continued. "You come from Mar-Storin; perhaps you are seeking Abion for yourself."

The color drained from the advisor's face as he stammered his response. "I-I-I can assure you nothing could be farther from the truth. You have many other, more important matters to attend to. I seek only to lighten the burdens you carry, and you make me out to be a traitor."

Morheim laughed at his obvious discomfort. "Do not forget that I, too can be dangerous," he warned. "Do not seek to cross me. I can promise you, it will end badly for you."

"If you have so little trust for me, then I shall step down from my position," he began.

"There is no need for that. When you have outlived your usefulness to me, I will let you know," Morheim said as he scratched at his neck. "I already know more than you think I do. For instance, I am aware that seven hundred years ago, one of Dramiol's sons disappeared from Mar-Storin during the bloody coup. His son was an heir to the throne."

"It is nothing, only rumors," the advisor protested. "Every good scholar knows that Dramiol's entire family was slain by his brother Dramios before he ascended the throne in Mar-Storin."

"So say most of the histories," Morheim admitted. "However, not all of them agree. There are a few sources that mention a single male child having been secreted from the palace in the early morning hours."

"I have read those records as well. They are not widely known nor readily accepted. They lack credibility. I name them fanciful myths at best."

Morheim smiled. "I wonder, how easy would it be for my enemies to write me out of the official history of this great city? Once they had ascended the throne, they could order the purging of records to remove all mention of my name, then ascribe all of my deeds to someone else, kill all of my relatives and any and all friends and acquaintances. Make it so no one dared remember me."

"Are you suggesting this is an active plot against you?" the advisor asked.

"Then five hundred years from now," Morheim continued. "Others would be having the same conversation we are about whether I really sat on the throne or not. The mention of my name in some forgotten manuscript would, in fact, be the truth, but the weight of lies stacked against it would cause most to suggest the truth were a lie and the lies were truth."

"Now I see where you are going with that," the advisor nodded. "Very good point."

"On the other hand, *you* would be very easy to write out of the records," Morheim continued. "Just as it would be easy to cover up the escape of one descendant of kings amidst the carnage and confusion of a royal coup."

"Impossible to prove," the advisor challenged.

"Difficult but not impossible," Morheim responded evenly. He stared at his advisor for a long time.

"What?" the advisor finally asked.

"How long have you been my chief advisor?" Morheim wanted to know.

"Almost seven years now," the advisor replied after a moment's calculation.

"And only recently have you begun withholding information from me. Granted, most things are minor at best and taken singly are no cause for concern, but taken together," he paused for emphasis. "They become quite alarming."

"I only seek to serve the king and further your goals," the advisor replied with a bow.

"You may still say that, but I have no plan from you to take Abion. Therefore, I will take matters into my own hands. Guards!" Morheim yelled loudly. The doors leading into the throne room opened, and six armed guards entered, "You will escort him to his chamber. See to it that he communicates with no one, either verbally or in writing. No visitors. *Is* that understood?" The guards answered that it was. "For the guard who fails in this task, your life shall be forfeit," Morheim added as he waved them away. "Bring the council to me," he bellowed. "And prepare a meal. This will be a late evening."

# White Chapter Six: The Snapping Of Threads

### The 15th of Lirinn, late afternoon

Arvendal worked feverishly over Balatiere, whose body was limp, his skin was pale, and his lips were blue. "Tell me what you saw!" he demanded. "Every detail! Leave nothing out!" His hands were steady as they prepared a salve in a small pestle and mortar. He listened intently to what both Elrynn and Draxin told him.

"Balatiere insisted on trying some tarts and said he would meet us at the far end of the square," Elrynn explained. "Then I heard him calling out to us for help, and by the time I found him, he was nowhere near the lady with the tarts."

"And I thought I saw a Dakirin and went to investigate; I had not taken more than twenty steps from the cart when I heard Balatiere bellowing for us to come to his aid," Draxin stated. "I did find an uneaten tart on the ground near him, though. Do you think he was poisoned?"

"Yes, I do, but I doubt it was the tarts," Arvendal clarified. "It would be too risky for a single poisoned tart to be kept handy for just the right person to come by. No, it is something else." He thought for a moment as he examined Balatiere. "So you three were separated for a brief time?" Both men affirmed that it was so. "When you found him, what did you see?"

"I got there first," Elrynn admitted. "Balatiere was lying on his back, his drawn sword still gripped in his hand."

"You saw no one else near him? Tending to him perhaps?" Arvendal asked.

"No," Elrynn replied. "Just some locals gathered around and staring."

"Besides the uneaten tart, I saw the same thing," Draxin stated.

"Did anyone else touch him after both of you arrived?"

"Only the tailor and his daughter who helped us get him to his feet," Draxin answered. "He said his name was Ryla something."

"His name is Rylabet," Elrynn replied. "I have met him before."

"Explain this," Arvendal demanded. He was still working on the salve.

"That day in Sivrellis when Telliken, Gilsarn and I first arrived in Elas-Tormas, we happened upon his shop while we were looking for this tower. His shop is in an out-of-the-way place, nowhere near the other tailor shops."

"And you are just now telling me this?" Arvendal asked.

"We did not think it important at the time," Elrynn replied. "I still do not see the importance."

"Do you think it mere happenstance that you met this tailor on your first day in the city? You and two other members of the mantle? And now, on this day, when another member of the mantle lies dying, he shows up again!" Arvendal shook his head. "We must find where he was bitten," Arvendal explained.

"Bitten?" Elrynn asked. "By what exactly?"

"Hopefully, just a gloom spider, but it may be a shroud spider," Arvendal stated as he lifted Balatiere's left arm and examined it closely. "Or a gravespider, the Weaver's Guild is behind this."

"Are you saying this Rylabet is part of the Weaver's Guild?" Elrynn shook his head in disbelief. "You have not seen him. He is feeble of body and dull of wit. How could he possibly be a danger to anyone?"

Arvendal glanced at him for a moment but said nothing else.

Shalamar stepped beside Arvendal. "How can I help?"

"Shalamar, look closely at any exposed skin; any bite would appear as a pair of tiny pinpricks. There may be small red welts in the area as well, but they can be easily overlooked. Take your time and examine him carefully."

"But why should the Weavers want to kill Balatiere?" Elrynn asked.

"Though he did not know it at the time, Balatiere witnessed a Weaver's Guild assassin kill the man beside him at Morheim's last night. This is no accident." Arvendal sighed as he placed Balatiere's arm gently upon the table and began to examine the left side of his neck.

"I think I found it," Shalamar exclaimed after several minutes, her voice shaking. She pointed to the right side of Balatiere's neck, and Arvendal, after coming to the other side of the table, leaned in close to inspect the area.

"You have done well," Arvendal proclaimed. "Now, let us pray that it is not too late for him." He took some of the prepared salve on his finger and gently painted it over the area of the bite, then he took a kerchief and, dipping it in cool water, dripped several drops onto the salve. "The salve works best when it is moist," he explained as he let a few more drops of water drip onto the salve. When he was satisfied that he had done all he could at the present, he suggested the others join him in the main room.

"I will stay and watch over him," Shalamar said. "In case he awakes and needs something."

"Re-apply the salve every hour and make certain it stays moist," Arvendal instructed as he handed her the pestle.

"I will stay as well," Fulcwin said quietly as he stepped beside Shalamar and put his arm around her. They remained hugging long after the others had left the room. Shalamar's soft sobs were the only sound to be heard.

Arvendal, Elrynn and Draxin joined the others gathered for a quiet meal. Several times which, Haendorn excused himself to check on Balatiere. On one such occasion, he took a small platter piled with food and drink for Fulcwin and Shalamar, and as he made his way back, the tower doors burst open. Kourakin rushed in, out of breath.

"Come quick! It's Gehm and Reesal!"

"What happened?" Haendorn asked.

"We found them lying in the street," Kourakin replied as he waved those carrying Gehm and Reesal into the tower.

Arvendal appeared and directed the men to follow him, "Tell me what happened," he demanded over his shoulder.

"I saw someone spying on us as we left the docks," Kourakin offered.

"Spies are everywhere these days," one of the men answered. "It probably means nothing."

Arvendal glanced back over his shoulder, his brows furrowed. "What else?" he asked.

"Gehm and Reesal must have gotten lost on their way back here," Kourakin answered.

"Then how did you manage to find them, and where is Perin?"

"Orendien and Tulikar knew of a more direct way to get here," Kourakin began. "Perin and Tulikar retraced our route from earlier while I went with Orendien. Not long after we parted with Perin, the sounds of fighting were heard, and we happened upon two bodies lying in the street. There must have been others because there were several trails of blood leading away from the area. We did not investigate any further once I discovered the bodies were, in fact, Gehm and Reesal. Afterward, we hurried straight here."

Arvendal nodded as he entered a room where several beds were located. In the corner were two immense stone baths; one had steam rising from it, and both were filled to the brim. Beside the baths stood a table with many white linens and bandages folded upon it, several small stone boxes and a tiny flask.

"Kourakin, it is good you found them when you did. Take Orendien and his men to the meeting hall, and please ask Paroch if he would join me." Arvendal instructed as he leaned close over one of the men, turning his head to listen for any shallow breath. He nodded his head and walked to the other bed, again leaning close. He walked to the table and grabbed a linen, dipping it into the steaming bath and then with it, he began to carefully clean the blood away. "Reesal, what happened to you?" he asked quietly.

Reesal's eyes opened wide, and he tried to sit up.

"Lay still, my friend," Arvendal instructed as he placed the red-stained linen on his forehead and gently pushed his head back down. Arvendal quickly retrieved the tiny flask from the table and returned it to Reesal.

"Is Gehm well?" Reesal whispered. He drew a ragged breath and immediately coughed a red spray into the air.

"I will worry about him now," Arvendal instructed. "Do not speak. Save your strength." He opened the flask and allowed a single drop of liquid to fall upon his lips. Within a few moments, Reesal was fast asleep.

Paroch entered the room, "I heard Gehm and Reesal were in trouble," he said as he stared at the battered bodies lying on the beds. "Will they survive?" he asked as he hurried to the table and, dunking a clean linen into the hot water, brought it to Arvendal.

"Ellonas knows," Arvendal replied. "But even if they do not, you must remember, all things work together for good to those who are called." There were no other words spoken between them as they worked first on Reesal, then Gehm, cleaning away blood, stitching split skin and setting broken bones. When at last they were finished, the floor was puddled with blood and water and littered with crimson-stained linens. What water remained in the stone baths was pink, the table was empty of linens and bandages, and the stone boxes were emptied of their ointment.

"The rest we leave to Ellonas," Arvendal said reverently as he stooped to wash his hands and arms in a third stone basin that Paroch had not noticed before. The water was cool and refreshing, and it was not long before both men were clean. "Let us join the others," Arvendal suggested as he left the room.

Paroch stood in the doorway of the meeting hall, mouth opened wide, the room was filled with several hundreds of men, and he looked on in amazement.

"Paroch, you look surprised," Arvendal laughed. "Do you not yet realize there is always room for one more in this tower? Neither is there any lack nor abundance; there is simply that which is needed at the time." He smiled broadly and entered the room.

Thinking back, Paroch had noticed a strange fact about this tower of Tergia: every room had one more seat than the number of people who entered. If ten people entered a room, there were eleven seats, but should another person enter, there were suddenly twelve seats. They were just there. The tables were always just big enough for everyone to sit at with one extra seat, but should that extra seat be filled, suddenly there was room for one more.

The room gradually grew silent as all eyes looked to the doorway and Paroch.

"How are our companions?" Haendorn asked.

"It is too soon to tell," Paroch replied as he took a few steps into the room, "but Arvendal would know more."

"I have done what I could," Arvendal agreed. "Still, it does not look good for any of them. However, there are pressing matters to attend to. As the armies of darkness close in upon this fair city, which way will you and the mantle go?"

"Perhaps we should stay and help defend Elas-Tormas," Elrynn suggested. "After all, we have the Kingsword."

"You have few allies in this city," Arvendal stated. "You would be fighting many others, not just those bent on the city's destruction."

"Then let us defend this tower. It is well-built. We could hold out for quite a long while, and besides, we need to wait until Gehm, Reesal and Balatiere are fit to travel," Telliken suggested.

"Undoubtedly, you would survive the initial onslaught and perhaps even many more attacks, but eventually, this tower would fall, and here you would remain." Arvendal shook his head. "Staying here would be folly."

"It seems to stay anywhere in the city would be folly," Paroch began. "That leaves but two choices: escape by land or by sea."

"The western road to Mirion is still open," Haendorn informed him. "If we leave soon, we could be out of the city and near the outer wall by tomorrow evening."

"If Morheim is watching this tower, you would not get very far into the outlands before he sent soldiers after you," Gedery said with a nod.

"Sailing has its own inherent dangers, but at this time, it seems to be our safest course of action," Perin countered. "We could sail around Mirion if need be."

The mantle was split; Telliken, Kourakin and Haendorn all wanted to travel to Mirion by land, while Perin, Draxin and Elrynn preferred sailing away in the dead of night.

After waiting for any other suggestions from the mantle, Paroch spoke again. "I intend to head to Mirion and speak to the Council at Elberon, but marching to the west would invite trouble, I think," Paroch mused. "Word would most definitely reach Morheim's ears, and he would send an armed host after us. Better to board ships quietly at night and make our way from Elas-Tormas as soon as possible." He nodded at Sarahin.

"Yes, we should head back to the ships as soon as possible," she urged.

"Arvendal?" Paroch looked to where he was standing. "Will you be coming with us?"

"I am the keeper of this tower. I must not shirk my duty nor abandon my post. Come what may, I will remain here."

Paroch nodded. "Members of the mantle, come with me so we can bring our wounded." He turned to Gedery and Sarahin, "We shall leave for the ships in just a bit."

An anguished wail was heard, and presently, Fulcwin appeared in the doorway. His eyes were red, and tears were on his cheeks; the sounds of sobbing could still be faintly heard.

"Balatiere?" Haendorn asked.

Fulcwin nodded his head. "He is with Ellonas now. He always imagined dying on the field of battle, but this…"

They followed Fulcwin back to Balatiere's room.

"Let us say our goodbyes," Paroch whispered, his voice cracking.

One by one, each member of the mantle entered the room. Some knelt beside Balatiere, others placed an open hand upon his shoulder, but all heads were bowed, silent prayers were mouthed, and tears fell freely onto the floor. Though they all looked at her, no one disturbed Shalamar in her grief.

"Who will carry him to his final resting place?" Arvendal asked as the last member of the mantle finished his goodbye.

Gently, the mantle lifted the corpse onto their shoulders and slowly followed Arvendal and Paroch as they led the way into the tombs.

Paroch began to sing softly, "Sightless, eyes have closed on this bright life." He blinked away the mounting tears.

"But on the other side, his eyes have opened to one much brighter," Fulcwin answered.

After a moment, Paroch continued, "Deaf ears have ceased to hear the sad and sweet song of life."

"But on the other side, his ears hear a melody much sweeter," Fulcwin sang, his voice cracking.

"Nostrils have ceased to breathe in the fragrance of this life."

Others began to join in, voices gruff with grief, "But on the other side, he smells something more pleasant still."

"Mouth has tasted the last of life's long feast."

"But on the other side, he takes his first bite of the never-ending feast."

"Hands no longer have strength in this life."

"But on the other side, they flow with new strength and vigor."

"His journey upon Kren is ended."

"Yet on the other side, his journey has just begun."

Arvendal stopped; on his right, the name Balatiere blazed forth from the stone above a wooden door. He opened the door and motioned the men inside. "Here is where we lay him to rest. May Ellonas have mercy upon him."

Once Balatiere had been gently laid upon the stone bed and last goodbyes were whispered, Arvendal spoke loudly. "Paroch, Herald of Light, lead the way from these tombs!"

As they climbed the last stairs of the tombs, Paroch suggested they check on Gehm and Reesal and make preparations to carry them to the ships.

Paroch went first to check on Reesal, placing his hand gently upon his chest. It rose and fell with each shallow breath. "Reesal lives!" he whispered before walking to Gehm's side. He placed his hand gently upon his chest, then after a moment, he bent low over his face and turned his head so he might hear the shallowest breath. There was no longer any breath in Gehm. Paroch touched his forehead and found it cool to the touch. He sighed heavily. Once again, the mantle gathered up a fallen member and carried him to the tombs below.

"I did not anticipate returning here so quickly," Arvendal said with sadness. No one replied. Paroch led them in singing their song of grief and hope, and again, they answered his every line.

When Gehm had been laid to rest and the mantle had emerged from the tombs, Paroch sent them to make Reesal ready while he spoke with Arvendal.

"I would ask that you join us," Paroch began, but Arvendal held up his hand.

"You do not realize what you are asking me to do. I will not break my oath. I am the keeper of this tower, and as such, I will stay here." And despite many pleadings and urgings to the contrary, he refused to accompany Paroch from the tower.

Paroch sighed and nodded his head. "I suppose you are right. Forgive my asking." He reached out his hand, and Arvendal grasped it firmly, and as they shook hands, Arvendal took on a distant stare as if remembering some long-forgotten thing.

"The days grow dark, but they will grow darker still before the light dawns once again. Know this Paroch, one seer yet lives who has not bowed the knee to Mazzaroth. Far to the north, in a lonely citadel, Sumertawn waits for you. He bids you come; Kolleleo knows the way."

Then, just as suddenly, he shook his head and looked at Paroch with a smile. "Time grows short. May Ellonas guide your steps and speed you on your way."

Paroch looked at him for a moment, "There is more to you than I first expected."

"Perhaps, then again, perhaps not. It all depends upon what you were expecting," Arvendal smiled.

Not long after, Arvendal stood at the door and watched as they headed for the docks; then, as the last person left the grounds of the Tergian Tower, he waved his hand in a complete circle before clenching his fist. He entered the tower and closed the door behind him.

The journey to the ships was undertaken with great caution. Orendien's men led the way, scouting out each intersecting road and alley to make certain there were no further threats and surveying every window to see if they were being spied on. Behind them, walking at a steady pace, followed Paroch and the mantle carrying Reesal on a litter and Tulikar and his men. It took a little over half an hour to reach the docks, and they were satisfied that their departure from the tower had not been noticed by anyone who cared. Paroch directed Perin, Kourakin, Elrynn and Haendorn to board Orendien's ship while he, Reesal, Telliken, Draxin and Fulcwin boarded Tulikar's ship. As soon as the last man had stepped aboard, both ships raised canvas and anchor and sailed several hundred yards out into the bay before dropping anchors to await the morning.

# Black Chapter Six: Intentions Revealed

## *The 16th of Lirinn, early morning*

Morheim waited in the throne room with his council. "I had hoped Queen Sarahin would see the wisdom of helping me obtain that sword of legend, but she has delayed in making her decision." He slammed his fists upon the table. "Should I count her as an enemy?" He looked at each of the five before standing up.

"If I am not mistaken, you gave her two days to decide what to do," one of the generals answered. "She may very well be waiting for the coming sunrise to deliver word of her agreement."

"That is a fair point, Eulix," Morheim agreed. "Send word that neither Queen Sarahin nor any of the men with her are to be harmed or obstructed in any way until the evening watch of this day. I wish to maintain Anar as an ally."

"Anar is broken, perhaps beyond repair," another general reminded him. "What strength is left to our east?"

"A broken ally who lends what aid they can is better than an enemy with no aid," the king replied as he looked out a window on the darkened city. He sighed heavily and resumed pacing, hands clasped behind his back. "Baldred, when will we know what has transpired?"

"My king, the moment the sword is retrieved, I have instructed the men to make all haste to deliver it to you," he replied.

Morheim furrowed his brow. "How many men did you send?" he asked again.

"Five hundred," Baldred answered. "Which is more than enough to take the sword if it will not be relinquished voluntarily."

"Unless they have barricaded themselves inside," Eulix contemplated. "Then we should have to attack them."

"Why should they barricade themselves inside?" Baldred wanted to know.

"I should hope it does not come down to armed conflict," Morheim shook his head. "It is for the good of this city that I go to demand the Kingsword be given to me."

"It is not simply by chance that the sword long lost has been found again in these dark days, and now it shows up within your grasp. It belongs in the hands of one of noble birth, not the hands of some commoner," Eulix insisted. "And after all, you are descended from nobility and are the rightful ruler of Elas-Tormas. It belongs to you. Take the sword and with it defeat the enemies opposed to us."

"And what about those in the Orders who were working against us?" Morheim asked.

"Their leaders will be dealt with. We have soldiers on their way to take them into custody now."

"How do you know where to find them?"

"You will have to ask the questioner that," Eulix turned to look at the man beside him.

"Your advisor was unwilling to talk with us, but with the right motivation, he became most informative," the questioner responded evenly as he stood.

"Is he still able to fulfill his duties as an advisor?" Morheim asked.

With a shake of his head, the questioner produced a small leather bag, wet with blood and tossed it upon the table. "I do not think that will be possible."

Morheim raised his eyebrows.

"I present his thumbs and his tongue."

"And why was this necessary?" Morheim asked.

"I told him before we began that being truthful was of the utmost importance. Then I explained that obstructing the king would cost a thumb but that lying would cost him his tongue. At first, he answered truthfully but denied obstructing your attempts to retrieve the sword. Then, after I pressed him on various details, he refused to speak to me any longer, which is, of course, obstructing the king, for you gave me an order." He bowed low. "That was when I took his right thumb. He became most willing to tell me the truth after this and finally admitted to obstructing your plans and aiding the Orders in their attempt to retrieve the very same sword you yourself are after. I thanked him for finally being honest before I took his left thumb, and of course, I reminded him of the penalty for lying."

"I should like you to question the leaders of the Orders when they are brought in," Morheim said.

"It would be my pleasure, Your Highness," the questioner smiled. "Shall I go and prepare my chamber for them?"

Morheim nodded, and the questioner left the room whistling a tune softly to himself. "What word do we have from the outer wall?"

"Many hundreds of thousands of soldiers are encamped just out of bowshot, and there has been no sign of any Falkiri or Dakirin," the general of the outer defenses replied. "Or any siege equipment," he added.

"Our enemy sits just out of bowshot, with no visible means to force entry? Perhaps his goal is to besiege us and starve us out," Morheim surmised. "You will ensure all the mounted legions are in the Outlands, where they can ride to the aid of any section of wall in need."

"Your Highness, with no siege equipment to be seen and none of the fantastical flying creatures that have been mentioned, is it wise to send all the legions out there? What of the defense of the city itself?"

"I have been thinking of a spoiling attack," Morheim began to speak. "Imagine if we were to open the gates at sunrise tomorrow and send forty thousand knights charging into the enemy lines. We could break this siege before it even begins."

"A wonderful plan," Baldred said aloud as he clapped his hands together. "They would never expect that."

"Better yet," Morheim laughed. "Let us attack from five gates at the same time. Eight thousand knights per gate. We will sweep the enemy from the field before noon."

"Your Highness, the more gates you open, the riskier this spoiling attack becomes. And what if they really do have those fantastical flying creatures fighting for them?"

Morheim frowned at him. "You remind me of my old advisor."

"Just making certain you consider all possibilities," the general said nervously as he cast several quick glances at the questioner's empty seat.

"Still, it is good to consider these things. I appreciate your concern; however, unless some news of flying creatures emerges between now and the morning, the spoiling attack will take place at sunrise tomorrow."

"Which gates would you have us attack from?" the general asked.

Morheim thought for a moment, then with a nod and a smile, he answered. "Let the attacks sally forth from the northern gate and the two gates to the east and west of it. Let us add two thousand foot soldiers to each gate as well; they can position themselves outside the gates until the knights return."

"We shall prepare for the attack as soon as it is practicable," the general replied.

"Practicable?"

"The movement of men into the right positions takes time; at the earliest, we should be able to attack the day after tomorrow."

Morheim frowned, "And if the day after tomorrow is too late? What then? I am not an unreasonable man," he stated. "But if no attack is carried out on the morrow, I will begin to question your loyalty."

"We have ten thousand men in position now to make an attack from one gate," the general explained patiently. "Your request for forty thousand more to join in is what will take time to get ready."

Morheim stared at the general for a moment. "An attack from one gate will not carry the field, but issuing forth from five gates at the same time will most assuredly drive our enemy from the field."

"I shall push the men to get into position as quickly as possible," the general explained. "Perhaps in the afternoon, we shall be prepared for your spoiling attack."

"Make it so!" Morheim turned to his admiral.

"As of last evening, enemy ships were spotted near the mouth of the harbor," the admiral reported. "They cannot approach the city undetected and seem content to try and blockade the harbor entrance."

"How many enemy ships?" the king asked as he rubbed his greying temples with the tips of his fingers.

"We cannot be certain of the exact number without getting closer, but we have counted several hundred in the distance. They are a motley collection of vessels, many of which look like they come from the Tav-Tar. There are warships among them, but not many."

"Have we the strength to defeat them?" Morheim asked.

"We are outnumbered, to be certain, and the battle would be difficult. But we have many warships of our own, and if we attack, we should be able to defeat them."

"Triple the guards on the docks this very evening and prepare to attack the enemy ships."

"It will be done."

"You see?" Morheim said as he looked at his general. "Our loyal admiral here is confident of victory."

"I, too, am loyal," the general protested. "I simply worry about the ramifications should this attack fail."

"Ramifications?" Morheim raised his voice. "If your attack fails, then you will retreat to the safety of our outer wall."

"And have our numbers for defense greatly lessened," the general said softly. "My king, I ask that you reconsider this spoiling attack. What harm could there be in delaying a day or two until we are in a position to carry out your orders?"

"As general of my armies, I should think you would have already laid plans to deal with any eventuality, and here we are with naught but a few preparations."

"I was entrusted with the defense," the general protested.

"Why have no plans for attack been made? Have you been away from battle for too long? Have you grown soft? Dare I say cowardly?"

"I am no coward!" the general roared as he stood and faced Morheim. "And I resent the accusation. I am as committed to the defense of this fair city as anyone here. If a spoiling attack is what you want, then you shall have one, but NOT before the men are ready and in position."

Morheim began to clap his hands slowly, "Not a coward to be sure, foolhardy perhaps, but not coward. You shall have your extra day, but I will not overlook your impertinence in this matter. It will be dealt with after this is all over."

"Begging your pardon, my king," the general said with a bow as he re-took his seat.

Morheim paced for a few moments. "We are surrounded; who among you will help me defeat the enemy that lies before us? It is true that in our history, we have never faced so daunting a challenge, but we are mighty, and we are fierce. Do not forget this: we will meet this enemy in battle, and we will emerge victorious. You have your orders. You are dismissed," Morheim said with a wave of his hand. "Baldred, please find out what is taking so long to retrieve my sword. Eulix, I would discuss a few matters with you."

***

Hammer kept peeking out the window, then pacing the floor before returning to the window.

"Would you please sit down?" Rose asked. "Your peeking and pacing will not bring news any quicker. Enjoy the wine."

"He has never been late," Hammer replied. "Since he first contacted us. Do you think something has happened?"

"If it has, we cannot change it," Rose replied as she sipped her wine. She sighed with satisfaction and smiled. "We have already decided that to try and take Abion here in Elas-Tormas was not the brightest idea. And with Morheim after it as well, it became quite dangerous. What we needed to do and still need to do is be patient. He will show up, and he will bring news."

"Perhaps he has been found out."

"By whom? Morheim?" Rose laughed. "He trusts his advisor, and were his advisor caught making a trip to a seedier part of town; it could easily be explained away as him trying to gather a bit more information. Your wine is getting cold."

Hammer turned from the window and looked at his goblet on the table before looking back out the window. "I am more of a beer drinker," he said over his shoulder.

"Suit yourself."

"I think something is wrong," Hammer persisted. "Maybe we should leave here while there is still time."

"Leave where? This room? This street? This city?" Rose laughed. "I have never known you to be such a worry-wart."

"Well, yes. At the very least, this building," Hammer urged.

"Let me finish my wine *at the very least*," Rose mocked.

"Are we certain Blade is dead?" Hammer asked as he craned his neck to see a bit farther down the darkened street.

"No, he is not dead, but when he awakens the day after tomorrow with his head pounding and his stomach heaving, he may wish he was. That much Nerium wine without the antidote is enough to knock out several men," Rose replied confidently. "Just because we of the Order of the White Rose have an aversion to weapons does not mean we are without defenses. Blade and his plans will trouble us no further. Come, take a seat."

"I will never understand why anyone would want to drink a poisonous wine." With one last look out the window, Hammer walked to the table and sat down.

"There are reasons, the least of which is the flavor. It is quite unique, don't you think?" Rose laughed. She placed her elbows on the table before her, goblet held securely between her hands. "Another reason would be that just the right amount of Nerium is said to enhance one's senses."

Hammer rolled his eyes at her.

"Some have experienced quite a dramatic effect," Rose continued. "Taste and smell are refined, sight and hearing sharpened, and one's sense of touch is increased."

Hammer laughed, "How can you increase the sense of touch? I put my hand on the table, and I feel the table; what else is there?" He placed his hand upon the table, and Rose quickly placed her hand upon his.

She looked at him for a long while before answering. "Can you feel the rough spot under your hand? Don't look!" she admonished him. "Close your eyes. Can you feel the rough patch? What about the various knots and the grooves of the wood?" Hammer closed his eyes. "You can feel them now that you are aware of them," Rose whispered. "This is the pull of Nerium wine; one can learn to feel things more," she hesitated for a moment. "Deeply," she added with a nod.

Hammer's eyes flew open, and he pulled his hand from the table like he was pulling it from an open flame. "Witchery," he breathed out as he stared at first his hand, then the table and finally at Rose.

"Perhaps it is an acquired taste after all," she smiled as she finished her wine. "Where are we off to?"

"Let us leave this building as quickly and quietly as we can," he urged. He took one last look out the window.

"Lead the way," Rose gestured to the closed door leading to the hallway.

Hammer opened the door and looked both ways before motioning Rose to join him. Together, they made their way down to the ground floor.

"I should think we have woken everyone in this place, what with all your tromping and stomping," Rose grumbled.

"No matter," Hammer said as he looked out the front door. He caught the growing glare of approaching torchlight and heard the sound of booted feet upon the cobblestones. "They are here, out the back door quick," he whispered loudly.

"Who is here?" Rose wanted to know. "And who are *they* here for?"

"I do not want to find out," Hammer said as he peeked out into a darkened alley. "Come on, we have a chance still." He grabbed her hand and pulled her along behind him as he navigated the narrow alleyway, turning left at the next alley and then right into the next one.

"I hope you know where we are headed," Rose whispered. "I am lost already."

"So the Nerium wine does not help with navigation?" Hammer asked as he took yet another left. "Fortunately for you, I do not need any wine to help with my navigation skills." He led her down another alley. "A few more turns, and we will be out of harm's way."

***

Five ships sailed into the eastern end of the harbor; not a light was to be seen either on deck or shining from any portholes below. Silently, they approached the docks of Elas-Tormas. When they were quite close, anchors were stealthily lowered into the water, making no more noise than the splashing of a jumping fish, and longboats were quickly lowered. Men clambered down rope ladders, and when each boat was full, paddles were produced, and noiselessly, they made their way to the docks.

Belenak growled at the men as they paddled. "Which of you will take my place watching over this boat?"

"None of us," one of the men answered bravely. "The fates have ordained that you be the one watching this evening."

"Curse the fates," Belenak growled. "I will offer three gold pieces to the man who takes my place." There followed several minutes of silence. "Five gold pieces," he offered. "Will no one relieve me of this drudgery?" he asked as a pier loomed into view.

"The fates have spoken," the same sailor replied. "The same fates that watch over us on the high seas. Who are we to tempt those fates?"

The longboat bumped into a piling, and Belenak hissed, "Alright, you already heard what the captain wants. Create havoc and spread fear."

"We bringing anyone back with us?" one of the men asked.

"No need to take any prisoners this evening unless, of course, she is beautiful." Several of the men laughed. "Get goin'," he barked. He tied the boat securely to the piling as the men clambered up the wooden ladder. Once up top, they fanned out in groups of three or four and disappeared into the night shadows. Belenak stepped from the ladder and crouched beside a few crates; they were empty, which allowed him to peer between the wood slats. To his left, he watched as another longboat unloaded its men; they, too, quickly disappeared into the night. Belenak waited and wondered what fun the others were having, every now and again cursing the fates for relegating him to such a mundane task. In the water below, he caught sight of several young night darters, fish that glowed in the depths of the sea. The young ones stayed close to shore where it was safer for them until such time as they grew larger, and they grew quite large. He smiled as he remembered a time when the ship he was on was far away from land on a moonless night. The crew had let down their nets to hopefully catch something for their breakfast and instead ended up in a life-or-death struggle with a huge night darter half as long as the ship itself and glowing a brilliant blue as it thrashed and lunged to break free of the nets. In the end, the nets had to be cut free, and the tired crew watched in amazement as the darter swam away, trailing torn nets behind it. Looking back to the darters below, they were not much longer than his hand, and their glow was not nearly as bright. He pressed his tongue against the back of his front teeth, forcing a stream of spit through the gap in his teeth. He watched the darters swarm to the surface to eat what had fallen atop the water. He was about to spit a second time when he heard the sound of approaching feet. Looking up, he saw a man with a hooded lantern walking cautiously toward the end of the dock.

"I am certain they came from here," he called over his shoulder. Two guards stepped up beside him.

"But there ain't no boats here," one of the guards said with a yawn.

"If this is some joke of yours..." the other guard threatened.

"I swear it is no joke," the man holding the lantern insisted. He took a few more steps toward the end of the dock, and then he pointed. "There, I told you?"

Belenak crouched as low as he could, hand on the hilt of his sword.

One of the guards looked down into the water, "A longboat? This is what you woke us up for. A longboat?" He turned and began walking back the way they had come.

The man with the lantern looked one last time before turning and hurrying after the two guards. "Don't you find it the least bit strange that a longboat is tied up at the end of this pier? There are no other ships around; where would it come from? And what of the people I saw running?"

The voices grew distant, and Belenak breathed a sigh of relief at his good fortune, breaking into a broad smile. He heard a creaking noise at the far end of the docks and cautiously peered over the top of one of the crates. The man with the lantern trailed after the two guards, but beyond that, he could see nothing and sat back down. Moments later, in the distance, he heard the sound of fighting, muffled at first, and then quickly it grew alarmingly loud. He swore softly to himself and peered above the crate for a second time. As he scanned the docks, he heard a noise in his right ear, and at the same instant, something splashed into the water behind him. He ducked lower, gripping the hilt of his sword, listening to the sounds of fighting. Torches were being lit along the whole of the dock as sailors and soldiers alike awoke to the noise. He glanced out into the harbor where their ships waited at anchor.

"I never did like sitting around and waiting," he murmured to himself as he looked from the ships to the longboat below him and back to the ships. The fighting was getting closer. He peeked over the crates one last time and suddenly fell backward into the water, a feathered bolt protruding from his forehead.

\*\*\*

"Where have you been?" Rylabet asked. He yawned once and scratched at the back of his head.

"Observing," Akina replied as she sat down at the table.

"What exactly have you observed at the Tower?" Rylabet demanded.

"Morheim's soldiers have surrounded the Tower and are busy hammering at the iron gate to gain access to the courtyard." Akina straightened her blouse and then wiped at a stain on her pants. "There was no opportunity for me to get any closer." She looked at Rylabet and smiled.

"Then the Kingsword is out of our reach, trapped inside the tower," Rylabet nodded as he contemplated. He stood and retrieved two mugs from a shelf on the wall, and after placing them on the table, he went to the fireplace. The embers had burned low, but there was still warmth. After a quick stir of the ashes and placing a small log upon them, he hung a kettle full of water.

"What took you so long anyway?" he asked suddenly.

"I was listening, following and observing," Akina replied innocently.

"Listening to what?" Rylabet asked as he spooned a spoonful of powder into each mug.

"To whom, you mean," Akina corrected.

Rylabet scowled at her, "What game are you playing at?"

"My dear Rylabet, did you think you were the only one with associates in this city? You may follow Vapir but do not forget that Jabitern has his adherents in most every city as well. It was from one of them that I heard whispered a most tantalizing clue."

"Vapir and Jabitern are both on the same side," Rylabet reminded her.

"Of course," Akina laughed in agreement.

"What was this whispered and most tantalizing clue?"

"A bunch of men were seen moving toward the docks and boarding two ships."

"A bunch?" he asked with raised brows. The kettle began to hiss and whistle, and Rylabet, after walking to it, tested the handle with his finger. After a moment, he nodded and grasping a scrap of cloth, he grabbed the handle and began to pour a steaming liquid into each mug.

"Hundreds of men left the Tower, including one being carried on a litter and several women. They moved quickly but with purpose, checking each doorway and cross-street for any would-be gossipers or spies."

"Obviously, they missed one," Rylabet remarked dryly as he sat down at the table and cupped his hands around his now-filled mug.

Akina nodded and continued. "By the time I got to the docks, both ships were out in the harbor, at least a mile from land and not easily approachable."

Rylabet nodded for a moment as he stared at Akina. After bringing the mug to his lips, he blew across it before taking a small sip and sighing with satisfaction. "What have you learned regarding the two ships?"

"They were recently arrived from Anar and rumored to be carrying royalty."

"Princess Sarahin, no doubt," Rylabet stated.

"Is she not the Queen now?" Akina asked.

"Princess or Queen, it makes no difference. There is no country left for her to be ruler of, my dear." He laughed at the thought. "How certain are you that Paroch and the sword are on one of those ships?"

"It stands to reason he is on one of them," Akina stated. "But where could he be headed?"

"A good question, seeing as his options are quickly diminishing. All possible land routes are blocked or at least will be very soon, and his only route across the water is also blocked. However, after careful consideration, I would say he intends to make for Mirion and try and disappear under the leafy boughs of that forested realm."

"And our plan would be what?" Akina asked.

"I am not exactly sure at the moment," Rylabet admitted. "It would not be good to get caught in the battle for this city." He sipped his tea.

"We are allied with the Darklord," Akina protested. "We can simply walk through their lines and go where we wish."

"My dear, in war, nothing is certain except that one side wins and the other side loses. While it is true the Weaver's Guild has allied itself with the Darklord, there are many within the ranks of his armies that do not know this, and many of those who *do* know that do not care."

"Are you saying we are in danger?" Akina asked.

"Our business is always a dangerous business," he smiled at her and sipped his tea.

"I know that, but you are suggesting we are in more danger because of the current hostility between Mazzaroth and Lepnar?" she clarified.

"This is no mere hostility," Rylabet laughed. "This is a war against all things Lepnarion. Many people are slaughtered in conflicts, not just those who have chosen a particular side. Your tea is getting cold."

She picked up her mug and sniffed it, then took a small sip, tasting it before swallowing with a nod.

"What is this?"

"Hyanor tea. Do you like it?"

"It is not what I was expecting," Akina admitted as she took another sip. "It is not bad, but no changing the subject, please. What is our plan?"

Rylabet smiled and nodded at her. "I appreciate your resolve." He finished his tea and then sat looking into the empty mug as he slowly tipped it from side to side, watching the few remaining drops roll across the bottom. "Hyanor tea has a calming effect on the mind and body, allowing one to relax in all but the most stressful of situations. It has been cultivated for over a thousand years now. Do you know where it comes from?"

"I do not," Akina sighed. She took another sip. "It has an earthy taste," she said after a moment. "But not overly so. A little mint, perhaps?" She held the mug under her nose and breathed in the rising wafts of steam.

"It comes from the deep woods of Mirion, the southern stretches where it is seldom cold enough for snow to fall, let alone accumulate. But the odd thing is the Hyanor tree needs a layer of snow before its leaves can be used to make this tea. And that same snow oftentimes kills the tree itself."

"I suppose they strip the leaves and haul them up north where it snows," Akina surmised.

"They tried that very thing, but the resulting tea was most sour and not very palatable."

"How often does it snow in the southern reaches of Mirion?" she asked.

"I would venture to say once every thirty years, give or take a few."

"The snow is needed to make the tea, but the snow kills the tree itself; how is there any Hyanor tea around at all?" she wondered aloud.

"The snow also serves one additional purpose: it freezes the stems of tiny seed clusters which fall to the ground, and when the ground thaws in a day or two, the seeds burrow into the soil and germinate with the warming temperatures of spring and tiny Hyanor trees begin to grow again."

"I suppose it is a good thing that it snows so infrequently, or there would be no more Hyanor tea to enjoy."

"That is precisely my point," Rylabet agreed.

"What is your point?" Akina probed.

"We must wait for the snow to fall."

"So your plan is to wait for the snow to fall?" Akina laughed. "Summer is already here, and I doubt the battle for Elas-Tormas will last until winter."

"Just as it takes patience for the Hyanor tree to grow and for the leaves to be ready for harvest, then comes the long wait for snowfall, so it will take patience to find the opportune moment in which to take the Kingsword."

Akina opened her mouth to say something; then she began to nod her head, slowly at first, then faster as she finally understood. "Opportune moment equals snow."

Rylabet smiled a broad smile. "Now, let us prepare to leave this city while we have the opportunity."

# White Chapter Seven: A Glimmer Of Hope

## *The 16th of Lirinn, midday*

The empty plate had just been whisked away from the table, Paroch was absentmindedly pushing the scattered breadcrumbs into a little pile, and Tulikar was just pouring a goblet of Tavanian wine.

"Even after the events of this early morning, there are still several hundred enemy ships blockading the harbor," Tulikar sighed as he sipped his wine.

"What happened?"

"Best we can tell, some of the enemy ships sailed in close to the harbor were spotted and set ablaze by the harbor defenses. I do not think any of the ships made it back to the blockade."

"Perhaps it was simply a diversion?" Paroch mused.

"Perhaps," Tulikar agreed. "But to answer your earlier question, we have absolutely no chance of slipping through to the open sea. Too many enemy ships to sail past during the day."

"What about at night, when there was a new moon?" Paroch asked hopefully.

"I doubt even that would enable us to make it."

Paroch nodded but remained silent.

"Fog might do it," Tulikar mused. "One so thick the helmsman cannot see the main mast. But of course, that makes it very dangerous for us as well; if they cannot see us, we would not be able to see them, and a collision would ruin everyone's day."

A soft knock interrupted their discourse. "Perhaps the enemy ships have sailed away," Paroch laughed. Tulikar opened the door wide, and Fulcwin looked in.

"Reesal is awake," he said as he leaned in. "He is asking for you."

Paroch stood from his chair and bowed to Tulikar, "Your hospitality is appreciated."

"See to your friend," Tulikar smiled. "The wine will still be here when you get back."

Paroch excused himself and joined Fulcwin as they made their way to where Reesal was resting. The gentle swells rolling under the hull caused both men to stumble as they walked.

"The sooner we are off of this ship and onto dry ground, the better," Fulcwin grumbled as he placed his hand on the low ceiling to steady himself. Telliken and Draxin were waiting outside the door.

"I would speak with him alone," Paroch stated and waited until each man nodded in turn before opening the door and closing it softly behind him. It took a moment for his eyes to adjust to the darkness.

"Where am I?" Reesal asked from his bed. His voice was weak.

"The Hooves of the Sea," Paroch replied. "How are you feeling?"

"A bit sore," Reesal replied after a moment. "Why are we on a ship?"

"It is safer for us here than in the tower. What happened that evening?" Paroch asked.

"I had too much of that Tavanian wine," Reesal answered. "I did not want to wait around for Kourakin and Perin to finish with Orendien and good old Gehm," Reesal laughed. "I owe him a drink when we heal up; in fact, I owe him several drinks! He kept trying to talk me out of leaving, but I would not hear of it. I had the fool idea to try some of the breads from the bakers we passed earlier. The bakers were all closed for the day; I should have listened to him. We were walking and talking and then realized we had missed our turn. We were about to retrace our steps when we were..." he paused. "Paroch, they were after the Kingsword!" he whispered.

"Who?" Paroch asked.

"I do not think they were with Morheim, but they were Lepnarion. Of that, I am certain. Where is Gehm?" he asked suddenly.

Paroch could see Reesal in the dim light, bandages stained with blood wrapped around his head and chest. "Can you remember anything else about the men who attacked you?"

"No, not really," Reesal replied. "I bet he is waiting right outside," Reesal chuckled, then he grimaced in pain and grabbed his chest. "Maybe you can have *him* come to me for right now."

"Gehm is not on board," Paroch answered.

"On the other ship then?"

Paroch shook his head.

"Then where is he?"

"Gehm was left back at the tower."

"He was hurt worse than I was?" Reesal asked in disbelief. "He will recover; he always does." Reesal shook his head. "There were at least twenty of them, if I remember correctly, coming at us from every direction. Too many to fend off. But I got a few of them at least." He smiled and shook his head. "Last I saw, Gehm had sent another one spinning to the ground lifeless, then…" he paused as he furrowed his brow. "I cannot remember more than that."

Paroch nodded but remained silent.

"So? Where is Gehm? Back at the tower, you say? When will he be joining us?"

Paroch simply looked at Reesal before pulling a chair close beside the bed and sitting down.

"Answer my questions if you please," Reesal demanded as he propped himself up on his elbow. He gripped Paroch's arm. "Tell me!" he hissed as he pulled him closer.

"Gehm did not survive the encounter," Paroch whispered.

"I do not believe you!" Reesal shouted. "Gehm!"

"Reesal, greater love has no man than that he lay his life down for his friend. There is nothing to be done now. You must…"

"You are lying!" Reesal growled.

"Reesal, I wish I were lying to you, but Gehm has departed from this world."

"Truly? Gehm is dead?" Reesal asked, his voice beginning to quiver.

"Yes," Paroch replied softly. "Gehm is dead and buried below the Tower of Tergia."

Reesal fell back onto his bed and stared at the ceiling of his room. There followed several minutes of silence before Paroch spoke again.

"Reesal, I am…We all are grateful to Ellonas that you are still with us," Paroch patted him gently on his shoulder. "Get some rest. I will be back a bit later."

Reesal did not respond, neither did he look at Paroch, but as soon as he was alone, a single tear rolled down the side of his face and pooled in his ear.

As Paroch closed the door behind him, he motioned for the others to join him. "We will need to keep a close eye on him," he warned.

"I will stay here," Fulcwin replied.

With both Telliken and Draxin following close behind, Paroch climbed the steps and stepped out onto the deck. The warm sun and a cool breeze greeted him, and he smiled. As he leaned against the railing, he watched Elas-Tormas and the activity on the docks. Many more soldiers were visible, some standing around while others were hastily moving trebuchet and ballistae into positions. On board many of the warships, there was activity as well.

"Something big is coming," Tulikar stated as he stood beside Paroch.

"Is this because of us?" Paroch asked.

"I should think not. More than likely, it is due to the skirmish from last night, but to be on the safe side, we should position ourselves a bit farther away." Tulikar motioned to a crew member who came running up. "Signal Orendien that we need to move from here as soon as possible." The crew member saluted and left to carry out the order. "Where are we going?" he asked Paroch.

"I have been thinking about that," he answered, never taking his eyes from the docks. "We must get to Mirion, but we are hemmed in on every side. I need to consult with all of my men, can you bring them over from Orendien's ship? And Lord Gedery and Leond and Queen Sarahin."

"Certainly," Tulikar replied, and he left to update his message to Orendien.

Both ships sailed slowly to the south and west of Elas-Tormas, and while the docks were still visible, one was hard-pressed to see what an individual might be doing. Once anchors were dropped, a skiff was let down from The Seamane, and presently Queen Sarahin's head appeared above the railing as she clambered up the rope ladder, followed by Leond, Lord Gedery, Perin, Elrynn, then Kourakin and finally Haendorn.

"How is Reesal? Has he awakened yet?" Haendorn asked almost as soon as he stood upon the deck.

Paroch shook his head. "Yes, he has awakened, and though his body is on the mend, his mind is in turmoil. He blames himself for Gehm's death."

"As well he should," Kourakin whispered loudly.

"Careful what you say, Kourakin," Perin hissed.

"You were there, Perin," Kourakin responded as he looked at those around him. "Many were the opportunities Reesal had to forego his rash decision, yet he refused. I only speak the truth."

"While it is imperative we speak the truth," Paroch began. "It is most imperative that we speak the truth in love." Sarahin nodded in agreement.

"Many of us have made rash decisions that have ended badly," Draxin agreed with a nod.

"And many times, the effects are not realized so quickly, but his rash decision cost Gehm his life," Kourakin persisted.

"You were not there," Haendorn spoke up. "None of us were there except Reesal and Gehm. Do not judge him harshly, for you do not know what transpired, only the aftermath."

"I deserve no love," a ragged voice said harshly. Reesal stood on unsteady legs, eyes blinking in the bright sun. "You have spoken the truth, Kourakin. I alone bear the blame for the death of Gehm."

"I only meant..." Kourakin began to speak.

"I alone bear the blame for Gehm's death!" Reesal repeated with as much force as he could muster. "And I will stop at nothing in seeking my vengeance." He leaned heavily against Fulcwin as a gentle swell rolled under the ship.

"No need to carry that guilt," Gedery spoke up. "You were not the one to strike the killing blow."

"I alone!" Reesal coughed and glared at anyone who would look at him. "Me! I bear this guilt! This shame! This...." he uttered before falling to his knees and sobbing uncontrollably.

"I tried to stop him," Fulcwin explained to Paroch. "He insisted."

Many were the hands that patted Reesal reassuringly on his back; each member knelt beside him and encouraged him. Reesal clung to each one for a moment, even as the tears continued streaming down his face. After a long while, Reesal at last stood on his feet again. "I have let the mantle down," he began. "Forgive me, please."

"Reesal, you are forgiven, but you forget your place," Paroch gently admonished him. "Is Ellonas not in control of all things?" Reesal did not reply but stood with head bowed. "You know this is true," Paroch continued. "Let Him carry your burden, for it is too heavy for you to carry alone."

"I, too, have carried a heavy burden," Gedery explained. "Let it go, my friend."

Reesal did not reply.

Paroch nodded and then, after a moment, began to speak. "We can no longer delay our departure."

"We cannot travel safely through the city, neither can we sail from this harbor," Fulcwin spoke up. "Unfortunately, our situation has not changed."

"I agree, we would not be safe within the walls of Elas-Tormas and attempting to break through the blockade..." he pointed. "Would not be without great risk, yet I intend to head for Mirion and the Council at Elberon this very evening."

"I am glad to hear this," Haendorn said loudly. "Many are the times I have trodden the paths we shall need to take. We shall be able to move swiftly and not be seen."

"Do not forget that we are with you, Lord Gedery and I and our men," Sarahin reminded them.

"I will lead us on paths seldom traveled, paths very few of my own countrymen know of. We shall be unseen," Haendorn boasted with a broad smile.

Paroch waved for Tulikar to join them. "We are going to make for Mirion this evening. How far west can you get us?"

"Not certain, really," Tulikar replied. "I believe Orendien has some knowledge of this harbor, so I will consult with him before I answer." He motioned to one of his men and sent him to fetch Orendien.

"It would be wonderful if we were put ashore near the Blackwood, and if not, then at the very least west of the outer wall," Haendorn nodded.

"Again, I am not certain, but I think we can get you far enough from the city walls that you will have a day or two headstart on any pursuers."

"Unless Morheim pursues us on horseback," Kourakin stated.

Orendien climbed aboard and joined them. "They want to know how far west we can get them," Tulikar explained. "And they want to leave this very evening."

"Can you sail us to the shores of the Blackwood? Or at least get us close?" Haendorn asked hopefully.

"Doubtful, especially sailing in the dark. If I recall correctly, the dockhands often warned newly arrived ships that the western bay was generally much shallower and difficult to navigate for deep-hulled ships. Shoals will be a constant danger, and if we were somehow able to avoid the shoals, then the ever-changing sandbars nearer to shore would certainly spell disaster for us." Orendien explained. "If you are determined on this course of action, we will do what we can to get you as far to the west as we can."

"Then it is settled," Paroch said. "This evening, we begin our journey to the west. Ready yourselves," he instructed them.

As the others left to prepare themselves for the long road ahead, Tulikar and Orendien discussed how best to bring their two ships safely to the west. Paroch stared out over the bay toward the city. Even from this distance, the activity on the docks was still evident, but it was something on the horizon that soon caught his attention. A fast-moving line of clouds, black as ink and growing in height as they rolled south and west, an ominous sight to behold. Soon, he was joined by others staring at the ever-growing wall of clouds.

"I don't think it wise to delay our departure," Tulikar warned after he stared for just a moment. Orendien quickly agreed and hurried to his ship. Both ships burst into activity; men scrambled across the deck and climbed masts, anchors were raised as were sails, and both ships began to move west. Paroch watched behind as the clouds swept closer. A tumult sounded from the city, trumpets blared, and bells tolled, then the docks were obscured, and moments later, both ships were battered by fierce winds and torrential rain as the storm hit.

# Black Chapter Seven: The Battle Begins

## The 16th of Lirinn, midday

It was nearing midday when a line of thick black clouds appeared on the northeastern horizon. Menacing even at that great distance, the clouds came on swiftly until the lower half of the sky was obscured in towering clouds of roiling black.

"The storm approaches," a voice cried out, quivering with evident fear. All eyes looked in the direction his quaking arm pointed.

"It is a bit intimidating," Tarbosar observed after a moment. He clapped one of the men on the back, "Just be happy this storm is not meant for you." He raised his voice, "Ready yourselves men!"

On the walls, many defenders could be seen peering with curiosity and pointing, but as the storm drew ever closer, the activity behind the battlements increased, trumpets sounded, and men began to scurry to and fro. The gentle wind that had been blowing from the west ceased, and a great quiet settled over the area. Then suddenly, the wind changed direction, howling in ferocity and carrying with it a wall of dust and leaves. Even Tarbosar ducked as the wind blew past, and overhead, the looming wall of darkness plunged his line of men into an eerie half-light. Flashes of lightning played in the clouds, and bright bursts of green and blue momentarily lit the ground.

"Remember men when the storm...!" Tarbosar's last few words were lost in a tremendous peal of thunder. The storm reached the walls, and Tarbosar raised his sword and charged forward. Drums began to beat wildly, a thousand trumpet blasts rent the air, and the men added their voices to the rising cacophony as they charged forward. Suddenly, a wall of green smoke appeared behind them and was propelled toward the outer wall by the wind of the storm. As the first bolt of green-tinged lightning scorched the outer wall, thousands of Dakirin sprang into the air. They swooped low over the charging ranks of men before climbing higher than the wall towers and then diving onto the battlements themselves. Wherever the Dakirin landed, the crenellations disappeared for a brief moment in a green fog and more often than not, only Dakirin remained alive atop the wall when the fog had cleared. The fighting for the towers, especially those nearest the gates, was exceptionally fierce, but there, too, the outcome was inevitable. By the time the first of Tarbosar's men reached the wall, the gates had been flung open.

"Make sure the towers are cleared," Tarbosar thundered as he leaned against the open gate.

"Them Dakireen cleared 'em out already," a soldier reasoned as he stopped to catch his breath. "Look!" he pointed to the thick plumes of green smoke pouring from the tower windows. The smoke quickly dissipated in the storm's strong wind.

"You will be checking the towers again anyway," Tarbosar roared and took a menacing step toward the man who, with a quick salute, hurried through an open doorway at the base of the gate tower. "The rest of you will form up two bowshots from the wall and await further instructions," he ordered the men rushing through the gate. He was about to follow after them when Vontar landed beside him, a broad smile on his face.

"The enemy flees," he shouted gleefully. "They have been routed along the entire wall, and it seems they are fleeing to Elas-Tormas."

"The entire wall?"

"The entire wall," Vontar repeated. "With the exception of a few towers down Hember's way," he added. "But our section is cleared completely."

"No one left alive in this tower," a soldier called from atop the wall tower. He looked down at Tarbosar and saluted again.

"It is as I have said," Vontar agreed with a nod. "The wall and the towers are devoid of any defenders."

A flash of lightning lit the ground momentarily, and Tarbosar noticed movement near the base of the wall. "What is that?" he asked.

"What?" Vontar followed his gaze.

"At the base of the tower, there," Tarbosar pointed. Another flash of lightning revealed a man slowly dragging himself away from the wall. "An enemy is trying to escape."

"He jumped from the tower when we landed," Vontar laughed. "Both of his legs are shattered. That one will give you no trouble," he assured him. "You can send your men forward; we will alert them to any enemy nearby." He laughed aloud. "I doubt there are many that will put up much of a fight; fear has taken hold in their ranks." He breathed deeply, "You can almost smell it."

"My ancestors fought many battles with Anar," Tarbosar began. "And always, the men of Elas-Tormas joined with them to defeat us. They are as cunning as they are strong in battle and cruel as well, never showing the slightest mercy to those they capture. It would be dangerous to leave him behind." As he was talking, Vontar strode over to the man with the broken legs and looked down on him.

"Where do you think you are going?" The man did not look up but continued dragging himself slowly through the mud. Vontar looked at Tarbosar, "I fail to see the danger in this crippled man, but so that you have no further concerns…" he placed his boot upon the back of the man's head and slowly pushed his face into the muck. Muddy fingers clawed desperately at his boot, and then, after a moment, the hands went limp.

"We Dakirin can also be cruel," Vontar remarked. "I trust this satisfies your concern about any defenders we may have left behind?"

Tarbosar nodded.

"Then let us press forward until we have reached Elas-Tormas," Vontar urged as he transformed and took to the air. He circled once just above Tarbosar's head, calling loudly before flying to the south.

\*\*\*

Erelis circled above the outer wall, most every defender had either been killed or was fleeing to Elas-Tormas. Only two towers were still in the hands of the defenders; they had repelled the first Dakirin attack and then managed to barricade the doors and windows. "Too costly for us

Dakirin to take, but definitely a job for Hember and his men," he chuckled. Another flash of lightning revealed less than half of Hember's command was advancing on the walls. He swore loudly as he banked into the wind and flew toward the first group he could see. Five soldiers were staring at the storm as it passed overhead.

"What is the meaning of this?" he bellowed as he transformed beside them. "Why are you not moving forward?"

"Our general is dead," one of the men replied and pointed to Hember's lifeless body.

"Many men die in wars. Were you not given orders to advance the moment the storm passed above the walls?"

One by one, each man nodded.

"Then why are you standing here instead of advancing?" Erelis demanded.

"We were trying to find who it was that killed him and take our revenge."

"Unless it was one of you who killed him," Erelis stated.

"Hember was like a father to us," one of the men explained. "It was a Lepnarion for sure."

Erelis looked at Hember's body. It was evident a spear thrust to the side had ended his life; there was no spear to be found, and any tracks the perpetrators had made would be washed away with the rain, and any that managed to survive would have been obscured by these five.

"Let me worry about those who killed Hember." Erelis stared at them for a moment. "There are two gate towers still in Lepnarion hands," he pointed to them.

"I heard you Dakirin were going to take the walls and open the gates for us," one of the men retorted.

"The walls *have* been cleared of resistance, and the gates before you are open. Now is the time for you to join in the fighting. You will take both towers, and then I will forget about your failure to carry out a direct order." None of the men moved toward the wall, but several of them cast sidelong glances at each other as hands strayed toward hilts. With a laugh, Erelis unsheathed his sword. "Die here by my blade or attempting to take those towers. The choice is yours."

"You forgot the third choice," one of the men said as he drew his own sword. "We kill you and head for home."

"Are you all in agreement?" Erelis asked. The only answer he received was the unsheathing of two more swords.

Erelis bowed slightly without taking his eyes off of them, then twirled his blade once before lunging forward. He stabbed one man through the neck, and even as his body crumpled to the earth, a quick swing of his blade lopped the head off another. He parried a clumsy strike, then removed a third man's swordhand, followed by his leg. He turned to the others. "You two still have a choice." A quick glance to the man screaming in agony, then to Erelis, whose red-stained blade now pointed to the ground was beginning to drip large crimson drops of blood, and without a word, both turned and sprinted toward the outer wall.

"The rest of you, forward! Take those towers!" Erelis ordered the others nearby. He watched as hundreds of men streamed toward the wall. Even in the dim light, he could see when one fell, clutching at a feathered shaft suddenly sprouting from leg or chest, but the defender's arrows were too few to make any real difference. It did not take long for scores of soldiers to reach the walls and the parapets and begin hammering on the tower doors. A roar was heard as one of the tower doors was breached, and the fighting intensified. With a nod of satisfaction, Erelis turned his attention to Hember once again.

*If I had dispatched this one, how would I evade capture?* He asked himself. He looked to the walls and then to the body at his feet, then he slowly turned to the river. Erelis transformed and flew into the sky, banking low over the western riverbank. He circled for many minutes before landing and examining a series of deep depressions in the sandy bank heading toward the water. Even though the wind and rain were slowly wiping away the evidence, he nodded. *Looks like footprints. Eight, maybe more. They were running and carrying something heavy.* His gaze went to the eastern riverbank; in the dim light of the storm, he could see nothing, but he stared nonetheless. He drew his dagger and quickly cut a strip from his cloak. Grabbing a dead branch, he tied the strip to one end, then plunged the other as deep as he could into the sand; the wind grabbed the bit of cloth, but the branch remained stuck fast. Satisfied, he transformed again and circling once, he made his way toward the outer wall.

\*\*\*

Pentar transformed in the air and landed next to Kinjal, whose horse snorted in surprise.

"She dislikes your sudden appearances," Kinjal laughed as he gave his mount a reassuring pat on her neck.

"She should be used to me by now," Pentar protested. He reached out his hand to let her smell him.

She whinnied and shook her head vigorously.

"I think she is," Kinjal laughed again. "But I do not think she likes you all that much."

"She does not like that I can fly faster than she can gallop," Pentar nodded knowingly.

"It is hard enough to ride in this wind," Kinjal said as he dismounted and faced Pentar. "How can you even fly in this weather?"

"It does take some getting used to," Pentar admitted. "But once you learn to fly with the wind instead of against it, it is not that difficult. The worst part is dodging any debris that might be carried by the wind."

"And the rain? Does it affect you at all?" His mount shook the rain off her back.

"Not one bit; water rolls off the feathers."

"It will take a week for me to dry out," Kinjal complained.

They were silent for a few moments, during which a long and loud peal of thunder sounded in the distance. The wind picked up, and with it, the rain began coming down harder.

"Did you stop by to gloat over your ability to fly in this weather?" Kinjal finally asked as his mount stomped on the muddy track.

"I have both good and bad news for you," Pentar laughed.

Kinjal shook his head. "Not interested."

"I shall give you the good news first," Pentar persisted.

Kinjal raised his brows, "Which is?"

"We have reached the last gate and begun…"

"You have the gate secured?" Kinjal interrupted.

"It is secure."

"Was the battle ever in doubt?"

"There was no fight," Pentar explained. "We found the wall and towers empty. Not a single guard to be seen. We have thrown the gates open wide."

"That is good news," Kinjal agreed. "Who is guarding the gate now?"

"There is no need at present," Pentar boasted.

Kinjal frowned.

"We have found no one even near the outer wall, and those we have seen are hurrying to the city. There are great crowds of people waiting to enter the gates of Elas-Tormas itself. The people are gathering themselves together for the coming slaughter."

"How can you be certain no one is trying to escape?" Kinjal wanted to know.

"I have instructed my Dakirin to make regular patrols between the city walls and the outer wall; they are to locate anyone attempting to leave. But we can make doubly certain once your troops arrive at the western gate."

Kinjal nodded, "I believe that is acceptable."

"Which brings me to the bad news," Pentar laughed. "You are still at least a day away from reaching the last gate."

"Only a day?" Kinjal grumbled. "With this confounded storm, it will add another day, I am certain. But what news of the others? Have they taken the wall yet?"

"The wall has been taken, and those surviving defenders are fleeing to the city as fast as they can go. Reports from everywhere bring the same tidings: victory for us and defeat for our enemies."

"Perhaps we will not need to do much more than reach the gate then," Kinjal pondered hopefully.

"I would think about that after you reach the gate," Pentar suggested. Then, he transformed and flew to the south and east.

Kinjal signaled for a rider as he mounted his horse.

"Sir?" the rider saluted.

"We will be marching through the night. We must reach the western gate by tomorrow. Ride to the end of the column and deliver my command."

"Yes, sir!" he saluted and immediately turned his mount and quickly disappeared in the driving rain.

Kinjal leaned low over his horse's head and whispered in her ear as he patted her neck. She nodded her head twice and began plodding south along the muddy track.

# White Chapter Eight: West Of Elas-Tormas

## The 16th of Lirinn, before dusk

"Never in all my years have I seen a storm with such ferocity!" Tulikar yelled above the wind. Paroch simply nodded as he clung to the deck to avoid being thrown overboard. He agreed; the storm *was* awesome to behold, oppressive darkness so thick as to crush all hope punctuated by myriad bolts of green and blue lightning striking indiscriminately, furious winds tore at the sails while enormous waves crashed over the rails, yet as the evening wore on and the sun sank lower to the western horizon, long rays of orange and red began to color the underside of the storm. Then, the orange disk dipped below the ragged line of distant clouds and hung there for a moment, a bright beacon of hope.

For a few minutes, Tulikar and Orendien were able to see a distant shoreline, and after a brief exchange of hand signals, both determined to attempt to land. The Hooves of the Sea led the way, and the Seamane followed as close as Tulikar dared. While the light lasted, both were able to safely navigate their approach to shore, but all too soon, the darkness returned and, with it, danger as well.

The Hooves of the Sea struck a shoal first and stopped abruptly, flinging several men overboard. The Seamane, following so close behind, only just missed crashing into the stricken ship. Tulikar spun the wheel, turning to port moments before the waves shoved the ship into the same shoal. Immediately, the Seamane listed dangerously and more so with the battering of each successive wave. Both captains feverishly worked to free their ships, shouting commands to their crew. As the wind blew harder, the main sail on the Seamane ripped in half, and then a tremendous wave crashed onto the deck, washing several of the crew overboard. At the same time, the tremendous sound of timbers cracking was heard above the wind and the roar of the waves as the stern of the Hooves of the Sea began to break apart. Without hesitation, both captains gave the order to abandon the ship. Those who could swim jumped overboard and made their way to shore, and the rest clung to barrels, crates or pieces of the ships.

Twenty minutes later, as the last of the men dragged themselves out onto the beach, the storm continued to rage all around them, with lightning striking alarmingly close, followed quickly by deafening peals of thunder. The rain had slackened. However, the constant spray of crashing waves kept those huddled on the land soaked.

Even with the howling wind, several resourceful soldiers soon had a fire blazing high up on the beach.

Paroch and the mantle gathered together around the fire. They were soon joined by Sarahin and Leond, Gedery and Tulikar and Orendien.

"Having a fire here will alert others to our presence," Leond observed.

"That may be," Paroch began. "But I doubt even the Dakirin are out in this. Does anyone know where we are?" Paroch asked hopefully as he rubbed his hands together. The fire sizzled and crackled as it licked at the soaked wood. Stronger gusts of wind threatened to blow the flames out completely, but each time when the wind subsided, the flames began to grow again.

"I have sent two hundred of my men on ahead," Gedery informed him. "Keeping the water on their left, they are to find the wall and secure a way out if possible."

"I have sent one hundred men with them as well," Leond added. He turned his back so the heat could warm him.

"This storm blew our ships on a westerly course for several hours before we made landfall," Tulikar explained. "But I do not think we are outside the outer wall yet." He knelt down close to the fire so that his wet clothes began to give off steam, wreathing his weathered face in swirling grey and white.

"We are still in the Outlands but much closer to the outer wall I should think," Orendien offered.

"I hope you are right about being closer to the outer wall," Paroch replied. "Let us gather the others and begin moving to the west. There is no telling how long this storm will last, and when it subsides, we do not want to be caught in the Outlands by Morheim or Dakirin."

"What of the fire?" Sarahin asked as they prepared to leave. "It will alert others of our having been here."

"The wind and waves will ensure it does not burn overly long," Gedery explained. "It will be out long before daybreak." As if to punctuate his comment, a wave rolled up to the base of the fire, causing it to hiss and sputter before the water retreated.

They formed into smaller groups and began marching to the west along the beach in the growing darkness. Many were the waves that crashed ashore, racing inland so that at times they marched through knee-deep sea water, then with great force, the water would drain back into the bay. More than once, an unfortunate was swept off their feet and dragged with the water, sputtering for air and crying for help, but each time, they were rescued by others close by. After an hour or so, the waves relented and did not carry as far inland; the wind grew less, and here and there, a weary smile could be seen. As they trudged through the clinging sand, there were many times the storm seemed about to end, the rain became little more than a sprinkle, and lightning lit the sky in the distance behind them, the thunder a mere rumble, then suddenly there would be a downpour such that they could hardly see even with their hands shielding their eyes and the lightning and thunder returned but not as close nor as loud as before.

During one of the lulls, Paroch and Sarahin spoke in quiet voices with each other.

"I had hoped to meet you again in better circumstances," Sarahin spoke as she glanced at Paroch.

"That was not the will of Ellonas," Paroch replied, his head bowed. "Besides, it is good that we met again, even under these circumstances," He smiled though he did not look at her.

"But I have lost everything," Sarahin continued. "I left everything behind when I fled Anar."

"Not everything," he countered. "Life is most precious. A gift."

"Of course it is," Sarahin agreed quickly. "I only meant that…" her voice trailed off.

"Possessions can be replaced, homes rebuilt, kingdoms reclaimed, but life….life cannot be replaced. Sarahin, in the coming days, we will part ways; my hope and prayer are that I can see you again no matter the circumstances."

Sarahin's reply was lost in another downpour. A fierce gust of wind blew her into Paroch, and he steadied her; his hand found hers as they continued along the beach. The torrent of rain lasted quite a long time and then stopped as abruptly as it had started.

Paroch looked at Sarahin and smiled, and he was about to say something when Gedery approached at a run.

"The wall is not far off now, maybe an hour at our current pace," he informed Paroch. "The others have turned north to find the western gate."

"Have they encountered anyone?" Paroch asked. "Either friend or foe?"

"No one," Gedery replied. He bowed his head once, then turned and jogged back to the front of the column.

"It is a mercy that our journey is almost over," Sarahin commented.

"Reaching the gate is just the first part. We shall have to ask Haendorn how far our journey into Mirion will be."

Sarahin nodded and gripped Paroch's hand just a bit tighter.

By the time they reached the outer wall they were greeted by several scouts. "The gate is but half an hour to the north."

"What of the guards?" Paroch asked.

"We found it open and unguarded," the scout replied.

"Perhaps the enemy has already passed through on their way to Elas-Tormas," Telliken offered.

"I do not know if that is the case," the scout replied. "I saw no signs of fighting; perhaps the guards fled in fear."

"Abandoned their post?" Fulcwin asked incredulously. "Highly unlikely!"

"It makes no difference," Paroch replied. "We must hurry to the gate as quick as we can." At his urging, the group hurried on. Those who were weary were supported by those who had the strength to continue.

When at last they reached the gate, it was just as the scout said he had found it. Both gates were thrown open wide, and not a single guard was to be seen.

"Paroch, we must leave," Haendorn urged. "We have another two days before we reach the outskirts of Mirion." He led the way along a wide road, climbing gently up a steep slope first to the left for a while, then doubling back upon itself again and again until, at last, they reached the top. Paroch stopped for a moment and, turning around, bid a silent farewell to Arvendal. "May Ellonas keep you safe until he gathers you home," he whispered.

Sarahin gently tugged at his hand, and with a deep breath, Paroch turned and headed toward Mirion. The now gentle rain hid the tear that fell down his cheek.

# Black Chapter Eight: Cleansing The Outlands

## The 17th of Lirinn, morning

Overhead, the tattered remnants of the storm of darkness were streaming to the east in a gentle breeze. The morning sun shone through breaks in the clouds. Elisad stood facing south, eyes squinting to see in the distance.

"Where I come from in the Tav-Tar," one of his men said as he walked up. "We get some bad storms in the spring, but I have never before seen a storm the likes of that one yesterday."

"I am not surprised," Elisad stated without looking at him. "That storm was created by Mazzaroth and sent to hurl his enemies into confusion."

"It worked well," the man said as he scratched the part of his hairy belly peeking out from under his hard leather armor. "No defenders were able to stand against us."

"That would have more to do with our Dakirin allies than with your fierce countenance, I should think."

"But we fought well, and they were defeated," he protested.

"Yes, you fought well, but consider this. How can one stand and fight when they are attacked from the front, above and behind? The Lepnarions are in disarray, but they are not yet defeated."

There were several moments of silence before Elisad pointed, "Do you see that?"

The man followed the direction Elisad pointed. "Beyond that hill with the solitary tree on top?"

"Yes, is that smoke rising?" Elisad asked.

"Could be," he replied, then after a few moments. "Yes, that is smoke. Probably refugees," he nodded.

"Carefully go and find out," Elisad commanded.

"By myself?"

"Take a few men with you, but remain vigilant. There are still many dangers to face before we reach Elas-Tormas."

"We are more than a match for soldiers, let alone refugees," he boasted.

"One man may stand against many, but without help, eventually he will be overwhelmed."

"You are in a fine mood this morning," he sighed with a shake of his head.

"Cautious," Elisad muttered more to himself than to the man beside him. "You have your orders; the rest of us will be along presently."

The man saluted and turned to walk away.

"Do not be overconfident," Elisad advised. The man waved his arm over his head, but he did not turn around.

As soon as the others were ready to march, Elisad led them toward the distant pillar of smoke. Less than an hour later, one of the men sent earlier came running toward them, his eyes wide with fear. He stopped in front of Elisad and bent over, hands on his knees.

Elisad raised his brows and tilted his head slightly as he waited for him to catch his breath.

"Knights…..a…..whole….army….of…them," he finally uttered, gasping for breath between each word.

"Where are the others that were with you?" Elisad demanded to know.

He shook his head, "I have…no idea…I stopped…to take… a stone….out of my….boot." he lifted his foot, wiggling his toes through the hole in the side of his boot. "I heard someone yelling and cursing, and then I heard the thunder of horse hooves followed by sounds of fighting, but it did not last long. By the time I crept to the crest of a hill and peeked over, my four companions were lying dead on the hillside."

"Where did this happen?"

"We came to a place where the road turned to the west around a tall hill. The enemy is encamped on the far slope."

Elisad nodded. After a moment's contemplation, he gave orders for his men to form in a line four ranks deep; spearmen were in the first and second line, archers in the third and axe and swords were in the fourth line. Anticipation of the coming battle was evident amongst the men, with excited whispers and a quickened pace. Less than an hour later, Elisad stopped his men; before him, the road veered to the west around the base of a tall hill; to his left was a line of trees and to his right, an open field. He raised his arm to order his men forward when a line of mounted knights appeared atop the hill. A trumpet sounded, and the knights charged.

The thunder of their approach spread panic among Elisad's troops. Few were the men who stood their ground, and for those who did, most were killed as the knights rode over them. Elisad tried to rally his men, but his commands went unheard amidst the din. Those men spread amongst the trees were able to unhorse a score of the knights and those they savagely attacked, hacking and stabbing. They fared better than their counterparts in the field, who were scattered and ridden down in turn.

Elisad grabbed a spear from one of the men standing beside him and hurled it at an approaching knight, knocking him from his mount.

"Rally men, rally!" he screamed until he was hoarse, but the fighting was spread far, and few men could hear him. Those who did hear rallied to their commander, forming a protective ring around him.

Suddenly, a jet of green smoke appeared beside him, and Kotkas emerged grinning.

"You started this battle without me!"

"Glad to see you, but where are the others?" Elisad asked.

Kotkas pointed into the air. "They will be along presently."

Elisad watched a group of thirty knights form a line, and as they spurred their mounts forward, pillars of green smoke began to erupt here and there until the knights were engulfed in a haze of green. Only three knights burst from the smoke, charging hard. Another fell from his saddle as a Dakirin transformed and crashed into him. The Dakirin was upon the hapless knight before he could stand up, thrusting his blade deep under the left shoulder. The two remaining mounted knights continued on, drawing ever closer to Elisad and Kotkas. With a curse shouted at his enemy, Kotkas charged forward, and a moment later, Elisad followed, yelling loudly. Elisad tried to dodge his attacker, but a well-placed lance caught him in the chest, and he fell on his back, eyes blinking rapidly as he stared into the sky. Turning his warhorse quickly, the knight drew his sword and swung at any unfortunate in his path as he thundered to the top of the hill, disappearing over the crest.

Kotkas dodged his attacker's lance even as his blade caught the horse in its side. With a loud neighing, the horse tumbled to the ground, but the knight was able to leap from his saddle and turn to face Kotkas. He advanced quickly away from the horse's thrashing legs, drawing his broadsword.

"Fly away," he taunted. "Or will you stand and fight?"

Kotkas raised his own blade in a salute and took several steps forward. "Leave him to me," he snarled as several of Elisad's men began advancing.

The Lepnarion smiled at him and then began his attack, swinging his sword at an upward angle, then with both hands bringing his blade down upon his enemy.

Kotkas easily dodged the first strike but was not quick enough to dodge the second. His eyes remained wide open even as he fell to the ground and breathed his last.

Satisfied, the Lepnarion turned in a slow circle, sword held before him at the ready. "Which of you will fight me?"

"Come on, we can take him," someone urged.

"This is most likely true; I am already tired. However, you should be asking yourselves: am I ready to die today? You may indeed kill me, but some of you will join me like your green-skinned friend here." He shoved his foot against Kotkas' corpse. "What will it be?"

Three men stepped forward, two wielding spears and the third an axe; the rest of the men began backing away. The fight began with one of the men thrusting his spear forward. The Lepnarion grabbed the shaft of the spear and, bringing his sword down upon it, cut it cleanly. In one motion, he threw the part of the spear he held, striking the man in the upper chest. He turned in time to take another spear thrust to his outer thigh; his armor deflected most of the strike; nevertheless, he could still feel blood beginning to trickle down his leg. He repeated the same process as before, grabbing ahold of the spear shaft and cutting it cleanly, but this time, he turned and hurled it at the one advancing with his axe raised. The axe fell from suddenly lifeless hands, and he turned to face the one remaining combatant. "The others have abandoned you. You heathens from the Tav-Tar always were a worthless lot. Only fighting when you were convinced of an easy victory over helpless prey." The Lepnarion laughed. "Without your green-skinned allies, you would still be trying to forge a way into Anar." He kept talking as he slowly advanced, and with every step he took, his enemy took two steps backward until he finally turned and ran as fast as his boots would carry him.

***

Aracelis ordered his men forward, then turning to Rakosa, waved him over.

"Good work yesterday helping take the gate. That was a tough fight, but you and your men fought tenaciously."

"The Lepnarions are fighting to protect their homes and families; I would expect nothing less of them," Rakosa replied. "And I and my men are fighting for our lives as well, so you should expect nothing less of us."

Aracelis nodded. "Today, I want you to ride around the town ahead of us and take up a position to block the route of those fleeing our advance. Prathin tells me there is some high ground just beyond that will serve our purpose well."

"I would expect many refugees to flee at your approach."

"They flee today so that they may fight again tomorrow," Niven explained.

Aracelis nodded. "Well said, and what of those who choose to stay in their homes?" he asked Niven.

"Obviously, they are planning on fomenting rebellion after we pass by," Niven replied with a laugh.

"Then they all must perish," Aracelis stated with a shrug.

"Women and children? The elderly?" Rakosa asked.

"It is like you have already said, Rakosa, these Lepnarions are fighting to protect their homes and families."

"How much of a threat can *they* be to your army?"

"Enough of a threat to find a permanent solution. Tell me, Rakosa, are you having second thoughts about this arrangement of ours?" Aracelis asked with a laugh.

Rakosa opened his mouth to answer but shut it again and shook his head.

"I thought not," Aracelis continued laughing. "Only after we take Elas-Tormas will you be given the antidote."

Rakosa looked at Aracelis and Niven, then saluted them and walked away.

As soon as he was out of earshot, Aracelis and Niven began speaking.

"You still want me to ensure he does not survive the taking of Elas-Tormas?"

Aracelis nodded as he watched Rakosa and his men ride slowly from the camp. "There is much more to that one than meets the eye."

"Will he carry out your orders?" Niven asked.

"I would expect him to. However, you should keep an eye on him to make certain he does fulfill them."

"Where is the antidote?"

"I have it stored in a safe place for now. After we take Elas-Tormas, I will have you deliver it for me."

"Why not withhold the antidote and let him die from the poison itself?"

Aracelis stared at Niven for a moment, then smiled. "We are men of our word, are we not? We shall deliver the antidote to the ones who survive. As far as Rakosa goes, it would be better for him to think he is saved from the poison and then when he is least expecting it to strike him down."

"That is a cruel twist," Niven said with a laugh. "Give him hope and then yank it away from him. This shall be great fun."

"Do not toy with him, Niven; he is dangerous," Aracelis warned. "When the time comes, be quick about it."

"I can handle him," Niven boasted.

"Bring me proof."

"I will bring you his body," Niven exclaimed.

\*\*\*

Kinjal was relieved when, at last, he saw the western gate in the distance. He spurred his mount forward until he reached it, and there he waited for his men. Pentar landed beside him and transformed.

"I trust the journey has not been too arduous for you."

"Once we make certain this gate is secure, my men will be ready to rest until the morning at the very least."

"Go ahead and rest up; the gate has been secured by my Dakirin," Pentar laughed. "Since we have been here, no one has managed to leave through this gate," he boasted.

"And what about before you arrived?" Kinjal asked. "I wonder," he mused as he surveyed the ground. "There are a lot of footprints here in the mud. They all seem to be heading to the west."

"They must have left before the attack began," Pentar offered.

"Except the rain would have washed away all prints. It looks like these were made recently." Kinjal followed the tracks with his eyes. "Have you sent anyone to check west of here?"

"I saw no need," Pentar answered. "We have been concentrating on the lands inside the gate, not those outside."

"Is it possible that people managed to flee before you got here?"

"Certainly, and if they did, they are most likely refugees, but no one has passed through since we arrived."

Kinjal continued staring into the distance, "What do you suppose is beyond that hill there?"

"I suppose the road continues into Mirion, though I hardly expect to find an army waiting on the other side."

"I would agree, but it would be good to know who has left so recently. I will send a detachment to the top of the hill there."

Pentar sighed audibly, "No need; I will send a beak to scout that area out."

Another Dakirin landed and saluted, "I bring word of two ships run aground in the bay. They look to be Anari vessels, but both are empty."

"How far from here?" Kinjal wanted to know.

"By wing, not far at all, by foot, maybe half a day," the Dakirin surmised.

"Is that all?" Pentar asked.

"There is something else; we found the remains of a large fire."

Pentar frowned as he rubbed the end of his nose. "Survivors of the shipwrecks, no doubt."

After a moment's contemplation, Kinjal spoke, "However unlikely this may be, I think we should scout the lands west of here to see if there are any large groups of Anaris running around near the woods of Mirion."

Pentar began laughing, "Why not? I suppose we will be venturing into that land sooner rather than later." He spoke to the one who had brought the report. "Take a beak and scout that road as far as the eves of Mirion. If you find anything of interest, report back to me immediately." As soon as the Dakirin left, he turned back to Kinjal. "Now, about a little rest after your arduous journey. The gatehouse there has several rooms that you can use. Not too large, mind you, but sufficient."

Kinjal nodded. "Many thanks, Pentar. Make sure to wake me when that beak gets back. I want to know what they find."

"You seem concerned," Pentar observed.

"Just a feeling that we might have missed something."

# White Chapter Nine: The Growing Fear

## The 17th of Lirinn, evening

Morheim stared out of his window to the darkened streets below. Nary a lit torch was to be seen, and the streets were deserted as far as he could tell. He glanced to the night sky. The storm that had wreaked so much havoc was beginning to break up, and for a brief moment, he was able to see a few stars. The door to his chamber opened, and a servant reported that his generals were waiting for him. With a heavy sigh, he turned and walked to where his generals and advisors were gathered.

The voices were loud and carried far in the stone corridor, but he could not discern what was being said. The soldiers guarding the room saluted him and opened the tall wooden doors.

"What news from the outer wall?" he asked those assembled.

"It has fallen," one replied quickly.

"In less than a day? Impossible!" Morheim was incredulous. "How did this happen?"

"They have Falkiri with them," another responded.

"Dakirin," another corrected.

"They were able to attack from above and overwhelm the wall. We had no chance!" the man continued. "Were this a normal attack using siege towers and ladders, we would have easily repelled it."

"Falkiri, Dakirin, bah! Do they bleed?" the king asked.

"Yes, but they are formidable foes," another general replied. "Every time our brave soldiers turn to fight, they are assailed not just from the front but from every direction."

"Have they never been surrounded before?" Morheim thundered.

"You must remember that these Dakirin fall from the sky into the midst of the defenders and…"

"Who among you will defend this fair city?" Morheim challenged.

"We all would," another general replied. "Will," he corrected. "However, we have never faced such an enemy as these winged Dakirin. There is no defense against them."

Morheim's brow furrowed, and his face reddened.

A knight stood and bowed to Morheim, "If I may be permitted to speak?"

Morheim nodded.

"I am the only survivor of the Fourth Knights," he began. "This morning, we numbered over five hundred and were defending just south of Acorn, facing many thousands of foot soldiers. Our first charge was successful, and the enemy was being swept from the field until the Dakirin began to appear." He paused a moment to collect his emotions. "There is not much a knight can do when, while he is charging, a foe from above dives into him, knocking him from his mount. This happened so quickly as to turn the tide of battle against us. The enemy before us rallied and turned again to face us while we were dealing with the Dakirin amongst us."

"How is it that you alone have survived?" Morheim demanded.

"I managed to keep my saddle, dodging several Dakirin that dived at me. I turned once to see where I could be of most use, but everywhere, the field belonged to the enemy. Riderless horses stood beside their fallen masters. I judged that living to fight another day would be far better than throwing my life away against such overwhelming odds as those." He sat down, head bowed.

"It is the same report from every sector," another general replied. "We have no defense capable of holding against the attacks of the Dakirin, and only those with mounts have any hope of ever reaching the safety of these walls."

"How many defenders do we still have in the Outlands?"

"We have lost contact with everyone except the Ninth Knights to the east. They are falling back slowly. Beyond that," he shook his head.

"Bring the Ninth back now. How many archers do we have to defend the walls?"

"None to speak of, m'lord. We had almost everyone deployed to the outer wall. There are no longer enough men to defend the walls of Elas-Tormas."

"How many men do we have?"

"The walls have room for forty thousand soldiers; currently, we have twenty thousand, maybe less."

"Are there no sections that could be held with fewer men?"

"If this were a normal battle, it would be possible for us to hold out and even defeat the attackers, but with Dakirin falling upon the walls and upon any other place a defense is attempted..." his voice trailed off.

"So we are defeated already?" Morheim asked. No one replied, and no eyes sought the king's face.

The doors to the room were opened, and a soldier rushed in carrying a wrapped bundle. He hurried to bow before the King.

"What business do you have with me?" Morheim demanded.

"While we were searching through the Order's quarters, we found this," he offered the bundle to Morheim.

"What is it?" Morheim asked; he reached for the bundle and then withdrew his hand.

"It looks to be the sword that we were searching for," the soldier answered excitedly. He began to unwrap the blade.

Morheim smiled for a moment, then he frowned. "Where did you say you found this?"

"In one of the Order's rooms."

"Which order?" Morheim asked impatiently.

"I believe it was one of the blade's rooms."

Morheim inspected the blade closely; it certainly looked like it could be Abion. But something was not quite right.

"Eulix, come and examine this blade," Morheim commanded.

Eulix bowed as he drew near. He placed his hands out, and the soldier gently laid the sword across his palms.

"With your permission," Eulix asked, and he tilted his head toward the windows in the room.

"Go ahead," Morheim said, and he followed him to the windows while the others in the room craned their necks to see if they could discern anything about the blade itself.

Holding it up to the window and the last rays of the setting sun, Eulix examined it closely, peering along its length and scrutinizing its pommel. He turned it over in his hands and continued his inspection. After a moment, he began to shake his head.

"What?" Morheim demanded.

"This appears to be nothing more than a clever forgery," Eulix began softly. He held the blade up for Morheim to see for himself. "Do you see here on the blade? The etching appears to stop and then start again, but there is an area where it does not quite match." Morheim nodded after a moment. "And here in the pommel and guard, do you see the way the gems are set? They are not quite even. In fact, they are not real gems at all but rather expertly carved blue glass."

Morheim swore.

"However," Eulix continued whispering. "Perhaps we can still use this to our advantage. From a distance, there can be no doubt that this *is* the famed sword of Abion."

Morheim frowned again.

"But, if those defending this city think that you wield Abion, they will fight all the harder for you." Eulix shrugged.

"And when it is found out to be a fake? I will be the greater fraud!"

"You can always say that in the heat of conflict, you were presented the sword, and it was a clever enough forgery to fool even you."

Morheim reached down, grabbed the sword and raised it high. He slashed the air with it several times. "This is a good blade, even if it is not the Kingsword."

"But it is real to those who are not aware it is fake," Eulix continued.

"You may have a point," Morheim nodded. "Was there no scabbard found with it?" he asked loudly for all to hear.

"No, m'lord," the soldier replied.

"Thank you for delivering Abion to me," Morheim shouted. "You are dismissed. But let everyone know Abion the Kingsword is in my hands, and with it, we will be victorious in the coming battle!"

Face beaming with sudden joy, the soldier bowed once more before leaving.

"Now, where were we?" Morheim asked as he approached the others in the room.

"We were discussing our options for defending Elas-Tormas," Baldred replied, even as he stared at Eulix with a furrowed brow.

"We have plenty of weapons in the armory," another general said quietly. "Perhaps we could arm every citizen."

"And you would expect them to stand and defend when our own soldiers cannot or will not?" Morheim shook his head. "No, I will not have the citizenry butchered in a vain attempt to keep what may already be lost. Abandon the Outlands, open the gates to all refugees seeking safety behind these walls, and for those who wish to leave, let them go," he sighed. "Scour the prison for any who are willing to fight in defense of this city, offer them pardon for their crimes. I will not surrender myself to the Darklord but let each of you decide what is best for yourself. If any man is willing to defend his King, let him remain with me. Send word to the soldiers that should the city walls be taken, our last bastion will be this palace."

Messengers were quickly dispatched, and within the hour, several thousand soldiers had taken up defensive positions upon the palace walls. What remained of the Ninth arrived just before daybreak, each knight leading his mount to the royal stables before joining in the defense. As word of Abion's recovery spread throughout the city, many thousands of citizens also arrived at the palace doors, eager to help in the defense of the city. In addition, four hundred criminals arrived from the prisons, barefoot and barely clothed, many still wearing shackles that had until recently been used to keep them confined. The armory was emptied, those who could wield weapons were armed, and those with no training were hastily trained on the use of a bow. In the end, just over ten thousand civilians joined in the defense of Elas-Tormas.

"The end must truly be here if we are forced to let criminals help defend the city," one civilian spoke loudly.

"If I must die for my crimes, then let me die in defense of Elas-Tormas!" a convict replied loudly. He raised his shackles and shook them so they made a great deal of noise. All around him, other convicts began shaking their shackles as well until, finally, a civilian approached with his hand outstretched.

"And our king has Abion! We will be the victors! I will fight alongside you," he said as he and the criminal before him shook hands. Other civilians came forward, and before long, the cheers of hope drowned out the noise of shackles.

"Can we have these shackles removed?" one asked his jailor.

"If you survive the coming battle, you will be granted pardon for your crimes and be given your freedom. Until then, they will remain upon your wrists and ankles."

"A just reminder of what we are fighting for," another convict spoke up, and the others around him cheered all the louder.

Morheim and his generals watched from an upper balcony.

"They certainly seem eager," one general remarked.

"That eagerness will last until the fighting is before them; then we will see how eager they are," another replied.

Morheim looked at the generals and shook his head. "I fear you are correct. Nevertheless, since they are eager, we should make certain they are of some use. Station them amongst the regular soldiers; perhaps they will not be overly quick to run when others around them stand and fight."

"They stand little chance," one of the generals replied. "But at least they will die fighting instead of huddling in a dark corner hoping to survive."

"Is it really Abion?" a general wanted to know.

"I can assure you it is," Eulix replied slyly.

"Then we have nothing to fear," Baldred replied.

***

"It is most fortunate that you knew about these tunnels," Rose whispered as she followed Hammer closely. In the dim light of the lantern, she could see the path they had been following. It was not more than five feet high and less than five feet wide in most places. The floor and walls were mostly smooth. In many places, tangled roots hung down from the ceiling.

"I said it is…" Rose began again.

"I heard you the first time," Hammer whispered sharply over his shoulder. "Please be aware that we are not so deep underground so as to avoid all detection."

nodded, though Hammer did not see it. After another half an hour of walking, the ground sloped down, and after a little bit, they came to a larger chamber where the ceiling rose high enough above them that they could stand up. There were four other openings for corridors stretching into the darkness.

"Here, we can talk for a bit," Hammer said as he stood up straight and stretched his back, hands on hips.

Rose followed suit but said nothing.

"Our path continues down that one there," he pointed to the second corridor from the left.

Rose shrugged.

"Come on, Rose, do not be angry with me," he pleaded. "I have no desire to be caught by the enemy or, worse, Morheim and his men."

Rose simply nodded in agreement.

"I do not think we are being followed," he ventured after a long listen back the way they had come. "There are no sounds of pursuit."

"That is good," Rose agreed. "But you did not expect anyone to follow us, did you?"

"Only if my attempt to hide the entrance to this tunnel was too hasty," Hammer boasted.

"How much farther do we have?" Rose asked.

"It has been a while since I was down here," Hammer admitted, "but if memory serves correctly, another day perhaps."

"Will our light source last that long?" Rose asked.

"This lantern? I should think so, but to be safe, I will lower the flame when we stop to rest."

"This chamber is a good place to rest," Rose observed. She lay down on the ground and stretched her legs out from her. "I do wish we could block the other entrances with something," she added. "I dislike the idea of someone or something happening upon us in our sleep." She turned on her side, left arm folded beneath her head and closed her eyes.

"I guess you want me to take the first watch?" Hammer asked, slightly annoyed.

"Suit yourself," Rose replied. "But as you already said, you are not expecting anyone to follow us down here, so do not bother waking me."

Hammer moved until his back leaned against the cool stone, turned the flame down until it was a thin tongue of blue and watched it dance upon the wick as he stretched his legs out in front of him.

Rose woke sometime later, her heart pounding nearly out of her chest and lay there listening to Hammer's shallow breathing punctuated by the occasional snort.

"Hammer!" she whispered, but he did not rouse in the least. "Hammer!" she said a little louder. His breathing changed slightly, but he remained fast asleep. She kicked him hard, "Hammer!"

"What do you want?" he asked sleepily.

"Something woke me," she explained.

"So go back to sleep," he advised with a yawn. His breathing became shallow again.

"Hammer!" she hissed as she kicked him twice. "Wake up!"

"Whatever is the matter?" he asked gruffly.

"Shhhhh!" she admonished. "Do you hear that?"

"I can only hear you at present," he replied. She kicked him again for good measure.

"You cannot hear that?!" she whispered, her voice trembling. "It is getting closer!"

With another yawn, Hammer picked up the lantern and increased the flame until the little room was bathed in bright light.

"Thanks for that," Rose complained as she shielded her eyes. "Now whoever is coming knows for certain we are in here! Not the brightest one, are you?" She was about to kick him yet again when a nauseating smell swept into the chamber. She retched twice, then vomited and even as she wiped her mouth with the back of her hand, the stench grew stronger.

"We have to get out of here," Hammer managed to say before he too began to retch. He grabbed Rose by the arm and half-drug, half-tossed her into the corridor, then reaching down he grabbed the lantern and hurried after her.

Rose looked back over her shoulder and saw several vines stretching into the chamber. "It cannot be," she said in awe.

"What?" Hammer asked as he prodded her forward. "Do not stop!"

"I have only heard of their existence," Rose continued. "I scarcely believed they could be real."

"Whatever are you babbling about?"

"I think we are being pursued by something called a Chantra!"

"And just what is a Chantra?"

"A living thing made from plants," Rose began to explain.

"No wonder you are intrigued."

"I am trying to remember what we were taught in school. Chantra are protectors of things. Long-lived. Immensely strong. They move about on appendages that resemble great vines, stretching, wrapping, gripping, and pulling. Highly intelligent."

"You are telling me those things are real? A giant thinking, stinking vegetable? And it is after us?" Hammer asked as he shook his head.

"Apparently, they are," Rose said. "Well, surely you, the Hammers, have some mythical creature or gemstone that no one believes exists."

"Now that you mention it, we do have the singing stones. These stones are said to have the most beautiful sound when struck with a mallet. The legends say there once was a woman who played the stones with such passion…"

"See? There you have it," Rose interrupted. "You Hammers have those things, too. So, do they exist? The singing stones?"

"Many of the rumors say they exist in one of the nights of Kulmaton."

"The city that has been lost for many thousands of years?" Rose asked. Hammer nodded, though Rose could not see him. "Of course it would be that," Rose continued. "No way to prove or disprove their existence. So those who choose to believe will look for things that bolster their belief, and those who do not believe will be doing the same thing. I was once in the belief that the Chantra were made up to scare little Roses into compliance…" her voice trailed off.

"I suppose it is that way with most things in life," Hammer mused. "That horrible smell seems to be growing fainter."

Rose looked to the darkness behind them. "I…did you see that!?" she asked, and she slowed to get a better view.

"Keep moving, Rose," Hammer implored.

In the darkness of the corridor behind, she saw two tiny points of red blink to light; they blinked off and then on again and suddenly began to grow larger, imperceptibly at first, but soon there was no mistaking it. "It is still chasing after us," she advised, and as if to bolster her statement, the stench began to grow stronger again.

"You said those Chantra are protectors of things," Hammer whispered. "What would it be protecting down here?"

"How should I know?" Rose responded. "You Hammers delved these tunnels. Have you heard rumors of some vast treasure being hidden away?"

"Here? In Elas-Tormas? I highly doubt it," the Hammer laughed for a moment. "Actually, I have heard a rumor that there is something hidden under the city. A ring or jewel that protects the harbor waters. But it was the Order of Miners that delved into these tunnels."

"Whatever reason it has for being here, I do not want to find out," Rose said. "You could go and ask it if you are that curious."

"Do they have a language? Can they understand our speech?"

Rose sighed, "I have no idea. I suppose they must have some sort of way to communicate amongst their own, but whether or not they can communicate with us?" she shrugged her shoulders.

"I'd imagine they could teach you a few things about growing plants," Hammer stated.

"Perhaps," Rose agreed. "How much longer will we be in these tunnels?"

"If I can find the right one, we should be able to emerge outside of the outer wall, which would be great; otherwise, we shall be in the Outlands, and who knows what will happen to us then."

"I can tell you if that Chantra catches up to us, you will not like what happens."

"What do you suppose can hurt them?" Hammer asked. "I mean, if it were to come to that."

Rose sighed again.

"You said they were made of plants, right?" Hammer continued. "A sharp blade should be able to cut through them."

"If its skin were as tender as a young sapling, I would agree with you, but you would need an axe, I think, to cause it serious hurt."

"What about fire?"

Rose nodded, "Fire might be very effective, though I doubt you would be able to get close enough with a lit torch." She laughed. "If you are that curious, why not head back to face the Chantra? If you survive, then you can share your knowledge of the encounter with me."

"Very funny, Rose," Hammer huffed. "I have no desire to fight that thing or anything or anyone else for that matter. Times like these are when we need a Blade with us."

"Well, Blade is no longer with us, and if we keep moving, we should be able to stay ahead of the Chantra, so no need to worry too much about fighting in these tunnels."

Not long after, the tunnel they were in stopped abruptly at a wooden ladder set into the wall.

"Do you know where we are exactly?" Rose asked as she stared into the darkness behind her.

"Only one way to find out," Hammer replied as he climbed the ladder and placed his shoulder against the trap door above him. After a third try, he managed to open the door, allowing a layer of dust and debris to rain down upon him. He shook his head and pushed the door open wide enough for him to look out.

"Thanks for that!" Rose grumbled as she wiped dirt from her face. "You could have warned me! Anyway, what can you see? Where are we?"

"I am currently looking at a pile of straw," Hammer replied. "I assume this is a barn, but where it is exactly, I am not sure." He climbed out onto the floor and turned to help Rose up. "Let's close and cover that door," he suggested. "Won't do any good to have that Chantra sneak up and surprise us."

"It will not pursue us out into the open during the day. Chantras dislike sunlight."

"I find that very strange indeed," Hammer mused. "Plants need sunlight, do they not?"

"Of course plants do, but a Chantra is not a plant," Rose replied. She laughed at the confused look on Hammer's face. "I will try and explain later," she continued. "But right now, I want to know where we are?"

"Hmmmm," Hammer intoned as he peered through a crack in the door. "I cannot tell for certain. We shall have to explore in a bit. No good rushing right outside, though."

Rose nodded, and she stretched herself out onto the floor. "Wake me before you go exploring."

"At the very least, I will wake you to take the next watch," Hammer laughed quietly.

# Black Chapter Nine: An Ember Extinguished

## The 19th of Lirinn

Five Dakirin stood on a tree-covered hill, staring at Elas-Tormas in the distance.

"It would be beneficial if Mazzaroth could spawn another storm like the last one," Burxon commented.

"There is no need for another storm of darkness," Tilden sighed.

"We should wait for the rest of the army to arrive," Vontar suggested to the others as he surveyed the city. "Tarbosar is moving as quickly as he can, but stragglers are a growing problem. Thousands of men a day are disappearing into the Outlands."

"Disappearing?" Tilden asked for clarification.

"They are present for dinner, but the next morning they are gone." Vontar continued, "Impossible to find unless they want to be found."

Tilden shook his head.

"Hember was slain before the battle even started, and without a leader, his men move far too slowly," Erelis acknowledged. "I doubt a single one of them will be here before the day after tomorrow." He laughed. "And any that do manage to arrive will be in no shape to fight."

"How did Hember die again?" Tilden asked curiously. "Fall from his mount?"

"He rode off by himself, and when his men found him, he had been skewered by a spear thrust to the side," Erelis explained. He hesitated for a moment before adding, "Probably a Lepnarion patrol."

"You hesitated?"

"There were no horse tracks save from Hember's mount, but I did search the river's edge and found what could have been footprints but could find no other sign of anyone. I marked the location so I could go back after the battle and search more diligently. It is possible that someone managed to cross the river heading east."

"As of now, I am in control of your murder. Take a claw and search for whoever made those tracks you followed. It does not matter if they are refugees, deserters, or enemies escaping to our rear; kill whoever you find," Tilden commanded.

Erelis nodded once, then saluted and left to gather his claw.

"Kinjal and his men are in position to prevent anyone escaping to the west," Pentar stated. "He only just got to the western gate yesterday," he explained. "What of Kotkas and Elisad?"

"Kotkas lies dead. The fool fought a Lepnarion knight by himself. I have taken control of his murder, and we are ready for the attack on Elas-Tormas. Elisad was also killed, and his men are scattered in the Outlands." Vontar replied. "I have tried unsuccessfully to round them up, but they are content to murder and pillage where they are."

"For now, let the stragglers be; they will help ensure that no resistance crops up behind us. We can deal with them after we take Elas-Tormas." Tilden stated.

"Are we waiting for any others?" Vontar wanted to know.

"Why?" Tilden asked. "Fear runs rampant through the city; we have enough Dakirin here to begin our attack within the hour."

"To lessen our losses," Vontar explained. "Even if they are not the best fighters, those troops from the Tav-Tar make great fodder."

"That is true," Burxon agreed with a laugh. "But Aracelis has at least fifteen thousand capable men that are near enough. They can join in the initial assault, let the rest of the stragglers be sent into the fray as they arrive."

"What about our ships blockading the harbor? Last I heard, there were over two hundred vessels gathered together." Vontar stated. "There must be many thousands of sailors that could join in the attack. They could be landed at the docks."

"Send a messenger if you wish," Tilden waved his hand. "It will take them far too long to be in position, and sailors fighting aboard a ship is vastly different than fighting an armed foe on land."

"It cannot be that different," Vontar persisted.

"Different tactics, Vontar. Fighting on the deck of a ship has certain physical limitations that are not present on land. I will hear no more. We have no need of any further help; we Dakirin will take the city! Have Aracelis move his men into position to support the taking of the main northern gate. Hopefully, he still has the use of Rakosa and his men. We attack within the hour! Be prepared to blot out the sun at my signal."

\*\*\*

Rakosa patted his mount's neck reassuringly as he surveyed the imposing wall of Elas-Tormas in the distance.

"We are to take that gate," he said to those nearest him, and he pointed. "And in return, we will be given the antidote for the poison flowing through our veins."

"I doubt any of us will be left alive after we attack," one commented. "How high are those walls?"

"The walls are seventy feet high with ninety-foot towers. The gates will be heavily defended. It is good that we have Dakirin with us, else their defenses would prove impregnable," Rakosa stated. "The Lepnarions will fight to hold that gate closed, and once it is open, we will ensure it remains open."

"Aye," one agreed. "But it is a shame that we are attacking those who, until recently, we called our friends."

"I am thinking only of today and my self-preservation," Rakosa snapped. "You would do well to do likewise."

"True, but you are Lepnarion correct? How is it that you come to be fighting against your own?" he persisted.

"By birth, not by choice. The Lepnar that I knew died at Kire. Those before me are my enemies as sure as I am now theirs."

"I only meant that…"

"I know what you meant! Now get ready to take that cursed gate!" He took a moment to compose himself, then turned his mount to face his men. Less than five hundred remained of the thousand he was given charge of. He scowled. "Men of Anar, you have fought bravely thus far. For that, I thank you." He waited for their cheers to subside. "We were given little alternative in this matter," he continued. "Join with the Darklord's armies or be killed without question. To ensure your loyalty, they made you ingest a poison with the promise of the antidote should we survive the taking of Elas-Tormas. We have endured the toughest fighting, and today will be no exception."

A cry sounded in the distance, long and shrill. The cry was quickly taken up by Dakirin near and far. The cloud of their transformation grew thicker as more and more Dakirin leaped into the air, thousands upon thousands of them all wheeling and turning in unison, casting a dark shadow upon the land wherever they passed. As one, they climbed higher into the morning sky, then, like a lightning bolt, they fell toward the walls of Elas-Tormas. The green cloud hovered just above the grass, and Rakosa yelled as he spurred his mount forward into the roiling fog.

"Now is the time to take the gate and be free!"

Instantly, the men with him charged forward into the fog. Through to the other side, their charge carried them ever closer to the walls, which were beginning to be obscured by the same green fog.

Rakosa yelled until he was hoarse, laying low across his mount's neck to avoid the increasing number of bolts and arrows that whistled past him. Many of those around him fell under the barrage of projectiles. Still, he held on until, at last, he was before the gates.

There were four iron-banded wooden gates; each stood forty feet tall and twenty feet wide. The two innermost gates were separated by a ten-foot wide section of stone wall atop which stood a fifty-foot tall tower, while the two outermost gates were both flanked by ninety-foot tall stone towers. Spanning the four gates and linking the three gate towers was a stone parapet upon which the fighting now raged. The middle gate tower was engulfed in green smoke, and the roar of fighting increased. Lepnarions inside the two larger gate towers began to concentrate their fire upon the parapet in an effort to help their beleaguered friends. Jets of green smoke erupted from the defense works, momentarily obscuring Rakosa's view, and then gradually, the fog dissipated to reveal more of the parapet in Dakirin control. From the towers came a steady stream of projectiles, arrows, bolts, and stones so thick that the Dakirin transformed and took to the air to regroup, which they quickly did. As soon as the Dakirin left the parapet, the defenders focused their missiles on the horsed riders waiting outside the gate.

"Where are we supposed to go?" one of his men yelled as he rode up. "The gates remain shut, and we cannot ride our horses over the walls!"

"We will stay right here until the gates open!" Rakosa roared as he ducked to avoid a heavy stone thrown from atop the tower. "Gather the others!"

"And help the defenders with their target practice, no doubt," the soldier complained. He gave a half-hearted salute just before an arrow slammed into his shoulder. His cursing was cut short as another sprouted from his neck, and he fell from his saddle. A sling stone struck Rakosa's helmet. He peered up at the battlements and saw another defender aiming a bow in his direction; he urged his horse to move just as an arrow grazed his leg. Rakosa raised his blade in defiance when suddenly both towers became enveloped in green smoke as hundreds of Dakirin landed atop each roof, beside barred doors and flew through open windows to transform inside.

Rakosa turned his horse in a circle as he watched the towers carefully. The green fog disappeared, and the sounds of fighting grew less, but still, he could not discern who was in control of the towers. He did take note that no arrows were being fired at him.

"Open the gates!" He cried out as he turned his horse again.

"Is that supposed to do something? Turning in a circle before the gates?" a voice asked from above him.

Looking up, he noticed several faces peering down at him as green smoke enveloped the wall and towers again, Dakirin faces.

"Open the gates; I am ordered to hold them at all costs," Rakosa explained.

"We will open them once all the defenders have been dealt with. We don't want any escaping."

"Open the gates. We can help you," Rakosa yelled.

"We have seen the way you fight; we have no need of that kind of help," one of the Dakirin stated.

"Perhaps, after the battle is finished, you can teach me the proper way to fight, but for now, open the gates!" Rakosa bellowed.

"I will open the gates for you, but the fight will be over before you can join." He disappeared from view.

Rakosa turned and hollered at his men to form up. "Remember," he explained. "We must ensure the gates remain open. There is no need for us to go fight inside the city."

Moments later, a great creaking sound was heard as the massive gates began to swing inward, and Rakosa saw a line of Lepnarion soldiers blocking the way, kneeling with spears and shields at the ready to receive a charge. Rakosa turned his mount from the gates and rode a bowshot's distance away before turning around again; without hesitation, he spurred his mount forward, followed by the rest of his men. The line of defenders disappeared in a cloud of green, and as Rakosa reached the gates, the fog dissipated, and he saw that the Lepnarions were scattered, with many of them lying dead. Rakosa raised his sword in thanks to the Dakirin nearest him.

"We will guard this gate with our lives," Rakosa informed him.

"There will be little need to guard this gate," the Dakirin laughed. "Lepnarions everywhere are fleeing like frightened rabbits looking for a way to escape." He transformed and took to the air before Rakosa could respond.

"What now?" one of his men asked as he rode up.

"Find a place to stable our mounts, and then let us guard this gate."

"The Dakirin said there would be no need," the man protested.

"Let us hope he is correct." Rakosa dismounted, gave the reins of his horse to the man and waved him away. "I need fifteen archers in each of those gate towers," he pointed. "And ten more in the smaller tower in the middle there. Then I want twenty men guarding the horses. The rest of you will form a defensive line across the plaza here."

When his orders were fulfilled, two hundred and seventy men stretched across the plaza in three ranks, with their backs to the open gates.

"What now?" the man beside him wanted to know.

"Now we wait!" Rakosa replied. "It is good that we who have survived so much have a moment of relative calm. Enjoy it; I doubt it will last long."

The men were quiet as they prepared to defend the gates; some attended to their wounds, gently applying salve and a bandage, while others sharpened blades or gathered arrows. As the sun began to burn hotter, the few surviving Lepnarions lying wounded on the plaza began pleading for water. No one replied or went to help, but each tried his best to ignore the piteous cries. After nearly thirty minutes, only one voice could still be heard persistently calling out for help.

When he could no longer stand it, one of Rakosa's men ventured toward a wounded Lepnarion and, kneeling down, propped his head up and gave him a drink of water. There quickly followed another score of men hurrying to help any of the wounded still living.

A small flock of Dakirin flying overhead circled once and then dived into the plaza.

"What is the meaning of this?" Burxon asked Rakosa as he transformed. Those Dakirin with him drew their swords as they fanned out.

"My men are simply bringing a little comfort to the dying," he explained.

"Bringing comfort?" he scowled. "I suggest you let them die, or you and your men will be counted as enemies." His hand gripped the hilt of his blade.

Rakosa did not respond.

"Stop them!" Burxon ordered his Dakirin. "If they resist, kill them."

"Men," Rakosa spoke loudly, "Return to our lines." His men dutifully began to return to their lines, but one lingered, letting the wounded man finish his drink. A Dakirin walked up and, without a word, struck the man, killing him instantly. His waterskin fell to the plaza just out of reach of the wounded man. Rakosa's men grew angry, and many of them drew their own weapons.

"Men, do not make things worse. Put up your weapons," Rakosa ordered. "You have made your point," he said to Burxon. "I suggest you and the others leave before things get out of hand."

Burxon laughed. "You threaten me? The traitor to his own and your band of brigands? One call and this plaza will be filled with enough Dakirin to deal with all of you."

"I want no bloodshed between us," Rakosa said plainly. "We are on the same side."

"I wonder about that," Burxon snapped. "Aracelis will hear of this before the day is over," he menaced. With a quick word, he and the other Dakirin transformed and took to wing.

The wounded man pleaded for help even as he stretched his arm to reach the waterskin. He cried out for several minutes, then remained still.

The ensuing silence grew overwhelming, and up and down the line, men began talking amongst themselves. They would grow quiet as a flock of Dakirin flew overhead but quickly would return to their conversations.

"Maybe we can get a hot meal tonight in one of the inns," the man beside Rakosa contemplated. "I have heard that the Golden Dragon is known for their food."

"As long as they are not owned by Lepnarions," Rakosa noted ruefully.

"So why have they let you live this long?" the same man asked. "Everywhere they conquer, they are killing Lepnarions, and you somehow have managed to survive."

"I cannot explain it myself," Rakosa sighed. "Sometimes I wonder what I am doing here."

"I think most of us can empathize with you on that point," the man agreed as he placed a hand on Rakosa's shoulder.

"We are all still alive, though," another joined in. "And that is most important, at least to me it is." He laughed, and others laughed with him.

"Do you hear that?" someone asked.

"Sounds like troops marching," another replied.

"Look," the first pointed. Several hundred Lepnarion soldiers were marching toward the gate. "Where are those Dakirin now?" he asked as he looked into the sky.

"You should not rely on them," Rakosa urged. "Rely upon your own strength, your training, your will to survive. We have no need of Dakirin to save us."

"We may need their help after all," another added as he pointed down a different street. A second group of Lepnarion soldiers were approaching the gate, though they were not as numerous as the first group.

"Towers! Do you see the enemy approaching?" Rakosa called out. Several of his men signaled that they could. "What are you waiting for? Release your arrows!" Rakosa growled. Moments later, the first arrows began to land among the advancing Lepnarions. With a shout born of desperation and hope, they charged forward.

"Here they come!" another yelled, and then the first Lepnarions slammed into Rakosa's line. The fray was sharp, and quickly, the casualties began to mount on both sides. It did not take long before Rakosa's line began to waver under pressure. But what had looked like professional soldiers from a distance turned out to be poorly armed and poorly trained militia.

"Hold the gate!" Rakosa roared. "Hold the gate!" He only narrowly avoided a spear thrust, and after killing the man who had wielded it, he paused for a moment. The man at his feet was elderly with grey hair and a kind face; it reminded him of his own father, long since buried. He opened his mouth to say something, but Rakosa could not hear. As the fighting swirled around them, Rakosa knelt beside the old man.

"Why are you fighting against us?" the old man finally managed. "You are Lepnarion as surely as I lay here dying."

"You would not understand," Rakosa answered after a moment.

"Then may Ellonas forgive you," he coughed once more, and then the light left his eyes.

"Ellonas cannot forgive me now," Rakosa whispered. He made sure the man's eyes were closed, then stood up. The Lepnarion attack was rapidly losing strength, and he saw no need to order his men to charge as the last few survivors melted back into the city. The gate remained in his control.

\*\*\*

It was late afternoon when Tilden surveyed Elas-Tormas as he soared on the rising currents of warm air. He banked around and between the thick pillars of smoke climbing from burning sections of the city. He no longer saw any fighting in the wide avenues and many plazas, but here and there, he recognized the signs of conflict as green fog billowed out of a building's windows and doors. To the north, he watched a ragged column of soldiers enter through the ruined gates, and he flew closer to investigate. The soldiers, probably from Hember's command, were searching each building on either side of the street. The frightened screams of women and children were plain to hear as he soared over the rooftops. He watched a soldier attempting to drag a woman into the street; she resisted pulling away with all her strength as the soldier laughed heartily. Then, a young child darted from the building and leaped upon the soldier's back, pulling his hair and pummeling his head in a vain attempt to help. Enraged, the soldier grabbed the child and flung them to the ground, drew his sword and even as the women pleaded for mercy, he killed them both with one swing of his blade. Tilden climbed higher into the sky, leaving the pillaging soldiers behind and turning his attention to the docks and harbor headed to the south. As he flew near the royal district, a Dakirin approached, informing him that the palace was surrounded and that they were preparing to force entry. Immediately, Tilden banked toward the palace and transformed as he landed. A large contingent of soldiers was milling around, waiting for direction.

"The enemy is holed up inside," he pointed to the palace. "Now is the time for you to show your loyalty to the Darklord."

"Haven't we done enough already?" one of them asked. "The city has fallen."

"The battle is not finished until every defender is killed or surrenders. Now breach those doors!" Tilden barked.

The men began hammering on the doors with their weapons.

"A hundred pieces of gold to the one who brings me the king alive!" he shouted. As the doors splintered and fell in, the fighting began and quickly grew savage as the Lepnarions sought to prevent entry. Slowly, they gave ground as more and more soldiers from the Tav-Tar pressed forward.

"Shall we join in?" one of the Dakirin close to him asked.

"Not yet," Tilden replied. "First, let the Tav-Tar bleed the defenders white. Scour the city and direct any soldiers you find to help in this fight."

Immediately, a dozen Dakirin took to wing. Soldiers began arriving in ones and twos and were sent into the fray as they arrived. An hour later, several hundred soldiers from both Hember's and Elisad's command marched past Tilden up the stairs and into the palace.

"Let us see how they are faring in there," Tilden said after a short while. He transformed and led a beak to search out the palace.

Flying was preferred over walking as the ceilings were lofty, the hallways wide, and the floor littered with corpses. They followed the sounds of fighting and soon came to a hallway where a few dozen Tav-Tar soldiers were gathered together, looking warily at the set of triple doors at the far end.

"What is wrong?" Tilden asked the men as he transformed.

"We forced them out of that room there," one pointed at the triple doors. "But they fell back to another room beyond. There is only one set of doors, and we lack the strength to root them out."

"I think it is the throne room," another added.

Tilden transformed and flew into the other room, returning a moment later.

Tilden nodded, "Their position looks strong. How many men do they have?"

"A hundred, maybe more," the first replied.

"Then let us burn them out," Tilden smiled. "Wait until we give the signal and then approach, marching in unison. Once inside, begin piling the wooden tables and chairs against the doors."

The men nodded. The Dakirin flew to the triple doors and began to transform multiple times so that a thick green fog began to fill the room beyond. They heard a shout from the defenders to barricade the door, and it was slammed shut. At this point, Tilden let out a shrill cry, and the soldiers from the Tav-Tar marched into the room. They hoisted a table between them and hurled it against the closed doors, and then another table followed until seven were piled high. Next came the chairs, and when they were all in a jumbled heap, Tilden transformed and, kneeling, lit them on fire. As the flames quickly grew, the heat increased in intensity, and grey smoke began to fill the room. Everyone scurried or flew out of the triple doors to the far end of the hallway to watch from a safe distance.

# White Chapter Ten: Nowhere To Run Nowhere To Hide

## The 19th of Lirinn

Baldred sighed heavily as he neared the throne room. His uniform was torn and stained with blood, some of it his own.

"Is it as bad as we feared?" Eulix asked quietly.

"Worse," he replied. "There is no use fighting in the streets; every time we make a stand, those cursed Dakirin appear, and the defense turns into a route with most everyone being slaughtered."

"Surely we are exacting a heavy price for every street they take?" Eulix asked hopefully.

"As far as I can tell, their losses are minimal, more wounded than killed, to be sure, but not enough of either to make a difference." After a moment, he continued, "I just came from the fighting on Governance Street just two blocks from here. Forty of us were prepared to defend the intersection, but moments after a single Dakirin flew overhead, we were surrounded; they landed all around us and in that cursed green fog of theirs, the fighting was fierce. I wrestled one of them to the ground and managed to stab him with my dagger," he shook his head. "By the time he stopped struggling with me, and I stood to my feet, the fighting was over. The dead were everywhere, and only a few of them were Dakirin."

Eulix nodded his understanding. "I suppose it is too late for us to escape?"

"There is no escaping this time, my friend," Baldred answered as he gripped Eulix's shoulder. "If this is to be our end, then let us die fighting with honor!" Again, Eulix nodded. He opened the throne room doors and beckoned Baldred to enter.

"Baldred, what is happening out there?" Morheim asked as he saw him enter. "Eulix, where are you slinking off to?" he asked as Eulix began to walk into the hallway. Eulix turned and followed after Baldred.

Baldred bowed low before Morheim and winced as he straightened. After a deep breath, he began speaking. "You already know that the walls were taken early this morning. The five eastern districts of the city have fallen, as have all seven of the northern and four of the southern districts. I heard rumors that some soldiers were holding out in the wharf district, but they were surrounded and will soon be overcome. The western districts remain in our hands, but for how long, I cannot say. No movement has been made against them as of yet."

"Can we advance to help those in the wharf district?" Morheim asked. "Perhaps join with those men defending the western section of the city?"

"This royal bastion is ringed by the enemy; no one can enter or leave without being seen," Baldred announced. "However, we have over a thousand men to help in the defense. Moreover, these walls are thick, the banded doors are sturdy, and we have enough foodstuffs for a year or more. Take heart, my king; we can hold out for quite a while, I am certain."

"Yes, like we held the outer wall just three days ago? Like we held the great walls of Elas-Tormas this morning?" Morheim bellowed.

"It is true the walls fell quickly and without siege equipment being used. But unlike the walls, we have a roof over our heads; the Dakirin must force an entrance," Baldred explained. "They will pay dearly to get in here."

"I am no dotard. I can see with my own eyes that our death approaches, my death approaches," Morheim stroked his chin, and his hand lingered on his throat. He swallowed hard. "This must be what it feels like for one condemned to death as he waits for the sentence to be carried out," he said to no one in particular. He stared at his hand, moving first one finger and then another, slowly twisting his wrist this way and that. "I find it strange that only now am I realizing the magnificence of life." He laughed ruefully and shook his head. "Only as death approaches."

"The men are aware there are but two outcomes, either victory or death," Baldred said with conviction. "They will fight with honor."

"Die with honor, you mean," Morheim challenged.

"M'lord, why are you not wielding Abion? That legendary blade can…" Baldred began, but Morheim interrupted.

"Abion? This?" He grabbed the sword leaning against his throne and, with a furious yell, flung it across the room. It clattered to the stone floor, sending fragments of blue glass into the air. "It is but a fake, a mirage, a delusion, nothing more than that." He glared at Eulix. "I never should have listened to you. The real Abion was within my grasp, and I allowed it to slip through my fingers."

"That is a shame," Baldred replied as he scowled at Eulix.

Morheim buckled his scabbard around his waist and fingered the hilt of his sword. "I should much prefer to charge with glory into death than to await death here in hiding. In dishonor," he added after a moment.

"The histories speak of death in battle being glorious, m'lord, but today, I have seen no glory in battle. There is only misery and death, only fear and hatred," Baldred acknowledged.

A moment later, the sounds of battle began to be heard, the faint ringing of steel and the crashing of shields, the yelling and cursing of men. A dull thud echoed in the chamber, followed by another and another.

"They have reached the outer doors. We have no way of escape," Baldred said knowingly.

"Soon, they will be at the throne room doors!" Eulix exclaimed. "My king, do not forget that there are catacombs beneath this palace. There may yet be a way to escape."

"Those passages, if they exist, have not been used in hundreds of years. Who knows what lurks down there in the darkness," Baldred explained.

"We can search for an entrance," Eulix replied hastily. "There must be a hidden door here in the throne room."

"There was never a need to use a hidden passage before now, and even if the rumors are true, we have no record of the location of any entrance. And there is no time to begin searching."

"So be it, if I am to die here, then let us fight to the last," Morheim declared as he drew his sword. "We will show them the courage of Lepnar!"

"I, I must go fetch something from my room," Eulix stammered suddenly.

"I see your courage has failed you already. Will you abandon your king at this hour of great need?"

Eulix's cheeks turned crimson. "I will return shortly," he promised.

Morheim waved him away.

Eulix walked slowly from the throne room, nodding at Baldred before closing the doors behind him, then hurried through the great hall to his quarters. Once inside, he rifled through the banded chest against the far wall, pulling out a small leather bag, tied closed at the top and filled to near bursting. It was quite heavy for its size. After another minute of searching, he brought forth a wooden tube sealed at both ends. Then he removed his royal robes and pulled on a pair of dark blue leather breeches; next came a dark brown leather jerkin and finally a black leather hood. He jammed his feet into his black leather boots, then grabbed a pack woven of coarse fabric, inside which he placed the few rations he had been saving and the wooden tube. Next came a coil of rope, a lantern along with two flasks of oil, a thick blanket, a waterskin and finally, the bulging bag. He took a last look around his room before clasping a cloak around his shoulders, dark blue with a white fringe. He buckled his scabbard around his waist, shoved a dagger into his belt and grabbed a sturdy walking stick from the corner. He closed the door to his room;

the sounds of fighting could now be plainly heard, echoing in the stone corridors.

Eulix began making his way back to the throne room, but as he drew near the great hall, he turned to the left down a narrow corridor. He ran heedless of any noise his footfalls made until he came to a small alcove. Then, looking around to make certain no one was there to see him, he placed his hand on the lit lantern, turning it to the left. Pushing on the stone wall, a door opened to reveal a set of stairs descending into darkness. He slipped through the door and then hesitated for a moment, raising his foot to step back into the hallway, but quickly changed his mind and pushed the door closed until he heard a muffled click.

In the dark, he grabbed the lantern from his pack and, after hanging it from one end of his walking stick, proceeded to light it. Leaning the stick against the wall, he pulled forth the wooden tube and unsealed one end, tipping it into his hand. Out slid an aged parchment, which he quickly unrolled to reveal the faded markings of a map. He studied it carefully for a few moments, then rolled it back up and slid it back into the tube, which he did not bother to re-seal. There was a thick layer of dust on the stairs, and his footsteps left obvious impressions for anyone following to easily track him.

"I cannot worry about that now," he whispered. Then he had a thought; he took up his walking stick, turned around and with a deep breath, set off cautiously down the stairs backward. The stairs were expertly carved and not too steep, and after ten minutes, he reached the bottom and smiled at the trail of footprints climbing into the darkness. He listened carefully for any sound from above but could hear nothing. He consulted his map again, then, with a nod, stowed the parchment in the tube and set off, facing forward this time. He traveled quietly, stopping every so often to take a drink from his waterskin. After an hour, he came to a place where if he continued straight, it descended another stair much like the first, but to his left, a hall stretched into darkness. The map did not show any stairs descending farther but only the corridor to the left. He studied the map again for a long while before deciding to descend the stairs. He did not put the map away but rolled it up and carried it in his free hand. This stair was much longer than the first, and after he reached the end, he stepped into a large cavern. He inadvertently kicked a stone, and it skittered away into the dark, but the noise it made echoed. Alarmed, he stopped until the echoes died away, and then he listened for a long while before he moved. He looked at the map again but, to his dismay, discovered that the sweat of his palm had managed to smear the faded markings. Gently placing the lantern on the stone floor, he spread the parchment out beside the light. He spent a long while trying to decipher the smudges, and when he was satisfied that he had finally figured them out, he rolled the map up and slipped it back into the tube. He looked behind at the stairs for a moment, then, with a determined shake of his head, set off again. He went slower now as he explored the cavern. He found a dark opening, but as soon as he smelled the dank air within, he quickly decided against exploring it further. He continued cautiously now. In the distance, he became aware of a soft blue glow, and his heart skipped a beat. He thought back to a day he had found an ancient tome in a forgotten wing of the royal library. As he poured through it, he came upon an obscure text that mentioned a ring of great power hidden below the city. No one he talked to had ever heard of such a thing.

Slowly, he made his way toward the blue glow. After a bit, the floor began to descend, and as the blue glow began to rise into the air, so did his hopes that it was indeed the Azure ring of legend. The blue glow was brighter now but did nothing to dispel the darkness in the cavern. Finally, the glow was almost directly above him. Before him rose a rough-hewn pillar of stone with a pile of bones near the base.

He knelt and examined the bones closely. A barbut lay on the ground nearby, and a set of rusty chainmail hid most of the ribs. A skeletal hand gripped the hilt of a broken blade. Looking at the pillar, he could see several marks where a sword might have struck. He was perplexed. As he stood up, he realized that one of the thigh bones was broken.

He studied the pillar farther, holding the lantern in one hand up as high as he could, then again using both hands. The pillar was only four feet in diameter, as far as he could tell, but he had no idea how tall it was. He took a few steps back, placed the lantern and walking stick on the ground, followed by his pack, and then he studied the blue glow again. Searching on the floor, he found a small rock, which he threw toward the blue glow. After waiting to hear the clatter as the stone landed on the floor, he judged the pillar to be about fifty feet high. He picked up his walking stick and, holding it like a spear, threw it, hoping to knock the ring off the top of the pillar. He misjudged badly, and his walking stick disappeared into the darkness of the cavern, clattering against the floor some distance away. Disappointed but undeterred, he reached into his pack and brought forth the rope and the small bag tied closed at the top. He tossed the bag in the air, catching it again. After judging its weight, he tied one end of the rope around it, then twirling the rope a few times; he launched the bag into the air. He held tightly to the other end of the rope, and quickly it went taut and then the bag hurtled toward him, landing on the cavern floor right beside him. The bag burst asunder, spilling gold and silver coins in every direction. He swore loudly and hurriedly began to gather the coins closest to him. Then suddenly, he straightened up, walked to the pillar and began to climb. He reached his right hand up, searching for a place he could grip, then bringing his left foot up to find purchase. Then he switched to his left hand and right foot and repeated the process. He was not an experienced climber and found the going difficult. Nevertheless, he made slow, if not steady, progress. He paused for a moment to catch his breath and looked to the top of the pillar. Craning his neck to make sure he could still see the glow of blue, his left foot slipped off the pillar, and before he could steady himself, he half slid half fell to the ground. It took several minutes for him to catch his breath and then several more for him to examine himself. The pain in his left leg was intense, and looking down, he saw his shin was a bloody mess, but he could wiggle his fingers and toes and move his arms and legs and counted himself fortunate indeed. As he sat on the ground, waiting for the pain to subside, he glanced up to the top of the pillar. It seemed to him that the glow of blue was just a bit brighter than before. When he was finally ready to try again, he limped over to the base of the pillar and began to climb. Every time his left shin scraped against the pillar, he clenched his teeth until the pain dulled. Even though he climbed slower this time, he was determined to have the ring for himself. He had not quite climbed as high as he had on his first attempt when he fell again. This time, he landed awkwardly and when he examined his dominant right hand, both his pinky and ring finger were bent at an unnatural angle.

After almost an hour of working up the courage, he finally grabbed his ring finger and pulled it until it straightened out. He screamed in pain. A while later, he attempted to do the same thing with his pinky, but he could not even touch the tip of it without excruciating pain. Above, the glow of blue grew ever brighter, or so it seemed to him. Glancing at his lantern, he realized it was burning low, so he made his way to his pack and fished out the flasks of oil. He tried to open one using his hands, but the pain in his right hand made any attempt useless. He finally resorted to using his teeth to open the flask, which spilled some of it down the sides and onto his left hand. He managed to reach the lantern, and as he attempted to fill the reservoir, the flask slipped from his hand and spilled on the ground. Frustrated, he tried again and managed to pour what little oil was left in the flask into the lantern. Reaching for his pack, he brought out his blanket, his rations and waterskin and, in the lantern light, figured he had enough food for a week, maybe two if he ate very meager meals. He rolled the pack up into a tight bundle and then laid down with it under his head. He stared up at the glow of blue; he figured he would rest for several days to regain his strength. He fell asleep, bathed in the glowing blue light, making plans for his third attempt to climb the pillar.

***

Morheim paced back and forth on the dais, looking up as the throne room doors opened. Baldred entered, leading several hundred men, many of which were wounded. Every uniform was torn and blood-spattered, but still, the men bowed before their king.

"The enemy has taken the lower halls. A score of men chose to stay and defend the broad stairs, but I fear they will quickly be overcome."

"Well?" Morheim asked. "Where is he?"

"He is nowhere to be found," Baldred replied. He dropped Eulix's royal robes on the floor. "Looks like he packed in a hurry," he added.

"I knew he would not return. The coward has fled!" Morheim fumed.

"But he has no place to go," Baldred pointed out.

"He was always snooping around," Morheim grumbled. "Perhaps he did find a secret way out."

"No matter, my king, we are here, and we are yet alive."

"Shouldn't we barricade the doors?" one of the soldiers asked, fear evident in his voice.

"Prepare to barricade the doors, but leave them open until we are certain there are no more survivors to join us," Morheim commanded. "Let us advance from the throne room and meet the enemy in the great hall."

Morheim led the men into the great hall, and they positioned themselves to receive the expected attack. Archers had a clear line of sight out of each of the three sets of doors, and plenty of soldiers waited on either side of the doorways. They could all hear the sounds of fighting far away at first but steadily drawing nearer. Then they heard running footsteps, and the archers took aim. Two Lepnarion soldiers appeared at the far end of the hallway, running hard, the enemy close behind. As the soldiers drew near the great hall, the archers released a volley right over their heads. Seven or eight of the enemy fell stricken, but dozens more dashed forward to take their place.

"Who dares enter my palace unbidden?" Morheim challenged, and the enemy slowed for a moment, giving the two Lepnarions just enough time to reach safety.

"We go where we will," one of the enemy soldiers shouted in reply.

"Their speech betrays them; they are from the Tav-Tar," Baldred stated.

"Steady yourselves," he encouraged those men with him. "We will teach them to fear Lepnar!"

The fight for the great hall began in earnest. The first enemy through the doors was cut down in turn but still more pressed forward. The fighting was fierce, and though they exacted a heavy toll on the attackers, the Lepnarions were steadily pushed away from the doors.

"Kill these heathens!" Morheim bellowed as he strode forward, striking down a soldier who got too near. The Lepnarions fought with renewed vigor and were able to reclaim the great hall. As the enemy retreated, Morheim took stock of the situation. Close to three hundred bodies lay upon the floor in heaps; too many were Lepnarion. The doors were ruined and could not be shut again. Already in the hall, he could see the enemy regrouping, gathering strength.

"Fall back to the throne room," Morheim ordered. "Fall back."

"What of the wounded?" Baldred asked. He was bleeding from a deep wound on his side.

"If they cannot defend me, leave them," Morheim replied.

"M'lord?" Baldred asked. "That is not how we treat our own."

Morheim stared at him for a moment. "Help the wounded," he said before turning and walking into the throne room. He sat upon his throne deep in thought.

Less than two hundred Lepnarions walked into the throne room. At Baldred's direction, they brought many wounded in as well.

"Those who can no longer wield weapons, take to my chambers," Morheim directed. He motioned for Bladred to come closer, "Do not let me fall into the hands of the enemy."

"I will protect you with my life," Baldred said as he bowed.

"I thank you," Morheim replied.

There was no talking amongst the men in the throne room, and only the muffled coughs and groans of the wounded lying in Morheim's chambers interrupted the quiet. The doors to the great hall were left slightly ajar so they could see those approaching the throne room. After a half hour of waiting and watching, one of the soldiers turned to Morheim.

"The enemy has not returned! We may make it out of here yet," he said hopefully.

"No, my son. The city has fallen. There is no help for us," Morheim replied dejectedly.

"Then we are doomed!" the soldier said in despair.

"Green smoke! Green smoke at the doors of the great hall!" a soldier peering through the doors suddenly yelled. "They are coming!"

Morheim moved on his throne so he could see the green smoke for himself. It was more of a grey-green, like the clouds in a particularly violent thunderstorm, and it was mesmerizing.

"Shall we barricade the doors?" the soldier asked. Morheim did not answer as he watched the roiling cloud approaching. "Barricade the door?" the soldier asked again with alarm.

Startled, Morheim stared at the soldier for a moment before suddenly shouting, "Barricade the doors!" He stood and drew his sword. "Archers, up here on the dais with me," he motioned for them to join him. "The rest of you spread out and prepare to meet the enemy." The soldiers in the room saluted him and scurried to carry out his orders. "Men. Fight with courage to save your king, and if you must die, die with honor!"

The shrill cry of a Dakirin rent the air, and fear began to take hold in their hearts as the sound echoed off the throne room walls. They heard the sounds of booted feet marching closer to the barricaded doors. Then, something heavy was slammed against them, and the barricade shuddered. Again, the doors shuddered.

"They have a battering ram!" one of the men exclaimed.

"No," Baldred replied after listening closely. "No, they are going to burn us out."

Every eye turned to look at Morheim, their evident fear growing.

"Is there no way of escape from your chambers?" Baldred asked.

"If the lower halls have been taken," Morheim shook his head.

All too soon, whisps of smoke began to drift into the room, and the crackling of flames was distinctly heard.

"We cannot stay here to die like this," Baldred warned. "Let us at least try the secret passage from your chambers."

Morheim nodded and stood from his throne. With shoulders stooped, he walked into his chambers, carefully stepping over the wounded, to a wood panel carved to show a king seated upon his throne. Pressing on the crown caused a section of the wall to open. Morheim stepped back and waved his arm toward the passage.

"The choice is yours," he said to those gathered around. "Die here with me or in the passage."

"You are still our king," Baldred stated. "Will you not lead us?"

"And what of these wounded?" Morheim asked.

"We will carry them if we must," Baldred answered. "Only let us hurry, for the flames are advancing."

Again, Morheim nodded. He stepped into the passage and began down the dark corridor. Behind him, he heard Baldred encouraging the others to show courage and to help the wounded who could no longer walk on their own. By ones and twos, the soldiers began making their way down the corridor. Morheim stood to one side and nodded at each man as he passed by. Already, the heat was increasing, and smoke in the air stung his eyes and burned his nose. Still, Baldred worked tirelessly.

"You are a good man, Baldred," he whispered. Looking back, he saw the last men beginning to enter the passage, one leaning on the other and Baldred bringing up the rear when a roar sounded. The passage was suddenly filled with hot smoke and burning embers. Morheim held the sleeve of his robe to cover his mouth and nose. Shielding his eyes, he took a few tentative steps back toward his chambers, but the way was blocked by debris, and the heat was unbearable. He turned and ran as fast as he could.

# Black Chapter Ten: Threads

## *The 19th of Lirinn, late evening*

Rakosa rode slowly through the streets of Elas-Tormas; smoke from the burning palace hung thick in the evening air. In the distance, he could hear the sounds of celebration, and soon enough, he saw drunken soldiers staggering into the night, singly or in small groups, looking for a place to sleep off their victory. He urged his horse down a darker street, farther away from the noise.

Rakosa kept his hand near the hilt of his sword; though the fighting was nearly ended everywhere, stubborn pockets of resistance still held out in a few sections of the city. This, despite Tilden's promise of clemency for any who would lay down their arms and Morheim's very public execution as a warning to those who refused. How he had escaped the burning palace was anyone's guess, but he had been dragged before Tilden, his robes in tatters, the skin of his arms blistered and black. However, this evening, he was not overly worried about fighting; in fact, he was looking for something in particular. He rode down streets lined with shops, all of which were closed and dark. He turned his horse down another street and stopped. The trees lining the pavement were not too tall that the upper levels of the buildings were hidden but tall enough to provide a little shade on a hot day. Most of the buildings looked abandoned, and there were not many shop signs to be seen. He was about to turn around when he spied a soft glowing light. He urged his mount on, and as he drew near, he noticed some light shining from an uncovered window, and there was no mistaking it; this was a tailor's shop. He tied his horse to a post and entered.

"Good evening?" a voice called from the back. "I thought I told you to draw the curtains, Akina!" the voice continued. "Good evening?"

"Hello," Rakosa replied.

"My good fellow," a man said as he popped out from the back. "We have no extra bed, but you are welcome to sleep on the floor; I have an extra pillow and a few blankets you can use. We have no extra food at present, but I can fix you some tea or coffee if that will suffice."

"I am not here for those things," Rakosa shook his head. "If you are closed, I can come back tomorrow," he offered.

"But you are here now. Rylabet is my name. How can I help you?"

"Thank you," Rakosa said. "As you can see, my uniform is a mess and…"

"I see; yes it is quite a mess." Rylabet scrutinized the man before him. "I am sure I do not have any uniforms right now; I could have one made in a few days, though," he added hastily.

"I was looking for regular clothes."

"Ahhh," Rylabet nodded. "You are Lepnarion, to be certain, but not from around here," he stated.

"I am indeed Lepnarion," Rakosa answered proudly. "And your ear is not wrong."

"How is it that you managed to survive for so long?" Rylabet asked as he rummaged through a stack of clothes folded neatly on a shelf.

Rakosa sighed, "I have no idea."

"So, you intend to purchase clothes from me in hopes of hiding your association with the military and making your way from the destruction of this city as a civilian? What is to become of me when it is discovered that I have helped you?"

"I have no need of a disguise and am not trying to escape the city," Rakosa assured him.

"Are you not being hunted?"

Rakosa began shaking his head when the door to the street opened.

"He is being hunted," another voice laughed as the door to the shop closed. "Now, Rakosa, why are you bothering this humble merchant?" Niven asked.

"I only stopped to see about getting a change of clothes," Rakosa explained. "This uniform is tattered and bloodstained."

"I can certainly help you," Rylabet said to Rakosa, then turning to look at Niven, he added. "I can help you as well."

"Are you following me?" Rakosa wanted to know.

"You have fought well, Rakosa, and you have my thanks and the thanks of Aracelis. Your prowess in the field has proven a great worth to our cause. The day of your freedom is drawing nigh."

"I and my men have fulfilled our obligation, so now you will give us the antidote?" he asked with anticipation.

Niven fumbled in a pouch at his waist before tossing a small glass vial to Rakosa. "Here is your antidote."

"Less than half of my command remains. Will this be sufficient for all of them?" Rakosa asked as he peered at the vial.

"The cost of your allegiance was certainly high," Niven agreed. "But they will be given their own antidote," he assured him. "Where are they now?"

"They are at a drinking establishment awaiting my return. The Golden Dragon, I think."

Niven nodded, "There is something else though."

"Another *errand* that is beneath you to complete?" Rakosa asked with disdain as he looked longingly at the dark liquid within the stoppered glass.

Niven's eyes narrowed slightly. "Every *errand,* as you call them, was essential to our success."

"Too difficult then?" Rakosa asked as he unstopped the vial. An unpleasant smell greeted his nose.

"Rakosa," Niven sighed. "The antidote is worthless to you."

Rakosa, who had the antidote up to his lips, pulled the vial back and peered at it and then to Niven. "Why is that?"

"The truth is you have outlived your usefulness to me." Niven chuckled as he walked closer and unsheathed his sword. "Put the stopper back in the vial and place it on the table."

Rakosa slowly pushed the stopper back into the vial and gently placed it on a neatly folded bright yellow cloth.

"You might want to go to the back," Niven instructed the tailor, watching him until the door to the back room closed softly. "Now then, where were we?" Niven asked as he turned to look at Rakosa.

"Why not just let the poison kill me?" Rakosa wanted to know.

"It might be interesting to watch your torment as the poison kills you," Niven nodded. "But I cannot wait that long."

Rakosa shook his head and drew his weapon. "I do not understand."

Niven quickly swung his sword so the flat of his blade landed atop the vial and the yellow cloth. The muffled sound of breaking glass was heard, and when he pulled his sword back, the yellow cloth was stained black. "If I am not successful this evening," he smiled a cruel smile. "You will still die, only not as quick and not as painlessly."

"Have I not proven I am trustworthy?"

"And how long do you think we would allow you, a Lepnarion, to live? We used your hatred of Fulcwin and Balatiere to our advantage. It is time; come now, just go quietly."

"I will defend myself," Rakosa stated as he backed up.

Niven shoved the table with his hip hard enough to send it into Rakosa, knocking him off balance and also knocking several large spools of thread to the floor.

Rakosa quickly recovered and moved to keep the table between the two of them.

"I am rather fond of you," Niven stated. "In another life, we might have made fast friends."

"Then why are you doing this?" Rakosa asked.

"Orders," Niven replied. "Orders, and I have a celebration to attend."

"Why not just tell Aracelis I am dead? You have already spilled the antidote; the poison will kill me anyway."

"There is that, but Aracelis will want proof that I carried out my order."

"Take my uniform," Rakosa pleaded.

"Then I shall have to lie to Aracelis, and he has informed me I am no good at it. It would be easiest to simply kill you. What better proof of your death than your lifeless body?" Niven lunged forward.

Rakosa easily parried the thrust and glanced to the front door.

"I bolted it when I entered," Niven advised.

"I can always slip out the back," Rakosa exclaimed as he looked to the backroom door.

"You would entangle the tailor in this?" Niven shook his head. "It is just like you Lepnarions to slink away when the fighting gets too tough for you."

"I trusted you! You showed me mercy!"

"Sometimes trust is misplaced," Niven explained with mock sympathy. "And mercy does not last forever." He continued walking around the table in pursuit of Rakosa. "My mercy has run out. You have no way of escape," he crowed before shoving the table again, sliding it against a tall shelf and blocking Rakosa's retreat. "Finally, the cornered dog turns to face his master," Niven gloated and took a step forward.

"You have this Lepnarion dog cornered. Now come and finish me!" Rakosa snarled as he raised his sword.

Niven's next step placed his foot upon a spool of thread, and he crashed to the ground.

Rakosa wasted no time; lunging forward, he stepped on Niven's sword arm, pinning it to the ground, and then he placed the tip of his own sword against Niven's neck.

"I showed you mercy," Niven pleaded.

"This dog will show no mercy," Rakosa whispered as he leaned on his sword and slowly drove its point into the floor.

Niven struggled mightily for a moment, mouth open trying to speak, eyes blinking furiously, and then, as his blood spilled onto the floor, he lay still.

A moment later, the backroom door opened, and Rylabet peeked out. "What a mess you have made of my shop."

"Not my intention," Rakosa replied. He pulled his sword from Niven's neck and, kneeling, quickly cleaned the blade on Niven's cloak.

"You have quite the dilemma," Rylabet stated. "I could not help but overhear the words between the two of you. What will you do?"

"I am not sure," Rakosa replied as he sat in a chair.

"You are a Lepnarion, right?" Rakosa nodded as he attempted to straighten out his uniform. "How is it that you find yourself in the employ of those seeking the destruction of Lepnar?" Rylabet asked as he pulled the table back to its original position and began picking things up off the floor.

"A long story," Rakosa replied.

"Then it is good that we have some time," Rylabet smiled. "Akina, fetch those two horses around to the back and keep them out of sight. Will not do to have your story marred by interruptions." He explained as Akina hurried past and out the front door.

Rakosa began telling his story, and all the while, Rylabet continued straightening things up.

"A map, you say?" Rylabet asked with sudden interest after Rakosa first mentioned the Empire Map. "I should like to have a look at that map myself," he exclaimed. Rakosa continued with his story. They both heard the back door open and close again.

"That would be my assistant, Akina," he assured Rakosa. "Please continue."

When Rakosa was finished, Rylabet nodded a few times. "The antidote?" he asked as he held the folded yellow cloth in his hand. The black stain had marred an otherwise beautiful piece of fabric.

Rakosa nodded and placed his head in his hands. "Without the antidote, I am as good as dead."

"Perhaps some tea will help you feel a bit better," Rylabet said as he peeked into the back room and asked Akina to heat the water. He sat back down and stared at Rakosa. "You have managed to kill this one that was sent to kill you."

"Yes."

"Surely this Aracelis fellow still wants you dead."

"Guess so," Rakosa replied.

Akina opened the back room door and brought out a wooden platter with three mugs and a steaming pot of water. She placed it on the table and sat down beside Rylabet.

"Try some of this tea," Rylabet said as he slid a mug over to Rakosa. He sipped his and sighed with satisfaction.

Rakosa picked the mug up, staring at his reflection in the stained water. The steam wafted up from the surface, obscuring his vision every so often.

"Would it surprise you to hear that I, too, have met Fulcwin and Balatiere?"

Rakosa clenched the mug, and he looked up at Rylabet.

"Yes, they were in this very store with several other compatriots. They claimed to be looking for something, but I got the impression they were looking to sell something valuable."

"The Empire Map," Rakosa whispered.

"I was unable to help them, and they left. But we did run into Balatiere a few days ago, actually."

Akina nodded. "It was in the market, but he was not doing very well. Ate a bad tart, I heard," she added, her eyebrows raised.

"Where was he staying?" Rakosa wanted to know.

"Some abandoned tower in the garden district," Rylabet answered.

Rakosa stood to leave and then immediately sat back down. He took a sip of his tea. "I am no longer free to roam about the city."

"Surely word of this one's death has not reached Aracelis yet. You could still have time."

"But my time is running low. As soon as Niven fails to report back with my corpse, Aracelis will send men after me."

"We may be able to help you with that," Rylabet stated.

"Help me how?"

"Akina, will you show our guest here what we are able to do for him."

Akina disappeared into the back room for a moment, and then Niven walked into the room. Rakosa jumped to his feet and drew his sword.

"What madness is this?"

"Please, have a seat, Rakosa," Rylabet urged. "You are in no danger. As you can see, the real Niven lies dead right over there."

Rakosa looked; it was true; Niven lay exactly where he had fallen. He looked at Niven standing in the room. "The resemblance is uncanny," he said slowly.

"Akina, if you would?" Rylabet nodded. She whispered a word and immediately changed back into her former self.

"Astounding," Rakosa admitted. "Simply astounding."

"Things are not always what they seem," Rylabet agreed.

"So, I would be able to look like Niven and Aracelis would never know?" Rakosa asked as he fumbled at his belt and presently placed a small bag of coins in front of himself. "How is this possible?" he asked as his hand covered the pouch.

"The spell is written upon a scroll," Rylabet explained. "Thinking about the person you wish to become as you read the scroll is sufficient to complete the transformation."

"How long do the effects last?"

"That depends on several factors," Rylabet began to explain. "Two or three minutes at a minimum, and up four or five days at most. How well you know the subject plays a crucial role in the longevity of the transformation."

Rakosa slowly nodded his understanding. "What else?"

"Of course, the skill of the scroll's creator. I can assure you I am one of the best masters of…"

"So I can walk out of here looking like Niven, but what do I do with his body over there? Any chance you can make Niven look like me?"

"As a matter of fact, we can," Rylabet boasted. "Though I would not be able to guarantee the effects much more than an hour. There is, however, the matter of cost."

Rokasa loosened the pouch's drawstring and was about to tip the contents into his left hand when he suddenly dropped the pouch onto the table. "How do I even know you are who you say you are?" he asked suspiciously. "Or her?" His right hand strayed toward his blade as he looked at first one and then the other. "You are definitely more than a simple tailor. And who knows what you really are," he said to Akina. "Perhaps you already know Aracelis!"

"First, we have not tried to kill you this evening, and second, you have little choice. However, I can assure you we are both just as you see us here and now," Rylabet spoke calmly. "We have no need of a disguise in our own shop, and as far as knowing this Aracelis," he shook his head. "We do not, but if we did, why would we allow you to kill this man?"

Rakosa scowled at him.

"We are trying to help you."

"So why help me anyway?" Rakosa asked as he settled down a little bit. "What is in it for you?"

Rylabet looked at Akina and shrugged. "I might as well tell you everything," he sighed. "When Fulcwin and Balatiere were in here, they stole something from me, from Akina, actually." Forlorn, Akina produced a slight frown, tilting her head and looking down.

"What did they steal?" Rakosa asked, anger evident in his voice.

"A cloak woven from the silk of a spider."

"To replace the other one, no doubt," Rakosa said more to himself than Rylabet.

"Yes, they mentioned that being the reason," Rylabet smiled.

"You have no other cloaks like that one?" he asked as he looked around the room.

"Cloaks woven from spider silk are extraordinarily rare and quite valuable, I might add. While it is true I have many fine cloaks to choose from; there is none as fantastic as the one that was stolen. So I would like to try and retrieve it from them. If you were to find Fulcwin, perhaps I would be able to reclaim what is hers."

"You help me, I help you," Rakosa frowned. "The last time I entered into that type of agreement, it did not go so well for me."

"This time will be different," Rylabet assured him. He finished his tea and stood up, "I tell you what, I will only charge you for the scrolls needed to disguise you and Niven here, and I will throw in a change of clothes in exchange for you letting us know where Fulcwin can be found."

"I may not be able to find him," Rakosa warned.

"I am willing to take that chance," Rylabet said.

Rakosa thought about that for a while. "How can I refuse?" he finally asked with a laugh and, raising his half-empty tea in a toast, drained it in one gulp, slamming the mug onto the table with gusto. "Where do we begin?"

Rylabet and Akina spent the next hour showing Rakosa various outfits and color combinations. In the end, he decided on a pair of baggy red pants, a white ruffled shirt and a grey tabard. He tucked each leg of his pants into his black boots and straightened up with a nod and a smile.

"How do I look?"

"Absolutely stunning," Akina crooned.

"Without a doubt," Rylabet chimed in.

So it was that as dawn began to lighten the eastern sky, a man looking very much like Niven mounted a horse and began moving down the street, leading another horse behind him with a corpse tied across the saddle; its ashen face looked very much like Rakosa's.

## The End of Grey: Book One

Made in the USA
Columbia, SC
26 January 2024

17f103e3-9533-4611-a564-1db2dd32f6e9R01